(more)

LEE SMITH

"Smith transmutes many of the elements of the Southern Gothic novel into farce, among them familial couplings and murder, feeble-minded cousins, loony aunts and lowdown tarts. . . . Do awful secrets lie behind Miss Elizabeth's lady-of-the-manor act? Could be. Unraveling the mystery, however, is secondary to the pleasures of Smith's wry comic vision."
Newsweek

"Even the minor characters are palpable and visible entities in the vibrant family pageant. It will be the rare reader who fails to become involved in the fortunes and future of this complex bunch and who fails to relax when the mystery of the murder is solved."
Publishers Weekly

"Welcome to FAMILY LINEN, Lee Smith's hilarious new novel. . . . A murder mystery that makes the reader laugh is rare indeed. In less capable hands, it might not work. . . . Lee Smith knows just when to draw back, and just when to stop."
Richmond News Leader

FAMILY LINEN

FAMILY LINEN

"A friendly book, easily read . . . The style is everyday, colloquial, distinctly American, casual. It is generally bent on humor, satirizing our lives, filled as they are with television adventures, daily murders, floods, plane crashes, fires, intrigue, and mayhem. . . . Amusement is Lee Smith's style and her greatest gift. The scenes between women often sparkle."

The New York Times Book Review

"Smith has given us an absorbing novel of family life—with all its intricate and linen-like interweavings. And she stands alone in her ability to capture in a sentence—often a mere phrase—the entire essence of a personality or situation."

The Charlotte Observer

"Smith finds the perfect balance of suspense, motives, and clues for the meticulously plotted mystery at the core of the novel. As a whodunit, FAMILY LINEN has a stunning opening chapter."

Houston Chronicle

FAMILY LINEN

Also by Lee Smith
Published by Ballantine Books:

BLACK MOUNTAIN BREAKDOWN

CAKEWALK

ORAL HISTORY

FANCY STRUT

FAIR AND TENDER LADIES

FAMILY LINEN

Lee Smith

BALLANTINE BOOKS • NEW YORK

FOR HAL

For their help in providing ideas and information for this novel, I would like to thank Laura Horton, Elizabeth Brown Taylor, Godfrey Cheshire, Dino Read, Martha and Willie Mason, and Dr. William Joyner. I'd also like to thank Margaret Ketchum Powell, Nancy Tilly, and Jill McCorkle for editorial assistance; Peggy Ellis for her help in manuscript preparation; Constance Freeman for her invaluable advice and support during the writing of this novel; North Carolina State University for granting me a semester's leave from teaching; and Liz Darhansoff and Faith Sale for their important roles in making all this possible.

THE PAST IS A FOREIGN COUNTRY:
THEY DO THINGS DIFFERENTLY THERE.

—L. P. Hartley
The Go-Between

SYBILL parks carefully at the curb in front of the hypnotist's house and stares at it for some time without getting out of the car, without even turning off the motor or the air conditioner. The hypnotist's white brick ranch house is not at all what she had in mind. She expected an office, with prints on the wall and a nurse. Maybe in a duplex, because of his business card, but still an *office*. . . . Sybill looks again at the hypnotist's card lying in the passenger seat beside her purse.

ROBERT T. DIAMOND, ACSW
Marital, Family, and Individual Counseling
Clinical Hypnosis
108 Mountainside Drive
Roanoke, Va. 24014
703-628-4366 By Appointment Only
Side Entrance for Consultations

After she called him up, the hypnotist sent her this card, with the time and date of her appointment penciled in at the bottom: 10:30 a.m., June 1, 1983. That's today—that's right now. Sybill doesn't know what ACSW means. Maybe he just made it up. He might be a con man. Diamond doesn't sound like a real last name, either. And you couldn't tell a thing from his voice, which could have been anybody's—a noncommittal noplace voice like a computer salesman, or somebody taking a poll, or an anchorman on TV. She and Betty got him out of the Yellow Pages, under "Hypnosis."

The plastic daisy air-freshener swings back and forth from Sybill's rearview mirror while she looks at the hypnotist's house. The hypnotist has not been out yet to get his *Roanoke Times*, which lies in the middle of the brick walk that goes straight as a shot from the boxwood hedge by the curb to his gray front door. Gray-green, actually. That color's in, now: the Williamsburg look. It's all over *Southern Living*. In the hypnotist's picture window, Sybill sees a big green plant, gold draperies, a round candlestand table with a pewter lamp on it. Sybill likes the lamp. Of course the hypnotist has got a wife, probably—why not? This idea makes Sybill feel worse, for some reason, instead of better. Then she sees the swing set in the side yard, beyond the rose garden. Children? Sybill has never liked children at all. But of course the children will be at school today, public school's not out until the twelfth . . . Sybill knows she's procrastinating, something she isn't prone to. But she would rather not go in. She would rather sit here in her new Ford Maxima and study the hypnotist's yard and consider whether she, if she were the hypnotist's wife, would or would not have put the rose bed in the side yard instead of in front of the picture window,

and whether she would have used so much ground-
cover by the walk which is beginning to shimmer,
incidentally, in the heat, as is the swing set beyond,
from this moist June heat or else from one of her
headaches coming on. They often start with that
shimmer, that special radiance just beyond the bound-
aries of vision. Unless they wake her up at night,
another problem.

Sybill approves, finally, of the hypnotist's wife. All
you have to do is look at her yard. Even if she has
children, she keeps order. Sybill approves of order
with all her heart. Finally she turns off the ignition
and puts the key in her purse which says SYBILL on it
in counted cross-stitch, and snaps the purse shut. A
big pretty willow in the hypnotist's front yard is beginning to shine, she sees, beginning—almost—to
twinkle. *Lord*.

Betty's nasal voice hoots softly in her ear: "Girl, you
haven't *got* a choice! I'd say you're right at the end of
your rope." Sybill is out of the car now and walking
up the hypnotist's walk, stepping smartly over his
Roanoke Times. She's a good-looking woman, forty-
seven although you'd never guess it to look at her, a
woman somehow almost military in the way she carries herself, the way her pretty graying hair is cut
and waved so short, the way her gold clip-on earrings
match the stickpin in the lapel of her navy blazer,
and the way her clear red lipstick is so precisely
applied. An attractive, efficient woman—people have
said she looks like Julie Andrews. Sybill's best friend
Betty put her up to this hypnotist thing.

Of course Betty believes in aerobics and astrology
also, dubious practices which she cited in urging
Sybill to try the hypnotist. "There are things beyond
our control I tell you, Sybill," Betty said, squinting

through her Salem smoke one morning last week in Sybill's dinette. "The fact is, a person can only go without sleep for so long unless becoming a zombie. The fact is, Dr. Rowland has as much as said he can't cure your headaches and said if he was you he'd go to a psychiatrist *muy pronto,* isn't that true?" Betty says things like *muy pronto* since she went on the Mexican tour. Sybill, sleepless and badgered, nodded.

But she didn't want to go, they both knew, to a psychiatrist. Sybill regarded her unconscious like she regarded her reproductive system, as a messy, murky darkness full of unexplained fluids and longings which she preferred not to know too much about. Except perhaps it *was* true, as Dr. Rowland apparently believed, that something down in there was out of whack . . . anyway, psychiatry was a real expense, and her Blue Cross from the technical school would only cover 60 percent of it. The hypnotist, Betty's idea, was a lot cheaper: twenty-five dollars per hour. Of course Sybill didn't know if Blue Cross would cover *him,* or not. But Betty swore a hypnotist could put you in a trance and ask you point blank what was the problem and you'd spit it right out, not have to go on and on for months spilling your guts at fifty bucks a shot. Plus Betty saw a lady hypnotist on the noon show one time who could cure just about anything, along with the videotapes of a woman who formerly stammered.

Sybill, walking, has reached the hypnotist's front door and has turned right, following the tidy brick walk around to the side of the house. Betty said that hypnosis, like astrology, is beyond the rational mind. Betty went on to say that if oysters are taken from the Atlantic Ocean and put into Lake Michigan, for instance, they will continue to open and close their shells in sequence with the tides in the Atlantic because the pull of the moon is so strong. Nobody understands it, Betty said, it's beyond the rational mind. Sybill stared hard at Betty, at Betty's close-set little eyes. "Betty," Sybill said, "we are not an oyster," and Betty blinked rapidly through the smoke and said, "No, of course not." But Sybill called the hypnotist, after all.

And now she's here, rounding the corner of the ranch house at 108 Mountainside Drive, feeling like a zombie. Normally Sybill would appreciate, for instance, these roses. But today she hates the Peace rose the way its colors run into each other. She hates that lavender rose with its petals shading to purple. Sybill likes a solid rose, red or yellow or white or pink, something definite. Up until now, she has been in control of every minute of her life.

Through a sliding glass door at the side of the house Sybill sees the hypnotist, his back to her, writing at his desk. His office looks like a study, like a professor's office, with bookshelves lining the walls, and wing chairs. Sybill feels the flush on her face as she knocks on the glass. Of course, it's so hot today, it's not a headache, they say there might be a heat inversion. The reflected rose bed shimmers in the sliding glass door, and right behind the reflection there's the hypnotist himself, unlatching the door and extending his hand, presenting himself on a wave of air conditioning.

And he's *short!* A little bitty rumpled man who comes up to Sybill's earrings. A small fat untidy man who looks like he might be wearing his pajamas, only of course he's not. That's just his short-sleeved shirt, his droopy little slacks.

"Miss Hess?" he asks. "Dr. Diamond?" Sybill responds. The hypnotist smiles. "Call me Bob," he says.

I won't, Sybill thinks. *I will not*—he wears round eyeglasses with pink plastic rims; his tiny hand feels like foam rubber. Sybill shakes it vigorously. He ushers her inside and seats her somehow, without seeming to, in the wing chair facing his desk. The hypnotist picks up a clean pad of paper and a ballpoint pen, the same kind Sybill buys by the dozen at Roses to grade her papers.

"Miss Hess, why have you come to see me?" the hypnotist begins gently, almost idly.

Sybill stares out the door at his wife's rose garden, framed now by an iridescence she doesn't much like. She closes her eyes, then opens them and looks directly at the hypnotist.

"Well, Bob," Sybill finally says, "I'm right at the end of my rope."

Bob smiles, a nice little smile which stays mostly in his eyes. He is not one bit scary. He would never do something like put you in a trance and then tell you that after you wake up, you will bark like a dog whenever you see chocolate. Sybill has heard of that somewhere.

"I have these headaches," she says.

"Tell me about them." Bob fiddles around with his ballpoint pen. He seems patient, real slow, like he has all the time in the world. Speaking of which, Sybill doesn't even see a clock in his office. How will he know when the hour is up? Sybill glances down at her watch quickly so *she'll* know, so she can tell if he tries to short her on time.

"Your headaches," Bob says.

Sybill takes a deep breath. She knows she has to tell it and tell it all, or else she'll be wasting her money. But instead she says, "This is so embarrassing."

Bob looks up. "Why?" he asks, a curious note in his mild little voice.

"*Well*—" Sybill doesn't believe he can't see this right off the bat. "Well, people don't just *have headaches*, or at least I don't. I mean I am not the kind of person who does something like this, surely you can understand that."

Bob smiles. "Headaches are hardly voluntary," he says.

"Listen here." To her horror, Sybill finds herself chipping away at her nail polish, something she never does, but she doesn't seem able to stop. "I manage a condominium complex, twenty units. The Oaks." Bob nods. "I teach at the Roanoke Technical Institute, business English, high-school equivalency classes, basic skills. I'm the head of Language Arts." Bob nods again. "I have twenty-six thousand two hundred dollars in my savings account and ten thousand dollars in my IRA." Bob blinks. "I play bridge and rook, I go to the health club, if I gain a pound I go on the grapefruit diet right away—" The words just come tumbling out now, Sybill can't stop them, she knows she's not making sense. "I go to church, Betty and I go bowling, I've been on a cruise before. I keep up with current events."

"You sound like a very capable woman," Bob says. Behind him, in the corner, the air conditioner hisses gently into the room.

Now Sybill smiles. "I am," she says.

"You live alone?" Bob asks. "In The Oaks?"

"Yes." Sybill drums her nails softly on the arm of the wing chair, thinking of her lovely apartment, which she keeps just so. It's a source of great pleasure to her. Everything is off-white, with dark, dramatic accents. But Sybill's nails look funny and ragged, red and flesh. Suddenly, she remembers a time years ago when she spent the night with her sister Candy, a big mistake. She had to get up in the night and clean Candy's bathroom before she could go to sleep, it was so messy. But Sybill can't see any point in telling Bob about that. She takes a long breath.

"Everything was just fine," she says. "And then suddenly, right after Christmas, I started having these headaches, and now they keep getting worse and worse. Sometimes they start in the daytime and I have to cancel my classes and go back home and go to bed. Other times I just *think* they're starting and I get so worried I can't do a thing. I thought I was getting one when I came in here, if you want to know, but I didn't. I just can't ever tell. I think about them all the time. Sometimes, and this is the worst part, they start at night and I wake up half dead with them and then of course there's no sleeping for the rest of the night after that. I'm getting so tired," Sybill says.

"It must be terrible for you," Bob says.

Sybill sinks back in her chair. He's really very nice, she thinks. He would never make you bark. Sybill tells Bob that the headaches are growing both more frequent and more severe, that she averages three or four a week now, and she worries about holding on to her job. She describes the headaches, how they start with her eyes, how objects and people begin to glow, to shimmer, before the light around them collects itself and strikes into her brain. "Just exactly like lightning," she says. Bob sympathizes and says, "Migraine, of course," which of course it is. She describes how the shooting pains start sometimes at her neck, other times at her forehead. Then the headache spreads out to cover her whole head, growing heavier, like an iron hat squeezing tighter and tighter. This is the point at which Sybill wakes up, if she has been sleeping. "Imagine waking up to that!" Sybill says.

Bob shakes his head back and forth, frowning, obviously moved by her pain. All in all he is one of the nicest little men she has ever talked to, a big relief. Usually Sybill doesn't talk to men at all, or at least not about anything very personal. But Bob, she can tell, is really *interested*, as interested as Betty or any one of her women friends. Plus he's not exactly a man, either, being a hypnotist. So she tells him all about the headaches and he writes down Dr. Rowland's name and a lot of other information such as her age, place of birth (Booker Creek, Va.), education (B.A., Longwood College), and so on, and then he says he wonders if she'll be a good subject for hypnosis.

"What do you mean?" Sybill asks.

"Well, some people are and some aren't. It depends upon what we call your suggestibility."

"You mean it might not work on me?" Now that she's here, Sybill can't stand to think she's gone to all this trouble and spent twenty-five dollars for nothing.

"Well, let's see." Bob smiles at her. "Why don't you just hold your arm out with your palm up, like this?" Bob holds his own arm out to show her. "Now, when you do this, I'm going to put a nickel on your palm. Okay?" He scoots his chair forward, away from his desk.

"Okay." Sybill holds out an arm which seems mostly unrelated to her, suddenly; she approves of the navy sleeve, the red cuff of her blouse, the gold bracelet.

"Now open your hand," Bob says, and she does, and Bob places the nickel on her palm. "In a moment, when I give you directions, your hand will turn over, and the coin will fall on the floor."

"It won't," Sybill says. "This is silly."

"We'll see," Bob says. He pauses—Sybill hears only the hiss of the air conditioner. Her arm is beginning to ache. His soft voice starts again. "Now your hand will turn over, and the coin will fall onto the floor. Observe your hand as it slowly begins to turn, turn, turn, turn—"

Sybill watches as her arm turns, as the coin drops onto the thick tan carpeting at her feet. This arm has nothing to do with her at all. Sybill feels special, like somebody on "That's Incredible."

"You did very well," Bob tells her. His voice is so calm, she sees why he's good at his job. "Now I want you to come over here." He stands up and walks to a dropleaf table in the corner, beside a door which undoubtedly leads into the rest of his house. He seats himself in a ladderback chair at the table and motions to Sybill to do the same. He puts a gold ring, with a string tied to it, on the table before them. Sybill is thrilled. "When I tell you to," Bob says, "I want you to pick up the end of this string. I want you to stretch your arm out across the top of this table, letting the ring dangle, and imagine that you are looking at a large circle which is in the tabletop. I want you to let your eyes move around and around this circle, until the ring on the end of the string begins to move in a circle also. The ring will move all by itself."

Lord. Sybill picks up the end of the string and holds her arm out, thinking that whatever happens from here on out, she's almost gotten her money's worth already. "Now," Bob says. Sybill lets the ring dangle while she looks around and around the top of the table, just exactly as if a circle were really there, although it's not, and she's not even surprised when after a while the ring starts to move too, slowly at first and then faster, exactly like one of those mechanical swings at the fair. "Now the ring will stop moving, gradually, it is moving slower, and even slower now, as you see. When it comes to a complete stop, you may place the ring back on the table again and resume your original chair."

And he's already there, in the chair at his desk, smiling at her.

"Well?" Sybill asks. Her heart is beating away in her throat, she feels like she might be having a hot flash, maybe it's time for the Change of Life. This whole thing might be nothing but the Change of Life coming on.

"I think we can work together very well." Bob looks concerned, sweet, tired.

"Then you can hypnotize me okay." Actually Sybill thinks this is not surprising. She's been good at everything she's ever tried her hand at, all her life. But she doesn't say this to Bob.

"We'll talk more," Bob says, "and I'll speak with Dr. Rowland. Next time we'll try a light trance and perhaps I'll begin to ask you some questions."

"What kind of questions?"

"Questions concerning your headaches and what events might happen to trigger them—sometimes the simplest events trigger complex emotions which we ourselves are not even aware of."

"I'm not here for any psychiatric," Sybill says. "I want you to leave my subconscious out of this."

Bob smiles. "You made your position on that issue quite clear on the telephone. Nevertheless I feel that there are certain facts which might be brought to light which could, perhaps, help us to understand the origins of your pain—"

"You mean my family?" Sybill asks suddenly. Her nails look just awful; she doesn't know why she keeps chipping away at them like this.

"Your family, yes. Perhaps."

"They're such a mess!" Sybill says. Now she's sure Bob will think they're more of a mess than anybody else's family is, just as she's sure that she's his most suggestible patient. Once Sybill goes into something, she goes whole hog.

"At any rate, I feel sure that I can offer suggestions to you which will help you, in the posthypnotic state, to deal more effectively with the headaches. Your anxiety level can certainly be reduced. Now there's one more thing I'm curious about," Bob says. "The rest will keep until next week. I wonder if you can think of any way in which your life since Christmas has been different from your life prior to that date. I wonder if any change has occurred at all, no matter how insignificant it may appear to you."

Sybill swallows hard. She might have known this was coming. She hasn't told anybody, not even Betty, because it's so silly, after all these years. Should she tell Bob, a perfect stranger? But Sybill reminds herself that she's here to get her money's worth, and that her Blue Cross might not even cover hypnotism. She might have to pay for this whole thing out of her own pocket. But is it even worth telling? It's nothing much, after all, just silliness. Still . . .

"There's a man in one of my condominiums," Sybill says after a while. "A widower, his wife died last spring, so he sold their house and bought into The Oaks. He's only been with us for two months, this old Mr. Edward Bing. He's not Chinese," Sybill adds abruptly, "in case you might have thought so from the name."

"No," Bob says gravely. "And?"

"And he wants to go out with me," Sybill says. "I can just tell he does. He's not *that* old. He's said . . . he's done . . . oh, he's done a lot of things. It's perfectly clear to me."

"Well?" says Bob. "After all, you're a very attractive woman, Miss Hess. I take it you're not interested?"

"Oh, heavens no!" Sybill laughs heartily. "Not in Edward Bing! Besides, even if I *was* interested, which I'm not for one minute, believe me, I couldn't very well have an affair with him, could I? I mean a date, of course—" She flushes and thinks again of the Change of Life—"I couldn't have a date with all these headaches, waking up in the night and all."

"I suppose not." Bob's eyes, like bright blue marbles behind his wimpy pink glasses, seem very intent.

"Well, that's all ridiculous," Sybill says. "Believe me, Ed Bing is totally beside the point."

"Let me ask you, Sybill"—Bob leans forward—"are you a virgin?"

"None of your beeswax!" Sybill rises abruptly, furious, but Bob apologizes so meekly that she finds she can't stay mad. Then she finds herself making another appointment anyway. She's gone this far, after all. Besides, she knows it's his job to ask questions like that. She's not paying him to be polite. Leaving, she notices again the door at the back of the study, the door to the rest of his house, and envisions his wife right there behind it, listening, jealous. How silly! But Bob thinks Sybill's a very attractive woman, he said so. She shakes hands with him; her hand would make two of his. "See you next week," she says. Then he slides the glass door open and the heat hits Sybill like a ton of bricks. She hesitates, squares her shoulders, and marches back out into the damp hot rosy world.

Betty is just as jealous as she can be, she must have asked Sybill about Bob a million times. Betty wants to be hypnotized, too. The two women sit at the shiny maple table in Sybill's dinette, as they do most nights, eating meatloaf, salad, and baked potatoes, while the TV plays on in the living room. Or the great room, as it's called in the glossy brochures that advertise these condominiums. Betty has a way of running her tongue around the inside of her lips which Sybill has never noticed before; it gets all over her, though. Sybill is worse off, actually, since she saw the hypnotist. She's had headaches two nights in a row and she's real nervous. "I'm just as jumpy as a cat," she says to Betty, who agrees.

"But Lord, why not?" Betty asks, waving her fork in the air. "If I had a strange man going down in my subconscious on Thursday I'd be nervous, too. Girl, I'd be more nervous than you! What do you reckon he'll find out?"

"Probably nothing." Sybill puts A·1 sauce all over her meatloaf. On TV, a blond reporter from California says that twenty-two volcanic eruptions throughout the world in the past year may have contributed to the current bad weather. "Or the cause may be El Niño, a fickle east-to-west countercurrent," the blonde says. "In any case, this rainy spring, which has caused deaths, floods, mud slides, and havoc, is one of the wettest on record for many parts of the country." The TV shows houses in Nevada and Utah, sliding down the muddy sides of mountains.

"Look at that," Betty says.

"I would never buy a split-level in the first place," Sybill says. "I wouldn't want to live on a hill."

"They say it goes back to your parents." Betty runs her tongue around the inside of her lips.

"What does?"

"Everything," Betty says. Sometimes Sybill just hates Betty, who only went to high school but acts so smart. Betty, who is a hospital receptionist, is a tall edgy woman with dark permanent curls and a jutting chin. Once Betty was married for three years, fifteen years ago. Now she claims she can't even remember what that was like.

Sybill looks at TV where they are talking about Alzheimer's disease which kills one hundred twenty thousand people annually and is the fourth leading cause of death. Sybill finishes up her meatloaf and lights a Merit and listens closely. Alzheimer's disease causes memory loss, confusion, speech impairment, and personality change. It doesn't say if headaches are a symptom or not. Huh. Sybill snorts. She doesn't believe in Alzheimer's disease because it doesn't make sense to her that a disease that major could have been around for so long without anybody even noticing it, or naming it, or talking about it, or anything. The first Sybill ever heard of it was last spring.

"It's just popular," Sybill says.

Betty lights up too, staring at Sybill strangely.

"That Alzheimer's," Sybill explains. "Like anorexia nervosa. You never heard of that either until it got popular, and then it was everyplace."

"I heard of it," Betty says.

Sybill knows for a fact that all Betty ever does at the hospital is give out Visitor passes. "Oh, come on." Sybill's patience is wearing real thin. "*Nobody* did." She gets up and snaps off the TV before the sports and weather come on, even though they always watch the sports and weather, and frequently "Family Feud." "I need to lie down," she says.

"*Well!*" Betty, miffed, stands to go. "It probably all goes back to your mother," she says.

"I love my mother, it's the rest of them I can't stand." Of course this is not quite true of Myrtle. But when Sybill thinks of her brother and sisters in general, she feels a sense of confusion amounting almost to nausea. Arthur, Myrtle, Lacy, and Candy—especially Lacy and Candy. Just being in the same room with Candy embarrasses Sybill.

"I can tell you're holding back," Betty says.

"I don't know who you think you are, Dr. Joyce Brothers or who," Sybill snaps. Of course she's holding back, she has no intention of telling Betty or any other real person about old Ed Bing whose condominium even now is visible right across the pool, who's probably cooking his own steak in his own dinette, this minute.

"*Buenos días!*" Betty leaves in a huff, and Sybill sinks down on her puffy white sofa and cries. Betty's her best friend, after all. Sybill feels her eyes swelling up; she can't get her breath. She's not used to crying like this—to be honest, she hasn't shed a tear since her Pekingese, Missy, passed away at the age of twelve, two years ago. Before that, it was all the way back to *Love Story*. It's not that she doesn't feel strong emotions, it's just that she rarely cries. A line from a song on the radio pops into her head: "Used to be I was falling in love, but now I'm only falling apart." Sybill can't remember the next line, but the verse ends with the line "total eclipse of the heart." Sybill thinks she's having a total eclipse of the heart. And she's not up to it, it's been years . . .

Because Sybill is the kind of woman who gave up all those ideas long ago, gave them up so gradually she didn't even realize she was doing it. As a young girl, she always expected to marry. As a young woman, she expected this, too. But she was in no hurry. It was a question of waiting for the right man to come along. While she waited, Sybill finished college and worked and dated others—such as the mathematics instructor at Douglas Freeman High School in Richmond where she first taught, a red-haired man who took her out to the Bonanza Steak House for dinner and even, on several occasions, tuned up her car, but somehow never got beyond that stage—nor, Sybill realized even at the time, did she want him to. Although kind, he was not Mr. Right.

For two whole years after that, she went out with Mercer Delaney, a pharmacist from Farmville, Virginia, that she met through a colleague at Douglas Freeman. This was the last time, looking back on it, that anybody ever offered her a blind date. Sybill and Mercer Delaney dated every other weekend when his sister came to stay with his mother, who lived with him. Sybill and Mercer attended many model airplane rallies—his hobby. Sybill spent a lot of time sitting out in the wind catching cold while Mercer tried to repair his engine. Finally it came to seem to her that Mercer would never grow up, that his mother would never die.

Sybill's most serious love, however, was illicit. A man who came to teach industrial arts at the technical school in Roanoke, where Sybill still works, began to show her a lot of attention—this was in 1975, close to ten years ago. His name was Joe Ross Miller. Joe Ross Miller started to drink coffee with Sybill every morning. He asked her opinion of world events. He confided in her about his wild son, his shy daughter, his neurotic wife. They had a lot in common, Sybill found, including a distaste for the messier, unrestrained elements of family life. They shared a sense of the way things should be. After a month or two, Joe Ross Miller's manner toward Sybill changed. He began to stand a lot closer to her, to brush her hand accidentally. He asked her leading, suggestive questions, such as whether or not she liked taking long hot baths. Although he was bald except for a fringe like a monk at the back of his head, Joe Ross Miller had eyes like Omar Sharif, dark and hot. He had big strong white workingman's hands, with dark curly hairs on the knuckles. After he had been at the technical school for three months, Sybill knew he wanted to have an affair with her.

But she was spared the big decision, after all. Sybill's father (or stepfather, to be exact) died that winter, in late December, and while she was at home helping her mother run the funeral, Joe Ross Miller gave notice at the technical school, citing "personal reasons," and disappeared. Sybill never found out what those "personal reasons" were. He might have found a better job; he was always dissatisfied, always looking. Or his neurotic wife might have had a complete nervous breakdown. Or he might have had one himself! What Sybill preferred to believe, though, was that Joe Ross Miller had left because of her, because he had decided to give her up. Since he knew they could never marry, seeing her that way, every day, had been too painful for him to bear. Actually, Sybill found, she was glad he made this decision. It was more sensible all around. When she returned to work after her stepfather's funeral, she cleaned out her desk and opened the window and stood in front of it for a long time, letting the cold winter air sweep her up like a benediction.

Since that time—and that was a long time back—a man simply had not occurred. And gradually even the *idea* of a man has stopped occurring, so that without realizing it, without making any conscious decision, Sybill has put those things out of her busy, useful life as firmly as she sets out the trash on a Tuesday morning.

Only sometimes there comes in even such a life as hers that kind of moment which comes to us all—a moment like a dark red leaf spiraling down through the summer air to land on the picnic blanket. So here's Sybill, crying on the sofa in her tasteful condominium, having just offended her best friend Betty Long. Sybill, crying because suddenly there are big jagged holes in this life which has seemed to her now for so long like a roll of fabric over at Cloth World, floral print polyester perhaps, rolling on and on forever in a perfectly straight even path—

Darkness is falling fast. Sybill stands up and presses her hot face against the cool glass of her sliding glass door and looks past her grill and the redwood railing of her deck, down into the pale blue glowing kidney-shaped pool below. Mr. Hollister is in there swimming laps, back and forth, as regular as a motorboat, leaving a regular wake. That young couple, the Martins, have put their baby in one of those round floats with a seat in the middle of it, in the shallow end by the steps. The Brown boys are swimming in the deep end with two other boys Sybill doesn't know. She'll have to speak to their parents, again. Some people will take advantage of you no matter how nice you are, abusing whatever privileges you care to offer . . . give them an inch and they'll take a mile. Momentarily, this thought cheers Sybill. But then she notices Marietta Billings, a divorced dancing instructor, over there in the darkness half hidden by a striped umbrella, not swimming at all of course, just sitting out in the heat with a man, probably a different man altogether from the one she had here this weekend. Sybill can't see his face. Marietta is wearing white shorts, which seem to glow out in the night. Sybill sobs to herself. Across the pool lies Ed Bing's apartment, #16A, and as Sybill watches from the darkness, she sees Ed Bing himself move past his lighted great-room door carrying—she thinks—a cup of coffee. Which pulls at her heart. A sweet man like that, fixing his own coffee, reading the paper alone . . . Sybill does not intend to tell anyone, not even Bob, what she did last week.

While Ed Bing was out of town (in Richmond; he'd told her he was leaving and given her the number where he might be reached) Sybill went into his apartment, using her master key, and *snooped around!* She looked at everything: his disorganized pantry, his shelf of mystery novels, the photograph of his wife, the pictures of his only daughter and her three children, his plants (overwatered), his inadequate spice rack. Ed Bing turned out to be fairly tidy, for a man. She opened the top drawer of the chest in his bedroom and horrified herself by suddenly burying her face in the sweet dark little mounds of his rolled-up wool socks. Then she went careening into the bathroom—it was all so strange, the floor plan exactly like her own, yet so very different, like being in her own apartment, but dreaming—and for some reason the sight of the little hairs sprinkled all over the creamy porcelain bowl of the sink made her feel suddenly, terribly nauseous, so that she backed out of the bathroom and ran through his apartment and back to her own with the headache right behind her already, lights flashing at the corners of her eyes.

Sybill, sliding open the door to her deck now and stepping out into the night, Sybill is so ashamed that she snooped in Ed Bing's condominium. Maybe she *would* like—go ahead, admit it!—to have a date with Ed. There's nothing wrong with that. To go to a movie, to have dinner (red wine, candlelight, a steak) at that new French restaurant out on the Williamson Road. She'd like to invite him in, after that, for a cocktail. But the very thought of him makes those lights start up, makes her massage her neck. . . . Ed Bing gets up, disappears, reappears, then sits back down in the reclining chair in his great room. Ed is tall, thin, and large, and looks, Sybill thinks, like Gregory Peck. He probably got up to switch the channels on his TV. It's nine o'clock; she wonders if he's watching "WKRP in Cincinnati." Below her, Mr. Hollister swims back and forth in the pale blue shining pool. The Brown boys yell and splash, and Marietta Billings, not caring a bit who sees her, kisses the man she's with. Sybill gulps, leaning into the night, too old for any of this. She wonders what's down there in her subconscious, if anything is, it's probably just the Change of Life after all, it's probably just her uterus exploding in all directions. She shakes her head. She looks up beyond the condominium complex to the sky beyond Mill Mountain, where stars appear. She's having a total eclipse of the heart. Sybill goes in and gets a glass of Mateus and comes back out on her deck and sits down in the sticky hot night to drink it, and after a while, a little breeze comes up which might even be the fickle El Niño.

* * *

On her second visit to the hypnotist, Sybill sits rigid, gripping the arms of the wing chair. Bob smiles. Outside, through the glass door, it's raining cats and dogs.

"Relax," Bob says. "It won't work unless you relax." Today he's wearing a little black shirt outside his pants and looks somewhat more mysterious, more astrological. Betty would approve. Behind him, over Mill Mountain, lightning flashes.

"Go ahead and start," Sybill says.

"Flex your fingers," Bob says. "Rotate your whole hand, like this, around your wrist. Now rotate your whole arm, like this, first one arm and then the other. Go ahead, that's good."

"Are you doing it?" Sybill asks. "Are you starting now?"

But Bob smiles his sweet tired smile. "No, Sybill," he says. "This is a relaxation technique. Now drop your head back, like this, and rotate your head. Now with your head still back, make chewing motions with your chin, like this." Bob's pink Adam's apple wobbles above his black collar.

Chewing motions! This is just the kind of thing she's been afraid of. "Listen," Sybill says. "Believe me, I'll relax. You just go right ahead and do it, I'll be fine." Sybill feels a strong sense of urgency; just last night, in the parking lot, Ed Bing gave her a long quizzical look that she felt was almost a proposition. Or an *invitation*, that's what she means. "Stop that chewing," Sybill says irritably to Bob, who stops immediately while Sybill says how sorry she is to be rude.

"An apology isn't necessary," he says. "Of course you feel a great deal of conflict and anxiety occasioned by what we propose to do here today. In one way, you want to let go, to give up your pain." Sybill stiffens in her chair. "In another way, you feel intensely violated. You wish to maintain your control, your privacy. You may, of course, stop this at any time. Just because we make a decision doesn't mean we can't change our minds. Sometimes our decisions are the wrong ones."

"Just do it," Sybill says.

"Sybill—" Bob leans forward gently, one hand on each knee, while a soft swish of rain blows against the door. "I can't just 'do' it, as you demand. I may not 'do' it at all. I'd like to chat a bit with you now, as a matter of fact, and then I may or may not feel that I want to try to induce a trance."

Sybill swallows. She woke up with a headache last night at three twenty-five, stayed awake until five thirty, slept until seven. "Shoot," she says.

"Well—" Bob leans back in his chair. "Why don't you begin by telling me about your family? We mentioned this briefly at our last session."

"I don't think that has a thing to do with any of this," Sybill says.

"Possibly not, possibly you're entirely right there, but let's just proceed for a moment along those lines." Bob puts the tips of his fingers together, making a little tent. "Your parents," he prompts her.

"Well, my mother is a lady, I mean a *real* lady, in spite of this little town she's lived in all her life, the town I'm from."

"And where is that?"

"Booker Creek, it's right outside of Marion. In the mountains, close to the North Carolina line," Sybill says. "Anyway, Mother always tried to give us culture and advantages all along. For instance, she writes poetry. She had a book published about twenty years ago, by the Colonial Press in Richmond."

"How old is your mother now?"

"Seventy-five," Sybill answers right away.

"And she lives alone?"

"Yes, well, of course she has some help but yes she does live alone, she's lived alone for the last ten years. She's so proud," Sybill says. "It's hard to do anything for her. And of course she runs everything in town." Sybill smiles and Bob smiles, too.

"Your father died ten years ago?"

"Yes, well, it was nine years ago I guess, and it wasn't my father actually, it was my stepfather, Verner Hess, who's the only father I ever remember, as far as that goes."

"Aah. And what was he like?"

"Oh, a sweet man, I guess. I mean everybody thought he was sweet, and I guess he was, he was a very popular man, but he wasn't very strong, you know, not like *she* is. He never had strong opinions on things, or knew very much, or laid down the law to anybody, he left it all pretty much up to Mother except for the actual running of the dimestore. He liked to be in the store, up front talking to people. He just loved that. But he wouldn't wear a sports coat, even in the winter, or if he did he took it off . . . He always wore a starched white shirt and bright blue suspenders, I guess you could say they were his trademark." Sybill is very surprised at the way Verner Hess has appeared in her head as clear as a bell, wearing those tacky suspenders. She's surprised by her warm rush of feeling. Sybill remembers herself at six, six or seven, snuggled down in a big box of pink cellophane straw in the basement of the dimestore while the "girls," as Verner Hess referred to the women who worked for him, made Easter baskets. Easter baskets didn't come prepackaged in those days. Sybill is really surprised to find herself with so much to say about Verner Hess since actually, throughout her youth, she thought of him as a source of mainly embarrassment, occasioned by what she perceived as his dullness, how ordinary he was, and how limited. When Sybill remembers Sunday dinners, for instance, Verner Hess seems about as important as the wood-work.

"My mother is such a lady," Sybill says. "Of course she's sort of bossy, and I suppose some people don't like her because of that, but you can't help *admiring* her. It was really a mismatch," Sybill says.

"But a long marriage . . ."

"Oh yes, let's see, it must have been thirty years. He worshiped the ground she walked on. So I sup-pose they were happy enough, as far as those things go. Of course, it wasn't the Me Generation," she adds tartly. "But I tell you, you're looking up the wrong tree here, I have a perfectly ordinary family I think even if some of them are of course obnoxious and my mother married beneath herself."

The rain has slowed down to a pale gray drizzle out there in the garden, where roses droop.

"Tell me about your real father," Bob directs.

"I don't know why I said that," Sybill says. "Calling Verner Hess my stepfather, I mean. Verner Hess *was* my father for all intents and purposes, and that's that."

"Yet he was in fact your stepfather . . ." Bob is like a cat, Sybill thinks suddenly, sneaking along a gar-den wall in the dark.

"Just forget it," she says. "I have these two aunts, you'd just die if you got a load of either one. I mean they're so crazy you could get papers on them in one minute flat."

Bob makes the tent with his fingers, looking at her, and Sybill goes on. "Fay and Nettie, that's them, and Mama hasn't had a thing to do with either one for years and years. As you might imagine. Neither do I, of course, if I can help it. They live out at the One Stop on Route 460, in two rooms behind the store. Nettie runs the service station—she must be, let's see, seventy by now. I can't believe it! And Fay, that's my other aunt, has never been right in the head. So she stays out there with Nettie. She used to live with Mother, years ago."

"And you mentioned, I think, a sister named Candy—"

"That's my next-youngest sister, Candy Snipes, who is a beautician by choice," Sybill says. "She could have gone on to school the same as the rest of us, but oh no. Too busy dating the boys, just couldn't be bothered with school. Ran away and got married. You can imagine how upsetting this was for Mother, for Candace to do that way. Candy is just infantile, even now. That's one reason I'm glad I live here, so I don't have to see Candy all the time. If Candy takes after anybody, it's Nettie. Certainly it's not Mother, I have to say."

"And your other brothers and sisters?"

"Well, there's Arthur, he's in his early forties now and pretty much of a mess himself, if the truth be told. He's divorced. And then there's Myrtle who married that nice dermatologist, Dr. Don Dotson, she's certainly the best of the lot, even though we don't always, of course, see eye to eye. But actually we get along fine." *Even though Myrtle has always had everything she wanted in this world and still does, without lifting a hand* ... "Then there's Lacy who's an intellectual. Lacy got all the brains from Mother, you might say, although she has never put them to any good use." *Imagine spending your parents' money on years and years of graduate school and then just up and deciding you won't even bother to write your dissertation! Imagine that!* "Arthur still lives in Booker Creek. So does Candy of course and Myrtle. Lacy lives in Chapel Hill, North Carolina. She's kind of an egghead, as I said. You know what I mean."

Bob grins. "Who's the youngest?"

"Lacy. And she's real pretty, too, or she would be if she kept herself up. They wear *anything* in Chapel Hill." Sybill squares her shoulders, in her off-white, linen-looking suit. You dress up to visit a doctor, that's one of the things her mother always taught her, just like you wear clean underwear every day and wash out a tub the minute you're through, and keep an open box of baking soda on the refrigerator shelf at all times, to absorb odors. Sybill is proud to be her mother's only responsible child—to be, in some ways, her mother's *only* child. Talking to Bob is fun, but this is Sybill's money down the drain. Suddenly, she's tired of fooling around. "Let's go for it," Sybill says.

"As I count to five," Bob begins, and Sybill is thrilled, really thrilled, he's finally *doing* it, she wishes Betty could be here, too—"As I count to five, slowly, you will fall into a deep, deep sleep. While you are asleep, you will have a dream which concerns your headaches. You will dream about that time in your life which is most closely associated with your headaches, that time which you cannot remember now. You will remember that time, and you will dream about it, and when you wake up, you will tell me your dream."

It won't work. Then Sybill wonders, in a moment of pure idle pain, why none of them—her brother and sisters—ever liked her. But of course that's foolishness, of course they liked her, they like her now, and look how things have turned out, anyway, most of them living such messy lives! *The way yours will be if you take up with Edward Bing.* Suddenly Sybill remembers the rush of cold air the day she threw up her office window, saved from love by the abrupt departure of Joe Ross Miller. She remembers how the cool air tingled on her face. *It won't work.*

"One," Bob says. He clears his throat modestly, apologetically. "You feel as if you have weights on your eyes, your eyelids are so heavy, your eyes are closing now of their own accord. *Two.* You are growing very, very sleepy. Your feet feel heavy, very heavy. It's time to let them go, relax and just let them go, let your legs go now, that's right, and your arms, Sybill, you're letting go, letting go, letting go. *Three.* You are asleep now. You are soundly, soundly asleep. *Four.* You feel yourself beginning to dream, to slip into the dream, to . . ."

"*Five.* You are almost fully awake now. You stretch, you yawn, you are waking up now. Your eyes will open when you are ready." Sybill knows the voice, that's Bob, but she can't really hear him because of the awful, awful pain in her head, just like somebody's taking an ax and chopping straight into her brain, it's so bad she can't even speak, she simply can't say a thing. From a long way away, she hears Bob's slow smooth voice . . . "your headache. You will not have this headache. You will go back to sleep now, now as I count *one* . . ." Sybill thinks she hears the rain outside; she sleeps.

Later, waking up, she's surprised to find she's so tired. *Lord!* is she ever tired, so tired it's all she can do to hold herself up in this chair. Sybill looks at her watch and it's four fifteen—three hours she's been here, doing what? *Sleeping.* A waste of time. A waste of money. Sybill wonders if he'll charge her by the hour, or just make up a flat rate for the day. She won't pay seventy-five dollars, that's all there is to it. It wasn't her fault she slept so long.

"Okay," Sybill says. Her own voice sounds funny, ringing in her ears. And outside it's still raining; it seems it's been raining for years. Sybill envisions huge modern houses sliding down cliffs into the ocean. But this isn't California, or Nevada, or even Utah.

"Tell me about your dream," Bob says. His black shirt is all crumpled; it looks like construction paper as he leans forward in his chair.

"In the dream I was real little," Sybill begins in a voice which is not her own, or at least it's a voice which she doesn't have anymore, that mountain twang she has so carefully gotten rid of. "I'm real little and I wake up in the night. I call for Mama but she don't come. I called and called for Mama but she didn't come, and it was thundering, and the thunder came into my window. The lightning came into my window too. I saw the lightning come into my window and it flashed in the mirror too, the one over the dresser, I could see everything then, Molly and the pillow too and my new silver brush-and-comb set, and the ruffle around the dresser. Fay made that."

"Sybill, who is Molly?"

"My doll, the one I got for Christmas. Christmas came before, and Molly was there, too."

"And what did you do, Sybill, when you woke up?"

"I got out of bed and put my slippers on, the fuzzy

29

ones, and I put my robe on too, and I tied the tie and me and Molly went out into the hall where it was dark and then I heard Mama downstairs, I heard voices, so I went down. I am not allowed to slide down the banister," Sybill says.

"And then?"

"They were on the back porch," Sybill says.

She went down the steps one by one, sliding her hand along the cool smooth wood of the banister, until her hand hit the hand-carved newel post and she knew she was on the rose-flowered rug in the hall at the foot of the stairs. She knew this even in the dark, and knew that the parlor was there to the left, and the dining room. Thunder crashed outside and then lightning came right after, lighting up her mother's big cabinet full of cut glass which sent out sparks of light in every direction. More light, real light, came from the crack under the kitchen door, and Sybill pushed it open, cautiously. "Mama?" she said. But the kitchen was empty even though you could tell they had just been there. The bulb in its wavy yellow shade hung low over the round wood table, swaying ever so slightly. The refrigerator hummed. Mister Cat, the cookie jar, sat on top of it, with his orange-and-white striped tummy full of oatmeal cookies. Fay made those cookies yesterday. The faucet dripped into the sink, Mama had been trying for days to get the plumber to come, and outside it was raining cats and dogs, beyond the blue-and-white figured curtains with the pattern of little houses on them, little red-roofed and yellow-roofed houses hundreds of them with smoke coming out the chimneys. The houses had blue front doors. Smoke hung in blue waves above the polished tabletop, her daddy must be home. But where were they?

"Mama?" Sybill said. The blue china clock on the wall chimed out but Sybill had not yet learned to tell time. About the clock, she would mainly remember the smiling face of the sun at the center of time and she would not remember at all what happened next. She heard a sound like a pig grunting, and a voice crying out which abruptly ceased. These noises came from outside, from the porch, beyond the cold-pantry. Sybill walked carefully across the yellow linoleum, sniffing the smoke from Daddy's pipe. It had a sweet smell to it, a kind of richness. She could smell the other smell, too, the way his breath was. *Liquor! Mama said.* "Mama?" Sybill said, and again she heard the sound like a grunt, like an "oof" noise in the funny-papers. *Oof! Ugh! Glunk!* Like little animals in the funny-paper, talking out loud. "Mama?" Sybill was not afraid. She opened the back door, slowly turning the cool white porcelain knob. She walked across the cold-pantry and opened the outside door. Air came blowing in cold, all around her. Freezing rain whipped across the wood planks of the porch. *Winter thunderstorm brings bad luck, Nettie says.* The cold March wind pushed and pushed, shutting the door behind her. Sybill put her hand to her eyes, and tried to look out in the yard. It was a night like nothing she had ever seen, a solid blackness swept by blasts of cold, by stinging freezing rain, drumming loudly on the tin roof, making it hard to hear or think: she couldn't see. *Boom! Oof! Thunk!* The thunder came then, rolling long and slow like a horrible horrible train, and then the lightning.

Then Sybill saw the figure out in the yard, with the long-handled ax upraised, and saw her bring it down again and again into the man who lay on the hillside in the streaming rain, the washing mud. Sybill saw everything: his face and hair all red with blood, the blood running down into the steep muddy yard, his black hat where it lay in the pouring rain, all that blood. *Thunk! Splat!* Sybill was so cold. She stood and saw when the lightning flashed but the storm was going away by then, the flashes fewer, shorter, the thunder a disgruntled kind of grumbling in the big black sky. Then they were together like some kind of enormous animal moving across the yard, moving across the rainswept hillside, toward the well. Sybill saw the red-shingled roof of the well in the flash of light, the rusty dipper dangling from the rope, the huge dark creature creeping through the rain. Then Sybil reached back and opened the cold-pantry door. She walked through it and into the kitchen, shutting the kitchen door behind her, and across the yellow kitchen floor and into the hall. She walked through the dark hall past the dining room and the parlor and across the flowered rug and then up the stairs, sliding her hand along the banister. Sybill was very, very cold. She walked into her room and took off her robe and her fuzzy slippers and put them back into the closet, shutting the door. Then Sybill got back into bed, pulling Molly to her, and closed her eyes and immediately slept, her face tight against Molly's smooth china cheek.

Sybill blinks, so slowly she can feel her eyelids open and shut like heavy garage doors. Sybill feels old, old: it's the Change of Life, for sure. She feels old, and sad, and sick. She doesn't feel like crying, though: a person has a duty in this world. So it was right, all along, that voice inside her that said, "Sybill honey, don't do it! Don't spill the beans!" *Lord*. Whoever thought it would be anything like this, though, anything like her own mother killing her own father, and all those years ago? Let's see, it must have been about 1940, because Mother married Verner Hess in 1942, although she never really loved him. Mother really loved Jewell Rife, who disappeared, but Verner Hess loved Mother. And so does Sybill, of course, or maybe she really hates her. Who knows what else is down there, after all? Sybill wishes she'd never let Bob step one foot down in her subconscious. She wishes she'd never come here. Sybill shakes her head to clear it, which she can't. It seems to be full of smoke, or fog, but at least there are no lights to tell the beginnings of headache. Sybill realizes to her surprise that Bob, the hypnotist, is holding her hand between his two pudgy white ones. Bob presses her hand.

"My dear Sybill," he says. But Sybill hates him! He looks like a crazy Kung Fu in that tacky black rumpled shirt, blinking his eyes behind the thick pink glasses. Probably his wife is just a sight.

"Betty'll have a fit," Sybill says. "It serves her right."

"I think you should proceed very slowly in terms of what you envision doing next," Bob says. "It's a far-from-foolproof process we have here, you know. The reason I directed you to recapture the experience through dream is so that you would repeat it aloud upon awakening, as you did, so that I would not be the only one of us who heard the explanation."

"I wish I'd never heard it," Sybill says.

"Well, I'm certain that's true, but there's a wide margin of error here, we must remember, in any of these interpretations. It's possible, you see, that you have simply repeated for me your worst fear, an early traumatizing fantasy." Bob releases Sybill's hand and sits back in his chair. Outside, Sybill sees that the drizzle has stopped and a pale wash of sunlight lies over everything. Beyond the roses, down the street, Bob's mailman moves like a robot from house to house.

Sybill thinks of her mother, leading the Elizabeth Nolting Parsons Study Group, writing poetry, planning the guest list for Myrtle's wedding, dusting the figurines, embroidering an altar cloth for the Episcopal church, rolling out tiny balls of dough for cloverleaf rolls. "I remember the whole thing," Sybill says. She knows it's always the one you least suspect. *I love my mother*, she thinks.

Bob clears his throat. "Sybill," he says, "I really feel . . ."

But Sybill has stood right up and now she's brushing off her skirt with that characteristic gesture she makes whenever she stands, a getting-down-to-business movement of the hands. "Listen, Bob," she says, "thanks a lot. I hope my headaches go away but whether they do or not, I'll have to get to the bottom of this." Then Sybill remembers something else, something perfectly dreadful: soon after that night, she took the long black flashlight from the high hook in the toolshed and shone it down the well. She remembers seeing her father's face there just for a minute, beneath the shiny black water. She saw his high pale forehead, his open eye. And not so long after that, the well was boarded up, and then cemented, as it has been ever since. Grass grows now where it used to be, on the mountainside behind her mother's house. "I guess I'll go home," she says. By "home," Sybill means Booker Creek instead of The Oaks.

"I would urge you to . . . " Bob begins, but Sybill brushes past him, toward the sliding glass door and the real outside. She's had enough of her subconscious, to say the least! Sybill is furious at Bob now, at her mother, at Betty, at everybody. She has a vision of Edward Bing, upended among these roses. Sybill slides the door shut behind her. Striding briskly down the hypnotist's sidewalk through the sweet moist air so heavy with roses and rain, Sybill sighs heavily, jingling her car keys.

MYRTLE is tired of going to parties where people ask, "What do you *do*?" She has noticed that this happens more and more lately, especially with the crowd from the new Racquet Club which they have just recently joined. As if you're bound to "do" something, like it's not all right anymore to be a homemaker. Nobody *used* to ask that. Myrtle says, "Oh, Don and the kids keep me so busy," and just lets it go at that. Sometimes she says she's thinking about getting a real-estate license. She doesn't believe in making a big deal of anything in public. She refuses to make a spectacle of herself. But Myrtle typed her fingers to the bone putting Don through medical school, and she's not about to do *that* again! The only degree she ever wanted was her "MRS," and she's got it, and that's good enough for her. As she told Lacy, their three children are her "PHD." Childhood sweethearts, Myrtle and Don married when they were still in college, sophomore year, and she dropped out then, and it's been hard work and happiness ever since. Myrtle has often thought that love is not easy. Children are not easy either. But she has never regretted a thing. Myrtle considers that she and Don have a marriage made in heaven, but that is also because they work at it. She doesn't mean simply the Couples Communication Course they took at the community college last year, either. She means *constantly*.

And Myrtle feels that it's impossible to maintain the quality of a marriage, over the long haul, with both people out there "fulfilling themselves" all the time. As soon as the woman goes out and gets a job, the quality of life goes down. She's seen it happen again and again. Of course there may be more *money*, but that soon goes for clothes and fast foods and day care, and you lose out on those moments you cherish—anyway, the money isn't the point. And she doesn't mean women who *have* to work, either, more power to them, she means women who simply *choose* to. You just can't do everything, is all Myrtle has to say, although she has many friends who work and of course she'd never dream of saying it to their face. It's up to the individual. Myrtle can only speak for herself. She knows she's lucky that Don is so smart and has done so well. On the other hand, she wouldn't have married anybody who *didn't* have those qualities, the potential for success. As Don says, that's what it's all about. There's nothing wrong with money. There's nothing wrong with wanting to be successful in your job or in your marriage either one. But if you want a successful marriage, you've got to *work* for it.

You can't afford to get fat, for instance, or let yourself go. You have to throw out your old lingerie and have sex in the afternoon. In general you've got to work to keep that spark alive between the two of you. Because the pressures of life are immense, and they'll put it right out, if you're not careful. Of course Myrtle doesn't serve dinner topless or meet Don at the door wrapped in Saran Wrap, as suggested by the woman who wrote that book. But she does try to have a really nice dinner ready for him every night when he comes home from the office, for instance, and she makes sure she's looking her best. Don has a right to *expect* that. And sometimes she'll have a little surprise for him, like the night Sean went on the ski trip with the church and she had a little picnic all fixed up for them to eat in the living room, on the rug in front of the fire. Those times are precious. "Occasions" are important.

And speaking of "occasions," it was the day before Myrtle's birthday when everything started to happen. But that's not quite right, either. That's when her mother had the first major stroke. Things had started to happen about a year before that, *in spite of everything she knows and thinks and feels*—because somehow Myrtle is able to hold two opposite things in her mind at the same time. She loves her husband, Dr. Don Dotson, the dermatologist, *with all her heart,* and they have three lovely children nearly grown, and one of the few truly successful marriages of the eighties. Don is not only her husband, he's her best friend. They share everything—their hopes, fears, plans, a laugh or two. But it's also true that Myrtle has days when she feels like her whole life is a function of other people's, and it's also true that her children have turned into problem children. Karen, the oldest, is a longhaired countercultural type who is majoring in folklore and living with her boyfriend, a computer whiz. Myrtle just can't *see* it—Karen, who used to be so cute. When Karen *does* come home, which is seldom, she's hard to talk to. It's like a wall has grown up between her and Myrtle. Karen really doesn't listen to anything her mother has to say, she stares out the window, and nibbles her lip. She doesn't want to go shopping. Theresa, the middle one, is even worse. She's come home from college this summer saying she won't go back, that she has no intention of it, that college "sucks." Theresa has announced that she plans to be a writer, for which she needs not classes but real life. Everything is ironic, Theresa says. And Sean, at fourteen, is the most incomprehensible of all—he's so angry, but no one knows why.

And it's also true that Myrtle has a lover.

She can't explain this at all.

Her lover's name is Gary Vance. He lives in a rented three-room cinderblock house south of town, toward the county line. Gary is an exterminator.

Myrtle was driving out there to break up with him when she saw the sign. It said LORDY LORDY MYRTLE IS 40! This was the day (June 1) before her birthday (June 2). This sign was up on the billboard which Clinus had put out in front of the One Stop, which is owned by Myrtle's aunt Nettie and which she has to drive past twice every time she goes out there to visit Gary Vance. Clinus is her aunt Nettie's second husband's retarded son. Although retarded, he's done just fine—he has an antique and junk business on the side—*literally* on the side of the One Stop, in a sort of lean-to he's rigged up. Myrtle heard he got his billboard in a liquidation sale. She's not even so sure he's retarded. At any rate, it's the kind of billboard where you can change the letters on it, like a theater sign. Sometimes Clinus does real well with it and other times his messages don't make sense, such as A STICK IN TIME, for instance. Mostly it's HAVE A GOOD DAY or SMILE. Myrtle sees them all, driving back and forth from Gary's house. Clinus gets her tickled, always has. Mother wouldn't let them have a thing to do with him, of course, growing up, or with Nettie or Fay either, for that matter. But Myrtle thinks they're all harmless. Don has always said that Myrtle's mother is anal retentive and lives in a fantasy world, which is neither here nor there. Don and Myrtle both think Clinus's messages are funny.

Or at least she *did*, until LORDY LORDY MYRTLE IS 40! showed up. How did Clinus *know*, anyway? Retarded people always know more than you think. She did not want Gary to see that sign whether she was breaking up with him or not. She did not want *anybody* to see it. Because it's true that if you don't look your age, which Myrtle doesn't, you don't want it broadcast around. And she has worked *hard* on herself. People simply cannot believe that she has a daughter twenty-two years old, or Theresa who is eighteen, or Sean, fourteen. They can't believe she's had three children at all. She's weighed one twenty-two for twenty years. So she was *furious* when she saw that message on Clinus's billboard. On the other hand, she didn't have time to stop.

Myrtle had been thinking, herself, about turning forty, and she had come to some conclusions. The main one was that she would break up with Gary as soon as she got to his house. They had broken up before, several times. Myrtle doesn't understand how she ever got into it, anyway. Of course she was practically a baby when she and Don got married, but that's no excuse. Childhood didn't last until twenty-five like it does now. And she knew exactly what she was doing. Still, they were very young. Myrtle had children herself when she was her own children's age. She was just a baby—Gary's just a baby now.

Myrtle and Don grew up together, as Don says. "We're still growing—" Don says this, too, to everybody. Don believes in lifelong growth, in constant flux and change. Myrtle knows she's lucky. She knows that's right.

But about a year ago, Myrtle began to feel that she had stopped growing along with him. Something happened—she couldn't pay attention anymore. She found herself just sitting in the family room, for instance, for hours. Or she'd come out of the Piggly Wiggly with her groceries and not have the foggiest notion in the world where she'd parked the car. She kept watching Dan Rather every night with Don, but she couldn't understand the news. Lebanon for instance did not make sense. She really started noticing the cellulite on her thighs, she got tired of cooking everything she knew how to cook. She locked herself out of the house five times in two months, which she had never done before in her whole life. Nothing was *wrong*, exactly, but she began to feel like she was missing out—on what, she couldn't have told you.

Of course Myrtle had missed the sixties entirely, while she was having babies. She used to hear the Beatles on the radio, that was about it. When she wasn't having babies, she was typing. She typed her way through the late sixties and early seventies. She never took part in a demonstration, or went to a big rock concert. She never knew anything that happened until she read about it in *Time*. She watched Vietnam and Watergate on TV, of course. But she never bought a pair of blue jeans before she was thirty. So she missed the whole thing. Then throughout the seventies, she cooked dinner, folded clothes, handed out pencils in her kids' classrooms for standardized tests, chaperoned busloads of fourth-graders on field trips to Natural Bridge, drove Karen and Theresa to ballet. Those things are important. And Myrtle and Don were growing up together. When they were first married, for instance, Myrtle used the *Better Homes and Gardens* cookbook, then she used the Fanny Farmer cookbook, and then she used Julia Child. Myrtle started off with lemon chess pie and moved to quiche. Plus she was happy—she had what she wanted, and she'd never wanted the moon.

Don finished medical school, then interned in Richmond, and then they moved back home for him to set up his own practice even though several people warned him against Booker Creek as a permanent location. "Listen, people have acne *everywhere*," Don said then. As usual, he was right. People come from miles and miles around to see him—he's the only dermatologist in this area.

But Myrtle is thinking about herself, about this feeling she got—or maybe she lost—last year.

For one thing, that's when gravity set in. Myrtle realizes that gravity has always been around, but she never noticed it until she was thirty-nine. Then right along her chinline, at either side of her mouth, something started to droop. Her breasts changed shape, hung lower. And her buttocks—which is probably what bothered her most, since Don is a self-professed "ass man"—really started to sag. Plus they had to have a new deck built on the house—the old one was just simply falling in. Anyway, gravity showed up, or at least Myrtle became aware of it. Once you become aware of something, you see signs of it everywhere.

The strangest thing about all of this is that Don didn't notice a thing. Nothing! He didn't notice her cellulite or the way she kept losing the keys. Their intimacy remained unchanged, remained, in its way, *total*, or perhaps it simply remained as total as it ever was. It made Myrtle wonder if all of it might—or might not—be simply *made up*. It made her wonder how anybody ever knows whether *anything* really happens, and if so, what it is, after all. Anyway, the intimacy remained.

One quality which Don has always had and which Myrtle has always loved is a kind of *paying attention*—it's the way he looks at you, how he cocks his head to one side, how he really listens to what you say. She's known Don since he was eleven years old, and he was already doing it then. Sometimes this quality makes her nervous, if she doesn't have much to say. But it's also one of the things she likes best about him, and she's sure other people do too. Sometimes Myrtle imagines Don at work, wearing his white lab coat, with his blond head cocked just that way, listening to one of his patients. It makes her jealous, it makes her wonder—anyway, Don continued to pay attention. Only he missed it all.

The deck fell in, and Myrtle got a new one, and during the course of all this, she called the exterminator to have it treated. The exterminator who came was Gary.

That old song "Breaking Up Is Hard to Do" was running through Myrtle's head when she pulled into Gary's front yard. His yard is not a yard at all, it's a junk heap. No grass—parts of cars, machines, and God knows what all just strewn around in the weeds. He said it was like this when he moved in, and he hasn't fixed up a thing. Gary's house is made out of concrete blocks, painted aqua. Then Myrtle thought of another song, "50 Ways to Leave Your Lover," which has lines like "Go out the back, Jack" and "Get a new plan, Stan." But Myrtle couldn't remember any more of the words. It made her feel sad to remember that back before she got married and started missing out on things, back in junior high and high school when she and Don were going steady, she was real popular and knew all the words to all the songs. Myrtle has always been popular, but that was the only time in her life that she ever knew all the words. Now she doesn't even know who the groups are. She parked her Toyota in a cloud of dust in front of Gary's house, next to his company car which has a large iron bug, orange, on top of it, and opened her car door, and the heat hit her like a sledgehammer.

This is one of the things Myrtle will always remember about going there, how hot it is in summer, how cold in winter, at Gary's house. Her own house has central heating and air, so she isn't used to these drastic changes. She isn't used to perspiring or shivering, since she never does either one of those things at home. Now Myrtle could feel the perspiration start to bead on her upper lip, she could feel her scalp beginning to prickle. Myrtle opened the torn screen door.

"Hello?" she called, and Gary said, "Come on in."

An armchair in Gary's living room has a broken leg which he has fixed by putting an upside-down saucepan under it. This is the best chair he owns. There's nothing in his refrigerator, ever, except beer and bean dip. He goes out to the 7-Eleven for everything, even coffee. That's what Gary's house is like. His brother used to live there too, before he moved in with his girlfriend. Every time they have a fight he comes back, and then they make up and he moves out again. Myrtle has never met him.

"I tried to call you, honey," Gary said, coming to

stand in the bedroom door. "I've got a job at two, we'll have to make it snappy."

"No problem." Myrtle stood there holding her purse. "I've been thinking, Gary," she said, "and I think it's about time for this to be over with, anyway."

"Come here, Myrtle," Gary said. She went over to him and put her arms around him and laid her head on his chest—he was barefooted, barechested, wearing blue jeans—and they stood there that way in the door. It must have been ninety degrees. Gary is slight, probably weighs one fifty or so, really just a boy. He's twenty-six. He has wispy brown hair which comes down below his ears, and a mustache, and a beard. Brown eyes which never look quite at you, a face you'd never notice in a crowd. Often Myrtle has trouble remembering what he looks like. That has always puzzled her. It has also puzzled her what in the world Gary's up to. He has no ambitions at all, that she can see. He works, goes to movies, drinks a lot of beer, and smokes marijuana. He does not seem to want to get ahead in the world. Sometimes he wears clothes which tear her heart out; when he's wearing them, Myrtle would not be caught dead with him. Blue jeans so old they're soft and sort of gray, fishnet T-shirts, running shoes she'd give to Goodwill. Of course Myrtle would not be caught dead with Gary anyway.

She has been with Gary Vance there in his house, on the bed and on the filthy floor. She has been with him out back of his house in the pine woods, and at the EconoLodge in Martinsville, Virginia, and in her own bed in her own house, she's ashamed of that. Myrtle has been with Gary Vance too many times to count, over too many months.

He ran his hands through her hair and lifted it up off her neck. "Whatever you want to do," he said.

Gary is always "laid back."

Myrtle went to bed with him in that heat, not meaning to but knowing it would be the last time, and then she showered and dressed quickly and watched while Gary put on his pest-control suit. She was crying. It was the suit he wears for major industrial jobs. It's white, made of heavy treated material that looks like linen. It flows out all around him when he walks, so that he looks like a cross between an Arab and an astronaut. When he puts on the hood, he really looks like an astronaut. Gary zipped his suit up and put the hood under his arm. He came over to Myrtle and kissed her on the cheek. "Call me if you want to," he said.

Myrtle always had the feeling that Gary had had lots of lovers, but he wouldn't talk about that. He didn't talk about much, in fact. A skinny boy with no knack for conversation, a boy whose face you couldn't recall. "If you want me, call me," Gary said. Myrtle watched him walk out to his car, looking larger than life in his spacesuit, she heard the CB radio crackling, the central office telling him where to go. Myrtle was crying when he pulled out, with that bug attached to the top of his car. It's a termite. Then she fixed her makeup, the best she could in that heat, and left. The air conditioning in her Toyota felt like heaven all the way home. She even managed to smile when she passed the One Stop, but really she felt like hell.

And Don was waiting for her in the foyer, looking serious.

He knows, Myrtle thought right away. Her knees were shaking.

"Myrtle—" Don took her hand. She wondered if he could smell it on her in spite of the shower. Usually she wears Estée Lauder, but she didn't have any with her. She was absolutely sure he knew.

"Myrtle, your mother has had a stroke," Don said. "Candy called here, and couldn't get you, and called me at work. They've taken her to Memorial Hospital." He hesitated—Don has the perfect, caring kind of face to break bad news. "It's serious," he said. "I'll drive you over right now."

"What about Sean—" Myrtle started.

"I left a message for him at school. Since Theresa's at the lake, I thought he could go over to Louise's" —that's Don's sister, who Sean hates—"for supper. He can stay until we get back."

"If he will," Myrtle said. You can't make Sean do anything he doesn't want to do. Myrtle wondered if he'd even go to Louise's. Probably not.

"If he will," Don repeated, smiling at her. They understood each other so completely. They always know, for instance, exactly what they mean about the children. Of course, taking the Parent Effectiveness Training class helped. "Come on, Myrtle," Don said. She loved him then so much! They stood in the foyer and Myrtle could see them both in the gold-leaf mirror. Don looks something like George Peppard. In high school, they were "Cutest Couple" twice, both junior and senior year. Don took Myrtle's arm and led her back out to the double garage and sat her down in the passenger side of the new BMW, which he drives. "Candy says your mother isn't conscious," Don said. They made the ten-minute drive in silence and it wasn't until they had parked the car in the Visitor lot and were walking through the revolving door that Myrtle thought, *This is my mother. My mother has had a stroke.*

By the time Myrtle and Don arrived, Miss Elizabeth was already settled in Intensive Care—in a way, Myrtle thought suddenly, Mother has been in Intensive Care for years. She's always been so concerned about her health. And now there was something *really* wrong, and she wasn't even able to make the best of it. It didn't seem fair. And she would have been embarrassed to see herself like that, and to be *seen* like that, by strangers—they had two IVs going, a nurse was checking her pulse, another nurse was writing something on a chart. Myrtle went to her side while Don stayed in the hall to talk to the doctors.

Miss Elizabeth's hair was all puffed out like pale blue cotton candy around her still, waxy face. Actually her face, without the makeup and the glasses, looked young and smooth and almost—strangely— carefree. It gave Myrtle a start. But her color was peculiar, a yellowish shade something like candles or magnolia blossoms. Myrtle had never seen her before without rouge. She was also surprised to see that her mother looked so *small*. One arm lay outside the oxygen tent, palm up on the tight white hospital sheet. She took her mother's hand, uncurling the wrinkled, papery fingers. This gave Myrtle the creeps! They had taken off all her rings. Myrtle couldn't get over her wrist being so small, so frail, her fingers so bony. She had always thought of her mother as a large woman, not so large as Fay perhaps, but a *large woman*—she couldn't get over seeing her without her earrings, her stockings, her gloves. Myrtle thought of how ashamed Mother would be, exposed like this. How embarrassed. Myrtle sat still and looked down at her mother's still face and couldn't help it that some part of her was, and she hated to admit it, *gloating*— because she gave me a time, Myrtle thought, she really did, she gave all of us a time except for Sybill. No matter how good we were, it was never good enough. Don, even though he was the quarterback, was not good enough for me to marry because he was an orphan. . . . A part of Myrtle was gloating, to see her mother so helpless. Another part of her was about to burst into tears. She felt like she was strangling on that one word "Mother!" in her throat. She knew if she said it, her mother couldn't hear. Myrtle had "mixed emotions," as she said later to Don. It was so horrible, yet so fitting, that Miss Elizabeth was there under that oxygen tent, where Myrtle could see but not *touch* her. As if she would have wanted to be touched.

Candy came in then looking like a nurse herself in her white uniform. But she's *not* a nurse, she's a beautician. Actually she doesn't look like *that,* either— everything Candy wears looks exactly the same, like something she just threw on temporarily to run to the post office, not like anything you'd plan to wear all day. Myrtle has always found this strange, since beauty is Candy's business. And she's good at it. Everybody in town goes to Candy. But you'd never guess it, to look at her! Candy is two years older than Myrtle and looks ten. Isn't it funny for a beautician to let herself go that way, to neglect her own looks? But Candy just doesn't care. She's always been like that, too—she wouldn't do her homework, either. Mother would get so mad. Mother was *always* mad at Candy. She didn't even speak to her for several years, from the time Candy eloped with Lonnie Snipes until the time he was killed in Vietnam. Mother felt sorry for her then, or had to act like she did, since the whole town was upset about it, with Candy pregnant and everything, but after Candy had the second baby and didn't mention whose it was, Mother pretty much gave up on her. Myrtle was embarrassed too, or she would have been, if Don hadn't pointed out that nobody expects you to be responsible for what your family does: "You can pick your friends but you can't pick your relatives," Don said. And this is true. It's a mystery how well those kids of Candy's have turned out, anyway. They've both gone to school on scholarships—Tammy Lee's an art teacher somewhere, and Tony's in law school in Florida. It makes you wonder. Because in Myrtle's opinion, Candy was just a terrible mother—all those kids ever did was play downtown on the sidewalk while she was doing hair. They never had any advantages to speak of. They raised themselves.

Anyway Candy came running in, short of breath—she looks like she's always running. She went right over to the oxygen tent and sat down in the chair and took Miss Elizabeth's limp hand, pressing it.

"Lord, she looks just awful," Candy said.

Myrtle knew that Mother wouldn't want Candy to hold her hand, any more (less, in fact) than she would want Myrtle to. Myrtle couldn't believe Candy would *want* to, either, after all that had passed between them. Candy's like that, however. Myrtle and Don don't see her socially, but she has good intentions and a big heart. She has never seemed a bit jealous of their success, for instance.

Don came in then with the doctors, Dr. Grissom and Dr. Grey, who is a member of the Racquet Club, too. Don put one hand on Candy's shoulder, his other arm around Myrtle's waist. Thank God she happened to look halfway decent. She was wearing her pale pink sleeveless blouse from Talbots, her matching rose skirt, the belt with the gold turtle buckle, and espadrilles. When Theresa accuses her mother of looking "preppy," Myrtle says she considers that a compliment. There's nothing wrong with being well dressed.

Candy looked at Dr. Grissom. "What do you think?" she asked.

Dr. Grissom is northern, cut and dry.

"I'm afraid the prognosis is the same one we gave you earlier," he said. "The CAT scan shows that your mother has suffered a cerebral hemorrhage severe enough to cause unconsciousness. Sometimes people regain consciousness and sometimes they do not."

"Can't you do *anything*?" Candy asked.

Dr. Grissom looked down at his clipboard, then back up at them. "In the case of a stroke," he said, "surgery is not indicated, so there's not much that we can do in terms of intervention. I'm sorry. It's hard to predict how things will go. Usually, as I said, there will have been premonitory symptoms—dizziness, numbness of the side involved, clumsiness, sometimes a blurring of vision."

Candy's whole face crumpled up. "When she was in the shop last Tuesday, she spilled a whole cup of coffee, and said that her wrist was weak, she thought she might have sprained it."

"There you go," said Dr. Grey.

Myrtle remembered other things—Mother's attention wandering, recently, while they were talking, the way she hesitated so long at the top of the stairs. "But she never complained," Myrtle said. "She never said a word."

"Well, Myrtle," Don said, "she wouldn't, you know."
As usual, he was right.

"For now," Dr. Grissom said, "it's just a matter of
watching and waiting."

The electronic lines of the EEG went up and down
again and again, a series of peaks and valleys, a
series of waves. Myrtle remembered when Mother
and Daddy took them to Virginia Beach and Daddy
got so sunburned, leading them one by one out into
the deep water. Verner Hess was small, red-headed,
fair-skinned. All he ever wanted to do was work—it
was like pulling teeth to get him to take a vacation,
but once he did, he went at it the same way he went
at the dimestore. He did everything too much. He
worked too hard. It has occurred to Myrtle that she
may have married Don because he's that same way,
because he has that same kind of "stick-to-it-iveness."
She remembered sitting in the sand at Virginia Beach
where the waves broke, sitting there until her bathing suit bottom filled up with sand, and building a
sand castle with Candy, and pushing Lacy's carriage.
Miss Elizabeth sat under the beach umbrella, wearing a white eyelet dress with puff sleeves. She studied the horizon. The heat made her feel faint, she
said. She went up to the green-shuttered hotel to lie
down, leaving Sybill in charge. Sybill was always in
charge. Myrtle remembered how sunburned she got
at the tops of her legs then, and how the Noxema
smelled. For some reason this, the smell of the Noxema
or the way she remembered it, and the way she
remembered the waves, made her cry. Mother is probably dying. They'll have to call Sybill and Arthur and
Lacy.

"Now honey," Candy said, hugging Myrtle. Candy

was soft, smelling like permanent-wave solution. She must have come straight from her beauty shop.

Dr. Grissom and Dr. Grey made little sounds in their throats, and left.

"Do you remember how we made pipecleaner dolls that time with those angel shells at Virginia Beach? We used their shells for skirts?" Myrtle's voice went up higher and higher. Mother, yellow beneath the oxygen tent, barely seemed to breathe. The lines across the EEG went up and down. In Myrtle's mind she saw Gary Vance walking across his junky yard in his big white suit.

"I'll stay here tonight," Candy said. Candy was speaking to Don. "If you all can call everybody up and get somebody to come over here in the morning." Candy speaking to Don like that, or maybe it was just being at the hospital, reminded Myrtle of what it was like when the children were born. They knocked her out with the first two (twilight sleep) and gave her a spinal with Sean, even though Don was all for natural childbirth which was "in" by then. "It's not *your body*," Myrtle said to him at the time. She wouldn't do it. But somehow, since Mother had had a stroke, Myrtle wished she *had*, she even wished she had felt all that pain. LORDY LORDY MYRTLE IS 40! she thought. But at least she doesn't look it.

Candy hugged her again. Then Candy pulled her back a little and looked at her hair.

"We need to touch up those roots," Candy said.

It was nearly dark when Don and Myrtle finally left the hospital. They stopped for a Hardees on the bypass. A thunderstorm had come and gone—you could still smell the ozone in the air. All the lights were off in Miss Elizabeth's house on the hill, Myrtle mentioned to Don as they passed it, and Don reminded her that Candy said she had already been up there and paid Mrs. Dwight and sent her home and locked up. Myrtle kept feeling like her life had happened to somebody else. Mother's house looked so small, up at the end of that long stone walk lined with boxwoods, looking down on the whole town. Myrtle used to think it was the biggest, most imposing house in the world. And now she and Don have their own white colonial in Argonne Hills, with thirty-eight hundred square feet, about double Mother's.

Sean was not at home. Don called Louise, who hadn't seen him. Then Don poured them each a glass of white wine. They like Principato. Myrtle tried to reach Theresa at the lake. Then she gave up on that and called Karen, whose computer boyfriend answered, and left a message. Karen says he's a genius. Then Myrtle called Lacy, who said she'd come right away, and Sybill, who wasn't home. She called Nettie and Arthur. "*Oh Jesus,*" Arthur said. Myrtle could tell he'd been drinking. Sean came in and refused to tell Don where he had been. Don treats adolescents all day long and establishes the best rapport. Sean just breaks their hearts. Myrtle was sipping her wine and dialing again when the doorbell rang.

Don went to the door and there was Sybill, all dressed up as usual—but tonight, she had a wild hard grim look about her.

Sybill looked exactly the way Myrtle felt.

"How did you know?" Myrtle asked.

"*Know what?*" asked Sybill.

I hate all this active-listening shit. Ever since they learned it last year in that class, you can't have a decent conversation with them. If you ever could. But now I mean you come home from school really pissed about something, I mean really pissed, and they say something like, "Gee, son, you're very angry!" and then if you say "Well yes, I am pretty goddamn angry" they say "Yes! Yes, you *are!* I can tell you're angry!" and *that's it.* Then they smile a big faggy smile and go off whistling or something, and you feel like shit. You feel worse than you did before. There must be some other part to it, some part they didn't learn or the class didn't get to, like in History the way they never finish the book.

The thing that really drives me crazy is how everything around here is so perfect and how they're so nice. They're just so goddamn understanding all the time. I mean if you leave a glass someplace, anyplace in the house, it gets automatically picked up like suction, and they're always going around asking you what your *feelings* are. Theresa and Karen were lucky. They got out of here before everybody got so rich and understanding.

Take my room. They say it's *your room,* right? They say you can do whatever you want in here, you can play your music as loud as you want, whatever. It's your room. We won't go in. But then she always does. She goes in and she's all disappointed and she says Oh honey, you'll make yourself sick it's so dirty, you've got to clean it up right away. So you say okay, and you *will,* but if you don't do it *right that minute,* like if you've got something else you have to do right then, when you come back she's gone in there and done it, she's been all in your private things, so you get pissed, and then she's all apologetic, and then she gets pissed too. You can't get any privacy around here. I'd say this is one of the biggest houses in town and you still can't get any fucking privacy. In your room or in your head. They want to know what you're thinking all the time. What you're *feeling.* I'll tell you, it's not like I'm feeling anything particular, if everybody would quit asking me about it. It's not like I go anyplace either.

Like that night, all I did was ride over where they're building that new office park, they've got an unloading ramp there that's real good, it's almost like a quarter pipe. I ride an aluminum frame PK Ripper with Red Line cranks. Dad says he's glad to spring for it, right, but then he goes into all this shit about being an orphan. So anyway I was riding up and down this ramp when the wind came up and the sky started getting purple. I love that. Anyway I could see all this terrific-looking sky through the two-by-fours, they have the building all blocked out against the sky. So I started riding up and down it faster and faster and when the rain hit, then I got under the edge of this place where they keep some tools and shit. Then I went by Jimmy Norton's trailer on the way home. Jimmy's a guy I used to go to school with before they sent me to the Academy. Jimmy and his little brother were just sitting in there eating white bread out of the loaf and watching a rerun of "Six Million Dollar Man" on TV. They crack me up. So I stayed over there a while and then I went home and got a lot of shit from Dad for *nothing*.

But I have to admit that the rest of the night was pretty interesting. Dad was sipping on his faggy white wine but you could tell he was upset, and Mom was on the telephone. Grandmother had had a stroke, that was the big deal. The old bat. If you think it's something over here, you ought to go over to *her* house, which is what they force you to do every Sunday afternoon. I hate it when people get all faggy and old and forgetful and they tell you how much you've grown and ask you the same thing about twenty times. They can't help it, probably, but you don't want to be around it. They start doing it early too, like when they're in their thirties. Mom and Dad do it all the time. Anyway that was it, and Mom was calling the whole family on the phone. Dad was giving me some shit for a while but then he kind of quit, you could tell he had his mind on other things. I went up and put on *Synchronicity* but then when I heard them yelling, I came back down.

My aunt Sybill was there. She doesn't like kids, so normally I disappear whenever she comes around. She's never had any kids herself, never been married either. She's a real faggy old bat whose best quality is, she lives pretty far away.

Anyway, this was old Sybill's big night. I was trying

to sneak my ass just quietly down the hall to watch TV in the den when I heard them all yelling. I *froze*. It made me think of that poem, Chicken Little. Sometimes I think of the weirdest things. But the shit was falling all over the place, man, right out of the fucking sky. It was awesome.

What Aunt Sybill said was that she had driven over here to ask Grandmother some very important questions, and that she just couldn't believe Grandmother had gone into a coma before she had a chance to do it.

"Questions about what?" Mom asked.

"Never you mind," said Aunt Sybill.

"Oh honestly, Sybill," Mom said. "What?"

"Just something about Jewell Rife," Aunt Sybill said, and they went on and on, Mom saying well what is it, and Aunt Sybill not ever coming right out and saying what she meant. Me, I never even heard about this Jewell Rife before, who turned out to be some first husband of Grandmother's back in the dark ages. I figured it was just about time for Aunt Sybill to hit the loony bin. She probably went out of her mind from horniness after all these years.

"Sybill, you're being ridiculous," Mom says. "If you have something to say, say it."

"Never you mind, Myrtle," Aunt Sybill says.

"Don't be afraid to say what you feel," Dad said. "Whatever it is. You're only harming yourself by keeping your feelings to yourself, Sybill."

"Oh, just forget it," Aunt Sybill said.

"Here she is, dying, and you come up with *this!*" Mom says. She gulped in her breath the way she does when she starts to cry. "I have to say, Sybill, it's just like you, to make as much trouble as possible for all concerned." Then Mom started crying.

"You *would* say that," Aunt Sybill said. "You want everything to go your way."

"Now let's not let this get out of perspective," Dad said. "We're all upset. Sybill, whatever the problem is, I'm sure Miss Elizabeth can answer your questions when she recovers. I'm sorry you won't share your problem with Myrtle and me. But let's get our priorities straight here. Miss Elizabeth is, as we have been trying to convey to you, gravely ill. Jim Grissom says he suspects she may have had a whole series of small strokes which have gone undetected over the last few years. So let's deal with first things first." Dad was using his Charlton-Heston-playing-God voice which I hate. He was rattled, though. He sat down in a chair and then he got back up. Mom and Aunt Sybill were standing in the middle of the living room. For the first time I noticed they look alike.

"I'll tell you, Myrtle, I don't want to hurt your feelings, but Mother is the only one I can talk to," Aunt Sybill said.

"Uh, oh," Mom said suddenly, in that voice which means she knows I'm listening. "Little pitchers . . ."

Jesus.

"What, Myrtle?" Sybill said.

"Little pitchers . . ." Mom said again. See, she never will just come out and *say* whatever she wants to say. It's like pulling teeth. She says everything else, see, and you're just supposed to sort of guess what's really on her mind. Unless it's something totally obvious and then she says it five or six times. She really does live in the dark ages. Nobody else in the world would have said "little pitchers," right?

I was moving out of there fast, on my way down the hall, when Dad put his hand on my shoulder.

"Son, this is a family matter," he said, meaning

59

don't spread this shit all over school. But I'm cool, I *know* that. Who wants to talk about their sick grandmother and their crazy aunt Sybill at *school*? It also pisses me off the way he calls me "son" whenever any big deal comes up, like I'm some generic son in the grocery store. I'm the only son he's got. Of course my real name, Sean, is faggy. If I could have any name in the world I wanted, it'd be Rick. Ricks are cool. Anyway I said I wouldn't say anything and Dad said, get this, "Mum's the word." I hate it when somebody says something like that, it's so embarrassing. The worst part is, he doesn't even know it's embarrassing. The last thing I saw, before Dad came to close the door where they were, was Mom standing in the middle of the Oriental rug crying and Dad putting his arms around her. Aunt Sybill was standing real straight by the window smoking a cigarette. She looked terrible.

I watched "Magnum" and thought about it. Magnum was trying to solve this mystery about two identical twins and one of them had put some dope in a suitcase or something. Somebody had died. I missed the first part. Both of the twins were girls, real foxes. The mystery was, which one was the hooker and which one was the lawyer, I guess. Magnum is real cool. I was thinking, now somebody might die here. Grandmother might up and die. But it didn't seem real to me. It didn't seem as real as Magnum. Then a bad guy was warning Magnum by saying, "Watch it, buddy, I've got a black belt," and Magnum said, "Hey, I do too" and pointed to his own belt, and while the guy was looking at it, he hauled off and hit the guy in the face.

Right above the TV there's this shelf which holds all Dad's old shit—his medals, his football trophies, pictures of him on teams. I don't do any dope, but I refuse to sign up for any teams, see. It kills him. But I can do without teams. And the thing is, he'd like me better if I was an orphan. But it's too late. I can't be an orphan, I'm his son. And I can't be his best friend, either. The thing is, you don't want your old man to be so good at everything and be your buddy too. He says he wants to be my best friend because his own father was not around to be with him. This pisses me off and makes me crazy. I mean the nicer he is, the more of an asshole I am. The whole thing pisses me off.

They were still down there arguing when I went to bed. I thought about going down there and saying, "Gee, Mom and Dad! Sounds to me like you're really angry with Aunt Sybill!"

That cracked me up.

I looked at *Playboy* for a while, all those foxes, and then I got up and got this stupid stuffed dog I got for my birthday one time when I was about seven or eight, don't ask me why it's still around. I got this old dog and listened to "Thriller" and thought about Mom and Aunt Sybill yelling. The thing is, and it says this in the stupid P.E.T. book too and it's really true, I hate to admit it but it's true, you're *not* really angry much, if you get right down to it.

And I could tell from their voices they were scared.

LACY was never prepared for the pain that kept coming over her: pain so bitter it was sweet almost, like a sore tooth which you have to keep touching with your tongue. She had felt it in the hospital as she looked at her mother, still elegant, still small. And it seemed so ironic—*because I am her daughter, in a sense, more than the others: more than Sybill, than Myrtle, certainly more than Candy. I am more her daughter in a way she could never understand, since I look, I suppose, so different; and since with her, appearances are everything. But the poetry took, with me. And how very strange, since she could never tell good from bad, poor thing, or see beyond the iron pink palace of niceness and illusion, of should and sweet, which she had constructed around all of us. She never knew any of us, really. I wonder if she ever knew Daddy, or anybody. Anybody at all. I wonder now if anyone ever does—and if we do, if it's worth it, all the trouble and pain, when it doesn't last—*

The pain came again as Lacy unlocked her car, got

in, and put her hand down on the lever to adjust the seat before she remembered it wasn't necessary. Nobody else drove this car now. The seat, already perfectly adjusted, felt burning hot on the backs of her bare thighs and somehow this pleased her, to find a real location for her pain. She switched on the ignition, then the air conditioner, waiting for Myrtle to come out and give her directions to the new grocery store. Miss Elizabeth's condition remained unchanged, so it looked as though Lacy and her daughter Kate would be staying longer than they had thought. Lacy felt a need for supplies, a need to draw her wagons into a circle and prepare for siege. But even after two days of it, two days of being here, nothing had really sunk in yet—not her mother's illness, not even the fact that she was here: that she had, dutiful daughter indeed, come "home."

For years Lacy had tried to put distance—real, emotional, and psychological—between herself and Booker Creek. Somehow this changed when Jack left her. It was no longer possible. She really thought she had struggled free of her childhood, of that shell that never quite fit, only to find, when Jack left, that she was caught fast in another sort of shell altogether. It was Jack's shell; Jack had made it and made her, fashioned her, too, in a way, but now Jack was gone. *It's worse to be abandoned if you were first rescued. Then you have nothing left except a void. Empty space.* Lacy felt raw, exposed, vulnerable. She could not seem to get her bearings.

She knew she'd get lost trying to find this new Piggly Wiggly, for instance. She knew she'd get lost even with Kate in the car, or especially with Kate in the car, and they'd have a regrettable scene. Kate was having her first period. Lacy was having an anxiety attack, a mild one, as she sat in her car in her mother's long driveway waiting for Kate, waiting for Myrtle. She could hear Myrtle's voice drifting from the open back door of Mother's house as Myrtle talked on the telephone, dealing tactfully, calmly, cheerfully with yet another of Miss Elizabeth's friends who had called to ask how she was "holding up." It seemed to Lacy that her mother's friends did nothing but call each other on the telephone all day long, greedy for medical gossip. Lacy hated to talk to them. She hated to answer the phone in her mother's house.

In fact this was the strangest thing of all, to be staying here at Mother's while Mother was in the hospital. Lacy felt like an interloper, a snoop, and sometimes—most unsettling of all—exactly like the malcontent, unhappy child she used to be. Sometimes it was as if all those years with Jack, the Jack years as she called them in her mind now, had never happened; sometimes it was as if she had never grown up.

Lacy had been nervous when she arrived, and all the clutter in her mother's house made her more nervous: she wanted to sweep her arm wildly across the surfaces of things, clearing off lamps, lace doilies, framed photographs of the adorable children they never really were, china ashtrays, ceramic animals, cut glass. Instead, for the past two days, she had been pacing through these cluttered rooms nervously, smoking cigarettes, or sitting at the hospital, smoking more cigarettes, or sitting out at the One Stop with Nettie and crazy Fay, drinking Coke, or sitting with Myrtle and Don in that house Myrtle was so proud of, among the ferns and wicker, the lime green and hot pink, drinking daiquiris which Don "whipped up" in the blender. At least, thank God, Sybill was not staying at Mother's too. For some mysterious reason of her own, she had taken a room at the Holiday Inn, which was a relief. It was clear to Lacy—clear to them all—that Sybill had something on her mind, but she wouldn't say what it was, nor would she leave Miss Elizabeth's bedside. Two days had passed since the stroke, and Miss Elizabeth did not improve, and Sybill almost never left her. Lacy had begun to wonder about Sybill's stability; Don and Myrtle, too, were concerned. But who's to say: Lacy wondered about her own stability, for that matter. Well, whatever happened, Myrtle and Don would certainly take care of it.

"Turn left at the old Raven Rock cutoff," Myrtle said now, giving directions. "You know, where we used to go out to the quarry."

Myrtle stood in Mother's driveway looking good. Looking young, blond, content, prosperous—looking, however, a little less certain of the nature of things than she used to. Lacy has always been not so much annoyed as simply astonished by Myrtle and Don: by their enormous blond beauty, their possessions, their health, their absolute invincible belief in human perfectibility. Their blandness. They are people like pound cake, like vanilla pudding. She used to feel—and still felt, post-Jack—that she could never talk to them about politics, or values, or money, or anything. Myrtle, however, had developed lines at the corners of her eyes now which Lacy thought she recognized—lines she knew something about. They had been drinking sherry together earlier that afternoon, sitting around the oak table in front of the old floor fan in their mother's kitchen. Miss Elizabeth kept nothing stronger than sherry in the house.

"Do you think you should go like that?" Myrtle

asked. "Like that" meant that Lacy was wearing her cut-off blue jeans. It meant that she—like Myrtle—was almost forty. Lacy chose to ignore this remark. Kate ran out of the house then like a bullet, hurtled into the back seat, and slammed the door.

"I'll be there at seven," Lacy said, meaning *at the hospital, I'll be at the hospital,* backing out.

Lovely Myrtle stood by the blossoming pink hydrangea and waved. Lacy remembered her waving just that way from—it seemed—countless floats. Myrtle was Miss Booker Creek, Homecoming Queen, Valentine Princess, while Lacy got good grades and sulked. Myrtle waved, getting smaller and smaller as Lacy backed away, with the mountains spread out blue behind Mother's house, beyond the green hillside. She backed onto the street and pulled into traffic. Although the town had sprawled in all directions, with malls proliferating on the outskirts, the downtown area had stayed exactly the same. Mother's house, on the hill at the south end of Main Street, overlooked it all, as it had for half a century. The house was symbolic of so many things: of the fact that she alone, of the three sisters who had grown up there, carried on the traditions which their own mother had tried to instill in them; of her own lofty ideas, ideals, and sensibilities; and of, finally, her profound isolation. Driving through town, Lacy thought of how they had all preferred, finally, in different ways, terra firma. How they all had chosen to come down the hill.

"I still don't see why I had to come," Kate said. "I could have stayed home by myself."

Lacy didn't reply, negotiating the traffic. There never used to be any traffic.

"Lois Emery stays by herself," Kate said. "But you

don't think I'm a person. You don't think I'm responsible. You think I'm some dumb kind of a baby."

"When you're sixteen," Lacy said in what she hoped was a light tone, "then you can stay by yourself." She turned left at the courthouse and headed out of town on the bypass, toward the new grocery store Myrtle had recommended.

"I could have stayed with Dad," Kate said, trying it out. "*Bill* is."

"Bill has a swim meet," Lacy reminded her. "He'll be at the club most of the time we're away."

"I could have stayed with Dad anyway." Kate was still trying it out. Lacy looked at her in the rearview mirror. They were all new at this.

"I guess so," Lacy said. She didn't explain that Jack was keeping Billy under some duress. And that, as a matter of fact, children are not always welcome in a love nest. "Love nest" made her giggle—it was a phrase from one of the *National Enquirer*s which Fay had had out at the One Stop. ALIENS ENTER LOVE NEST, FRIGHTEN ILLICIT LOVERS was the headline. Fay was still, as always, nuts. But that was the situation: Jack and Susan, back home in Chapel Hill, living in their love nest. Sooner or later, Lacy would have to make some decisions. She supposed she'd have to sell the house.

She watched the land slip by on either side of the congested road. "Don't be a stranger, now," was what Nettie always said when she left. The old country goodbye. But Lacy did feel like a stranger now, driving through empty space. Daddy dead, Jack gone, Mother in the hospital. And Kate nearly grown up, so suddenly, so mysteriously: Kate's period had started. Even those mountains, which Lacy always loved, looked different. How many times, in how many other places, had she closed her eyes and summoned them up before her? She has always had a Romantic, Jack called it Wordsworthian, attachment to them—she has always been more attached to the *place,* perhaps, than to her own family. That's one of my problems, Lacy thought, that tendency to get more attached to the idea of the thing than the thing itself. *Oh, don't be a stranger now.* The mountains seemed older, softer, and somehow sad—or perhaps it was only this particular wet June, so much foliage, the haze. Lacy considers herself an old hand at the pathetic fallacy. And she had not been back for three years. When she was a girl, there was nothing but trees and sky along this stretch of road. Now they passed McDonald's, Long John Silver's, a K-Mart, a string of used-car lots. She turned left.

"There used to be a sign here that said Raven Rock, three miles," she said.

"*I don't care,*" said Kate.

"No kidding," Lacy said, and then Kate surprised her by giggling. Kate was moody, lovely, exasperating. She had had a hard time, too, and Lacy hadn't been able to help her much, consumed, as she had been, by her own pain.

The Piggly Wiggly, when they arrived, was as huge, as new as Myrtle had promised. As modern as anything in Chapel Hill, or even Raleigh. Booker Creek was changing and very little remained of the old ways—except those cabins you still saw high up, driving down that long valley through the mountains into town, those cabins so high and strange, and the isolated farms in the valley, and except the people, of course: like Nettie.

According to Myrtle, this Piggly Wiggly was owned by Lewis Ratliff, who had been in Lacy's class at school. He owned it and three others in neighboring towns. Lacy supposed that this made Lewis Ratliff a grownup, which she was not. She imagined how Myrtle and Don, and Candy, and even Arthur must have kept in touch with lots of the people from school. How they must run into these people day after day, year after year, as all of them married, had children, and aged. These lives seemed continuous, while hers did not.

A "Rodeo of Values" was in progress at the Piggly Wiggly; pennants fluttered all around the enormous parking lot. A country band played while cloggers in red-and-white checkered outfits danced on a raised wooden platform. A flea market and pony rides were, a sign said, out back.

"Yahoo," Kate said sarcastically. Kate was used to Chapel Hill, which is not the real world, in Lacy's opinion. Not that there's much advantage in the real world, either. Then Kate said, "Do you think they've got any games?" and headed into the Piggly Wiggly alone. Kate wore a man's hat and dangling silver earrings; she went to the Friends School, and looked like it.

Lacy locked the car and pulled her cut-offs down in the back. She needed staples—milk, cereal for Kate, some frozen dinners. She had no idea how long they'd be here, how long her mother would be in the hospital, what they'd do about her when she got out, whether Mrs. Dwight would be able to stay with her full time. Of course, in most cases, someone in the family would take over—Nettie, the logical one, would come to live with her. In most families. But for as long as Lacy could remember, her mother had had as little to do with Nettie and Fay as possible, for reasons the children never knew. Their father used to laugh a little and shake his head when they asked him about it, bemused and delighted, as always, by his Miss Elizabeth, by whatever vagaries and affectations she possessed. On the side, he gave them money; Lacy knew that. He had helped them through the long hard time when Millard Cline, Nettie's second husband, was dying of cirrhosis, before Nettie married and then buried her third husband, Dutch Musick, who owned the One Stop. *Gothic*. It's all so Gothic. Lacy remembered in college, when she read Faulkner for the first time, the way it all made perfect sense. Yes, she thought then. *This is how it is*. It was like coming home, in a way in which she had never been able to. Don't be a stranger now, Nettie said.

The country band at the Piggly Wiggly wore short-sleeved black shirts with glittering red cuffs and collars, and huge black cowboy hats. They were doing an old Kenny Rogers song, "Don't Take Your Love to Town." Lacy thought again of the things she planned to buy. Suddenly she remembered a disastrous dinner she had cooked sometime during the early years of her marriage. She had known, serving this dinner, that something was wrong with it, but she hadn't been able to figure out what it was. "Lacy," Jack had said after a moment, "it's all *white*." As indeed it was: fish with a cream sauce, rice, cauliflower, homemade rolls. Lacy used to tell this funny story to their friends. But now it seemed unbearably sad to her. It seemed like so many other things almost independent of herself and Jack, of their enormous good will, things that could not in any way have been foreseen or avoided. It's something that wouldn't occur to you, a white dinner. Thinking of Jack, Lacy saw herself again in the picture she had been looking at the night before, at her mother's: she and Jack, hand in hand, at a beach. In the picture, her mouth is a wide dark bow. Jack's eyes stare fearlessly into the future. That picture had been taken nearly fifteen years ago, at Wrightsville Beach, when they were in graduate school at Duke, before they married. When they were in love. And now Jack was in love with somebody else—Susan, another graduate student, ten years younger than he was. Doing it all over. But you *can't* do it all again, she wanted to scream at him. You can't have it twice, and you can't get it back— Although Jack himself looked exactly, she thought, the same: thin, bearded, the lopsided grin, the warm brown eyes. She couldn't imagine where those years had gone.

Lacy leaned against a battered blue camper to catch her breath as it all—flying pennants, whirling dancers, jostling crowd—blurred and swam, for a minute, before her eyes. She noticed that the guitarist was staring at her. He was a heavyset man of sixty or so, with a snake tattooed around his arm. "Ruby, for God's sake turn around!" he sang in a high nasal voice.

Suddenly Lacy realized that this Piggly Wiggly stood on the site of the old drive-in movie theater where she came with Louie Scuggs, the first boy who really loved her, and with Red McClanahan who touched her breasts and then never asked her out again. She hadn't liked Louie because he was too much like she was—too smart, too vulnerable, never quite "in." Lacy was the spelling champion, for instance, instead of a majorette like Myrtle. Louie Scuggs brought olive-and-cream-cheese sandwiches to school. But Red McClanahan! He was the kind of boy Candy knew. Lacy couldn't believe it when he asked her out; she still couldn't believe it, twenty years later. Myrtle had told her that Red spent six of those years in prison, that now he sold linoleum and carpet for Sears.

Lacy remembered three things about the night Red touched her breasts: *Thunder Road,* starring Robert Mitchum, was playing at the drive-in; she wore a white sundress, with spaghetti straps, which she had made herself in the 4-H Club; and little Linda Milligan, her distant cousin, fell from the top rung of the jungle gym and landed on her face in the gravel right under the giant screen, splitting her chin wide open. Just as Red touched Lacy's nipples, Linda Milligan ran between the rows of parked cars screaming bloody murder, while Robert Mitchum drove wildly across the huge pearly screen behind her. Robert Mitchum's job was running moonshine through the woods. It was, Lacy remembered, a really good movie. Linda Milligan grew up, got married, moved to northern Florida. And even now Lacy could almost feel Red's hands on her breasts.

The guitarist with the tattoos kept looking at her. "Ruby, I know I'm not half the man I used to be," he sang with the band, "But Ruby, I still need some company." Lacy started to giggle; she couldn't help it. The band took a break, and a little wind whirled the trash at her feet. Lacy knew she should do her shopping. But the guitarist was moving forward. "Listen miss," he said, "listen," in her ear. Then suddenly he was right in her face, with his gray-black stubble, his flat light eyes. "Now you're Verner Hess's girl, aren't you?" he asked deferentially. "I ain't seen you since you was grown."

"Yes—" Lacy's voice sounded strange to her in the sudden lack of music.

"Well, I don't know if you remember this or not, but I had a son, Donny Dodd? and he was sweet on

you? and we, me and the missus, took you with us
water skiing it must of been at least two times, over
to Holston Lake. We had us a boat then, for the boys.
We used to go over there every Sunday in those days.
I'm Ernest Dodd," he said.

"Oh sure," Lacy said, when in fact she didn't remember any of it, not Donny Dodd's face, or this father of
his, or the missus, nothing at all of those Sundays
spent water skiing on Holston Lake. No, wait—there's
"Rambling Rose," sung by Nat King Cole, coming
from the small black transistor radio on the green
blanket. Transistor radios were new then. Lacy saw
again the wide shining lake, the circle of hills, and a
boy coming up at the end of a ski rope, suddenly and
totally out of the water. But she couldn't see this
boy's face: all she remembered was "Rambling Rose,"
and the way your nose feels when you get it too full
of water. *Oh, Jack,* she thought, suddenly furious.
Oh, Jack darling. Because he had left her, and left
her open to all of this.

"That was fun, that water skiing," Lacy said to Mr.
Dodd, edging past him toward the store. "Please tell
your wife hello."

"Died," he said. "Cancer. She was all eat up with
it."

"I'm sorry." Lacy shook his hand, squeezing the
snake. "Take it easy," she said, and, "I think you all
are real good," meaning the band.

She found what she needed and went to stand in
the checkout line behind a man and his wife and
three little sobbing girls. *Sweet on you,* she thought.
The Dodd boy was sweet on you. The clock over the
automatic door said 7:05. Back in North Carolina, her
lover would be having a martini, probably, or running. He runs five miles a day. Visiting hours would

73

have started at the hospital. Candy would be there already, smiling softly, in her crinkled white uniform. Arthur might be there too, scowling in a corner, permanently ill at ease. Sybill would have her mouth pursed, legs crossed at the ankle. Out front, Mr. Dodd's band was starting up again. After Lacy paid, she went to stand by Kate at the line of video games. Kate was playing "Nuclear Holocaust."

"This is the last American family," Kate said. "See, the thing you have to do is get Timmy past these dorks. *Whoops,*" she said.

"Come on now."

"*Mom,*" Kate said, but then the screen went dark. The air had cooled off, and the violet arc lights were glowing softly all over the Piggly Wiggly parking lot. Mr. Dodd's band played "Orange Blossom Special," with a skinny rat-faced boy hunched over the fiddle. A big woman with a long black pony tail ran forward from the crowd and started dancing all by herself on the pavement. Lacy felt old and tired; she knew she could never keep up with her running lover.

"Weird music," Kate said. As they waited to turn into the main road, Kate asked what would happen if she got pregnant.

"Well," Lacy said, "that would probably be really unfortunate, because it would be so bad for your health, as well as for the baby's, so I guess we'd all have to sit down together, that is, with the boy, and his parents, and your father, and we'd just have to decide what would be the best thing to do under the circumstances, and then—"

But Kate flipped the radio dial, not listening. Finally, Lacy stopped talking. She always tends to answer their questions too fully, to give them more information than they need to know.

"I *could,* you know," Kate said after a while.

"Could what?"

"Get pregnant now. Couldn't I?"

So that's it.

"Sure you could," Lacy said. She waited for a break in the line of cars.

The early evening air smelled new, green, and full of possibility. The haze was gone. Beyond the bustling parking lot, the mountains rose; high above them, the sky was clear and luminous. Lacy couldn't understand what she remembered and what she didn't—why, for instance, the theme song from *Thunder Road* kept running through her mind. Robert Mitchum's face, dark and strong, was as big as a house on that shining screen—that screen which used to be *right there* behind the Piggly Wiggly where the pony rides were. Red McClanahan had coarse brown hair and yellow-green eyes. When he kissed her, he kept them wide open. *Life before Jack.* Lacy rolled the window down, over Kate's protests. She found herself smiling, on the road back to Mother's house.

*L*ACY is just so pretty, every day she brings me these flowers. They are blue. We put them in my vase, my swirling vase from Clinus who brings me things too. Lacy is not my baby. Clinus is not my baby either, or Lacy who says these grow up on the hill, Fay, out behind Mother's house. They grow on the hill by the split rail fence which runs up to the barn, won't you come out Fay to see them? The whole hillside is blue. Here, we will put them in a vase, but won't you come out in the car? It's such a pretty day, Lacy says, it's so dark in here. Can you see them, Fay, how blue they are, in your vase? Can you see in here? Nettie says leave her be, Lacy. She's okay. I say I'm okay, you're okay too and Lacy laughs. I laugh too, ha ha!

I keep up. I don't need to go anywhere, that's what I tell Lacy. It's so bright out there it hurts my eyes. Sybill is such a loud person. And don't I know how the hillside looks, and those flowers, and all that blue? I know, Lacy, but thanks I say. Thanks a million ha-ha.

But oh Lacy is pretty, she looks like Princess Di. It's that haircut she's got. Candy come to cut my hair. And I was such a pretty girl myself and Elizabeth put a bowl on my head then and cut my bangs. Elizabeth is very sick, Nettie says. Listen. Pay attention. Elizabeth is very sick, that's why her daughter Lacy is here who looks like Princess Di who has lost twenty-three pounds on her amazing diet, you can too, you can share the Royal Secret, how she lost four pounds in forty-eight hours and ten pounds in just one week right after the birth of the Prince. Mealtime is an exciting time on Princess Di's diet. This diet would not work of course for Kenny Rogers who spends two thousand dollars a week on barbecued ribs he has them flown in to wherever he's performing, for the whole crew, such a generous man. While Sue Ellen on the other hand keeps her blender on the set where she whips up seven types of grain, bananas, and raisins in hot water for a very healthy snack. Sue Ellen has a young lover now. You can't blame her either, JR is so mean. Some men are just mean. It was awful for Pamela when JR dug up her first husband and accused her of bigamy right in front of Bobby. That was awful! And Pamela poor thing had that miscarriage. Some men are just so mean. Oh don't I know how it looks out there, so bright, and all the flowers? Listen, honey, Nettie says. Listen here. I've been there, is what I tell Nettie. I'll take care of it, okay? If I can find it and send it off.

Speaking of bright, honey, did you hear about the electric housewife who makes sparks fly wherever she goes? This forty-one-year-old mother of three was

ironing a dress when it just up and burst into flames.
Now she has to take three showers a day and wears a
copper bracelet on her wrist and a long piece of wire
tied to her ankle to ground her at all times. Some
women are mean, too. Sybill is turning mean in her
age like Elizabeth, Nettie says. Asking so many questions like that. And I say ha ha! Sybill was never a
child at all, just a spooky little grownup like the ones
who have that disease they're born old and by the
time they're eight they're ninety, all bent over with
arthritis and God knows what. They have little old
bodies and nappy white hair. I have it too but it's
pretty and soft, Candy puts Spun Sand rinse on it to
keep it so nice that's why I look so pretty. I don't
know how it got so white. But if Sybill was my baby
I'd of drowned her, ha ha! Of course I would not, it's
a terrible death, what a way to go, just look at Natalie
Wood. If she had enough sense to take off her jacket
she'd be right here with us today. Clinus has a joke,
What kind of wood won't float? The answer is Natalie
Wood. Ha ha. And of course it was the height of
tragedy leaving Robert Wagner and those three children. Called RJ by his friends. Natalie and RJ had
been married for years and years, don't ask me how
they met. You never can tell, when you meet somebody, whether that mysterious chemistry will occur.
See here. It was love at first sight when I served him
a fake hamburger, I was working in a Denver lun-
cheonette when a man gave me this rubber burger
for a joke and so I gave it to Johnny R a twenty-nine-
year-old truckdriver who happened to be my next
customer. He got mad at first but then he took me to
the movies and five years later we are as happy as
clams. The Wacky Way I Met My Mate by Louise
Nettles, oh we've all had a little romance. In fact,

those flowers. Nettie says listen Fay. Don't worry! I tell them. Ha ha! It's nice in here and cool and dim. I like it cool like this with lots of atmosphere. It's wacky and bright in Hollywood otherwise known as Tinseltown. I'll take care of it! I say.

See here. If you're in trouble get in touch with Reverend Al and the prayer family of Fresno, California. Check the appropriate box for better job, more finances, I am worried, my health is bad, people talk about me, happier marriage, I need more confidence, I am not understood, someone to care for me. You will receive a beautiful rugged leather cross and a special prayer handkerchief and he will meet your needs. Yes he will! If Clinus will get me a stamp. Nettie won't. Sometimes Nettie is mean. JR was so mean to dig up Pamela's first husband it was as Elizabeth would say in poor taste. Listen honey. Elizabeth is very sick. The way I met my mate was just so wacky. Put a check by my health is bad and get me a stamp honey and don't worry I'll take care of it.

ARTHUR went by the One Stop on his way home from work, he'd been drinking maybe a little. The air conditioner was busted in his car and his shirt stuck flat to his back like a creepy wet skin. Arthur had come to a low pass anyway. He's done it all in his time, a jack of all trades you might say. Now he's a house sitter. He got out of the car. Clinus was out there by the gas pumps fooling with something. Clinus never seems to get hot or cold either one. He wears khaki pants and a khaki shirt year round, Nettie buys them a dozen a time at the Army-Navy, that's all he wears. His pants are too short. He never sweats or gets cold. If your brain stops, everything else does too, Arthur could use some of that.

"Howdy," Clinus said. He squinted at Arthur, grinning. His dog Bert lay flat out in the dirt beside him.

"Howdy," Arthur said.

Bert didn't even move.

Clinus wore his cowboy hat with the feathers in front, he's got a lot of hats. Clinus sat flat on his ass in the dirt with some kind of a thing in front of him, between his legs, and his tools, and his feet stuck out straight as poles on either side of the thing and the tools. Arthur got a big kick out of the way Clinus was just sitting out there.

"What you doing?" Arthur asked him, mainly to pass the time of day. Arthur doesn't give a shit about much of anything now.

"Coffee grinder," Clinus said. His fluffy gray clown hair poked out from under his cowboy hat. "Looky here." Clinus held it up and that's what it was all right, an old coffee grinder. Arthur figured he'd probably sell it for seventy-five dollars when he fixed it up. People are nuts for antiques. People will buy anything, too. "That's nice, Clinus," Arthur told him, and Clinus grinned his big grin, like he'd really done something this time, like he'd got the whole world by the tail. Maybe he had. "Nettie here?" Arthur asked, and Clinus put the coffee grinder back down on the ground where it landed with a soft little splat kicking up little puffs of dirt that hung in the air all around. He jerked his thumb toward the store.

It was real hot. Arthur could feel his blood pressure up in his ears when he climbed up the wooden steps and pushed on the screen door. He needs to get back in shape. He's got high blood and a bad heart, a weak stomach, low back pain and hemorrhoids and a terminal case of despair. Ask anybody. Arthur has come to a sad pass recently, done in as he says by Inez Nation, a low woman with shameful behavior. He's on Elavil and Dalmane, he drinks Mylanta like it was water. Arthur stopped in the door and looked around, wiping his face on his sleeve. He's still a good-looking man and in his ravaged face you can see the boy he used to be, the handsomest boy in town. Now, his niece Theresa says he looks like Lawrence of Arabia.

"Nettie," he said.

Nobody was in the store there, where they haven't changed the signs or the merchandise in years, or if they have you can't tell it. No way to run a store, thinks Arthur, who has had some experience. The old ceiling fan going like crazy, all it did was stir the dust. Arthur has told Nettie a million times, things could be done with this place. You ought to put in a motel. You've got a prime location here. Nothing doing, says Nettie. You can't tell her a thing. Well if you all want to live out here like Negroes, it's all right with me, Arthur says. He looked at the counter, Chapstick and Little Debbie oatmeal cakes, Nerds, and the gumball machine, Kleenex, Rubiks Cubes, key chains, pickled eggs. And nobody home. So he went over to the drink box, an antique just like that coffee grinder, and opened it up and got him a Sprite, chugged about half and put him in a little sweetening to go with the rest. He could hear the TV going in the back. He knew that was Fay back there, watching her stories. All Fay ever does anymore is push those little buttons to change the stations, the whole thing freaks Arthur out.

But hell, at least it's cool, and he went back there too. This is, you might say, the living room. Full of big heavy dark furniture with fringes on it, Nettie's last husband's first wife bought it before she died. Plus Fay of course has got *her* stuff around in there too, the whole coffee table full of *Star*s and *Midnight*s and *National Enquirer*s. Which she was looking through real careful, paging through like a person who knows what they're doing. *Wrong.* Fay keeps the lights real low and the window air condition was going like crazy. The TV was too. Only she wasn't watching it, just paging through all careful and real slow. Somebody had brought her some flowers. You'd have to cry, going into that room, if you didn't have to laugh. And Fay getting real heavy now, like a big white slug that never sees day. It freaks Arthur out. Although he ought to be used to it, he's been there enough.

But one of Arthur's problems is, he never gets used to a thing.

"Nettie," he yelled.

Fay didn't even look up.

"Come on back." Nettie's voice came from the kitchen, over the sound of Fay's TV.

"And how are *you* today, Fay?" Arthur asked but she was just turning the pages real slow, and mumbling. Hadn't said a whole sentence since about 1975. As far as what else she does, her functions, you can't afford to think too much about that. She sleeps right there on the couch. Nettie and Clinus sleep in the back. Plus whoever Nettie has taken in this week. Nettie hires boys and then she raises them. Been doing it all her life.

It's a damn loony bin out there at the One Stop.

Arthur went on back.

Nettie's last husband owned the store, and then he got married to his first wife, the dead one, and added another room right behind the store, and then a kitchen on back of that, and then when he married Nettie and inherited Fay, you might say, he put two more rooms on behind the kitchen. So it's a shotgun all the way, straight back. Then when Clinus's real mother died he went out there too and built that stuff on the side. Where the antique business is, only it's mostly a junk business if you ask Arthur. But it pulls them in. Any Saturday, half the county is out there, seeing what Clinus has got. Shows you what there is to do in Booker Creek on a Saturday, too.

"How are you?" Nettie said.

She looked at Arthur once, sharp, he knew she knew he was drinking. Nettie doesn't miss a trick. And she has had some drinks with Arthur in her time. Years back, growing up, Arthur was out at the One Stop more than he was at home, for a fact. Or else he was on the sofa over the florist shop, in town, when she was married to Millard Cline. Nettie damn near raised him, or tried to. Nobody finished the job. "The thing about you is, Arthur, you are infantile," Inez Nation once said. She said this before she ran off with all of Arthur's money and the driver education teacher from the high school, plunging Arthur into despair. "At least I'm not an extravagant slut," he should have said. But you never think of what you ought to say until the time is past. Arthur's got his whole head full of them, the right lines from his whole life, which he never said.

Nettie was canning beans. She's a little old woman now, looks like a Indian, wrinkled from working in the garden year after year and pumping gas. Wears a man's shirt and jeans and running shoes. Nettie looks like hell. But she's had some husbands in her time. Nettie was smiling at him. Arthur sat down on a high round stool.

"Well, how's it going?" he asked her, and she said, "Fine, honey." Nettie would say this if the house was on fire. Arthur sat there a while watching her boil the jars and then put the beans in them and turn them upside down on a clean kitchen towel by the sink. You can't find a woman who'll care to do a thing like that today. They're all into women's lib. Even Alta, that he loved with all his heart, got to where she would rather go to Taco Bell than cook when she was working. Nettie was whistling a tune through her teeth. Arthur got another shot and after a while he started feeling better, and then the phone rang.

He thought how good it was drinking in the summertime. After a while all the light and heat gets up in your head to where things look good again and you get this kind of whispering in your ears. Makes you feel like you're in on something. Winter is different, nothing you own runs right. You get cold, you get mad, you go ahead and get drunk. You can stay drunk most of the winter if the weather is bad enough. But in the summertime if you do it right you can pace yourself and drink all day and stay right all day long.

Nettie was talking straight into the phone. Then she got the dishrag and started wiping her hands off while she talked, holding the phone to her ear with her shoulder. She was wiping her hands off like she meant business. Arthur thought, uh-oh. But he couldn't hear much due to this nice pleasurable buzz in his ears, and Fay had the TV going, it was a game show. Then she changed the channel to "General Hospital." Arthur was thinking, It's not such a bad life, Fay's. You don't have to hear anything but what you want to. You don't have to see anybody but stars. They say Fay used to be different, but Arthur doesn't know. He can remember, himself, when she talked. But he can't remember a thing she said.

Nettie hung up the phone. Then she turned around to Arthur, and it seemed like she turned real slow in that hot kitchen. He knew it was bad news. Nettie opened her mouth and it took her a year. Out the window he could see the old Chevrolet, puke green, which Clinus had been working on for two years, and his red pickup, and a big old white refrigerator. The grass was real green.

"Arthur!" Nettie said. "That was Myrtle, calling from the hospital, and she says Elizabeth has had another stroke, a real bad one, and they're going to try to get her on a pacemaker. But she don't stand much of a chance. I guess we'd better get on over there."

Now this hit Arthur hard. He wasn't expecting it. He fully expected his mother to get well and get her one of those machines that glide you up and down the staircase and that'd be the end of it. In fact he could just see her, gliding up and down the staircase like a queen, all dressed up.

Nettie's face looked like it was carved in wood. "Get yourself together now, Arthur," she said. While she went out the kitchen door, going around to tell Clinus and Roy Looney, the boy who works for her, what was up, Arthur thought about that. If he was to get himself together he'd have to go all over the Tri-State area to do it. Not to mention Florida. He poured himself a little drink. Nettie came back in and said, "Come on, now," and Arthur followed her back into the store where she got some Pringles and took them in and left them with Fay in case Fay got hungry while she was gone. Fay wasn't paying her any mind, reading those magazines. Arthur and Nettie walked out in the sun in front of the One Stop where Roy was pumping gas for some hippies in a van. Clinus's billboard said GET WELL SOON. Clinus sat in the dirt fiddling with his coffee grinder, Bert beside him. "I'll drive," Nettie said, looking at Arthur. Nettie is real little. Arthur put his keys back in his pocket and went around the side of the One Stop and they got in the pickup and took off in a cloud of dust like a western movie.

Nettie drove and Arthur looked at things. When you're driving, you miss a lot. Going in toward town they passed the fancy entrance to Argonne Hills, the new subdivision where Myrtle and Don live. Myrtle and Don remind Arthur of that Rickie Scaggs song you hear on the radio now, about the people who sit around in their hot tub and talk about the things they've got. Although they haven't got a hot tub, yet. Although they have been damn nice to Arthur, Don in particular. Sometimes he's so nice, you wonder what *he's* getting out of it, being that way. Don was always nice. In high school he was the kind of guy that wore a white short-sleeved shirt and got Best All-Around. What do you expect, though, an orphan raised by a preacher and a deaf woman? Don's okay. So they passed by Argonne Hills, full of those rich young marrieds that moved down here with Burlington, and young doctors and lawyers. This is one thing Arthur never could understand about Mother. Where she got those ideas. Why she thought she was better than everybody else in town, when you've got the Harrisons who send their sons to Yale, been doing it for a couple of generations. Or the Bentons who have owned Long Valley for two hundred years, not to mention all these young marrieds in Argonne Hills. It never made sense. Their grandfather did well in the lumber business, of course, years back, but then he lost his shirt. And Miss Elizabeth ended up without a thing but the clothes on her back and that house. Even if she never would admit it.

Nettie turned onto Main Street and there it was on the hill at the end of town, Arthur used to have to trim the damn boxwoods and clip the grass between all those goddamn stones in the walk.

Nettie drove by the new post office and here came two girls walking along in jeans and those stretch halters they're all wearing this summer, laughing, eating ice-cream cones. You could see their nipples jiggle up and down. Arthur got hard, then. He has followed his cock all his life, and see where it's got him to. He gets hard riding in a beat-up pickup truck with his seventy-year-old aunt while his own mother's dying in the hospital and he's looking out the window at the tits on high-school girls. It's shameful. He has followed his cock too far, he's a psychological misfit and as Alta once said, a scumbag. Alta actually said that, "Arthur, you are a scumbag." God knows he was, too, in that case, but he wished she hadn't said it. Later, he tried to make amends. Arthur can hear her right now saying it. He was losing that nice little buzz.

Alta when he met her was that age, not long out of school, and he was working for Buddy Lewis's daddy in the tire business and playing music part time in the band they had then, the Hot Licks. Verner Hess wanted to send him to college but Arthur was too hot to make big money in those days. And hell, it was all he could do to get out of high school. Arthur wasn't the college type. Then Verner Hess wanted him to go into the dimestore business with him but Arthur was too hot for that too, Verner had some idea about him learning the business from the bottom up. It would have been a sure thing. Arthur didn't want a sure thing. Arthur didn't want to be in the dimestore business either. He wanted the big bucks and a fast break, he drove a baby-blue Corvette in those days.

That was when the Hot Licks was going good, too.

The Hot Licks was a going concern. They had jobs everyplace, around Booker Creek and over the state line in North Carolina, over in Tennessee. They had as many gigs as they could handle and still hold down a regular job. And girls—girls will just as soon fuck you as look at you, in a band. They used to fuck girls all the time. This was Arthur and Buddy Lewis that Arthur was in his daddy's tire business with, and Fuzzy Ledbetter who died in Vietnam, and George Lee Wilfong that did go on to make it in a manner of speaking and was in jail in Tennessee the last Arthur heard for income tax evasion. Buddy still has the tire business, and a kidney-shaped swimming pool in Argonne Hills, and looks the other way now when he sees Arthur coming up the street. He thinks Arthur is bad news. It breaks Arthur's heart. Because there's nothing as sweet as when you've got it right, like that night in the Pearl Tavern or any one of a hundred other nights Arthur could mention when it was just so right, they used to do "Shout" and Buddy would get right down and slobber on the floor. He'd deny it if you asked him today. Now he's the head of the Heart Fund. They'd do shit like "The Wayward Wind." Before they were the Hot Licks, they were the Great Pretenders, This Side Up, and the Long Valley Boys. Not in that order. Arthur has forgotten the order.

The trouble was, they didn't have a format. First they were country, then they were folk, then they were country again, then they were rock. Folk didn't last anyway but they should have stuck with country, look where they'd be today. Country is big. Look at Willie Nelson. You can be old and still be big in country. Finally they stuck with rock. The trouble with rock was a serious lack of Negroes. There's not many of them around Booker Creek anyway, and none of them could play shit at that time. Arthur has often thought since, if they had had a couple of Negroes and a format, they could have made it. Why not? They were hot. They used to wear long hair and pink silk shirts they bought down in Charlotte, North Carolina. Miss Elizabeth used to look at them and cry. She would have died for sure if they'd had a Negro in the band. But more Negroes in town would have been good for her, in Arthur's opinion. It would have given her somebody to rise above, besides her own family.

Anyway the Hot Licks had it so right for about eight months there, before Buddy's daddy made him quit and George Lee went to Nashville and Arthur fell in love. They had their shit together for a while. They used to drink all night long and smoke dope before anybody else even heard of it.

They were the vanguard.

Hell, they were just boys then, twenty, twenty-two years old. They'd fuck anything in a skirt. A lot of times this would go on in cars, they'd drive out someplace after the show, park, you've got the picture. Hot sweet summer nights. All those pretty girls.

Sometimes now when he's in the Piggly Wiggly, say, Arthur will notice some fancy housewife come in there with her linen dress on, or he'll look real sharp at the gray-haired woman behind the counter, not any older than he is, or he'll check out the classy lady with the sunglasses and the little tennis outfit, and he'll wonder, Did we ever do it? Hard to say. He'll look real close. Cars still get him horny, to this day.

But he never had Alta until he married her, which is why he did. Not that he minded either. He wouldn't have done one thing to upset her. Even now after all the hard times and bad shit that have fallen between them, Arthur can think about Alta and cry.

Now, Alta is a postal inspector in Vero Beach, Florida, searching for cocaine. But you should have seen her then.

Arthur saw her the first time across a crowded room as they say, noticed her as soon as she came in. The Hot Licks were playing Paul's Pizza Den over in Clarkston, near the lake. Buddy had quit by then. Alta came in with some girlfriends, two of them, and sat down at the little table in the corner under one of those hanging Tiffany-type lamps, so the light fell right down on her hair. Which was blond and went damn near down to her waist. *Shit*, Arthur thought.

He was in the middle of singing "The Twelfth of Never," he tried to put something special in it.

Alta was laughing and talking to her girlfriends. Arthur couldn't catch her eye. They were eating pizza and drinking Coke. It was summer. She wore a pale blue sleeveless dress, a dumb kind of dress really, like you might see for sale in a K-Mart. A prim dumb kind of a dress that buttoned up the front. Arthur loved it. Everybody else in the place had a tan, but Alta's neck rose up out of her dress like a white column on a mansion, her arms were the purest, palest white you ever saw. Long arms, but real round. She was fiddling with her straw.

"Look at that," George Lee said, nodding his head at her while Fuzzy was doing the lead vocal on "Sea Cruise."

"Forget it," Arthur said.

George Lee grinned at Arthur.

George Lee knew Arthur was hooked.

And before he knew it, Alta Wood had him settled down.

She was the only child of real old parents, Ruby and Forrest Wood. Arthur always thought that was pretty funny, Forrest Wood. Forrest Wood didn't think so, though. He was the kind of old man who does not have a sense of humor, and writes down everything he's got stored in the attic. He was real religious, too. Alta's mother turned out to be a dingbat. At first Arthur liked her, back when she liked him. But then she changed, so Arthur did too. There's no percentage in it, after a while. Arthur came to his senses and saw her as a dingbat, in the end. At first, when he first started courting Alta, Ruby was taken with him as women generally are and she stayed on his side for a long time after they got married and Forrest turned on him. But then she turned on him too. Forrest Wood and Arthur were somewhat alienated from the word go. But that would have been the case with Forrest Wood and anybody his daughter married, probably.

Since they didn't have Alta until they were real old, she was the light of their life. They tried to keep her, too. They had sent her to a Christian academy over in Buncoe, run by a bunch of born-agains. They aimed to keep her pure. Which they did, too. Alta was as pure as the driven snow, it was like she had come from another world. Then when she got out of high school, they got her a job keeping the books for her uncle, who ran a plumbing supply business in Buncoe. This was her Uncle Dink. He put her in a little room in the back of the plumbing supply, where she wouldn't meet anybody and get distracted. And she probably wouldn't have, either, except for plumbers and preachers, who Ruby and Forrest approved of and who used to come courting her all the time having seen her in church, if she hadn't gone out for a pizza with her girlfriend the night in question, the night she met Arthur.

Alta was young but ready. Alta was ripe for it, as Fuzzy Ledbetter said later and Arthur hit him for it. Now he's sorry, since Fuzzy died. Arthur was hot-headed in those days. But there is nothing so sweet as a born-again virgin with a certain curiosity. And Arthur loved her. Alta Wood used to wear a blouse with a sailor collar, and red lipstick. She used to giggle. He swore off drinking and then he swore off rock-and-roll. The Hot Licks were breaking up by then, anyway. Their time had come and gone.

Before Arthur knew it, he'd bought her a ring, and right after that, they got married. In the Woods' church, of course. Ruby planned the whole thing. Since Miss Elizabeth wasn't consulted, she got her feelings hurt, and she claimed later that she nearly fainted dead away at the extreme tackiness of Arthur and Alta's wedding. Miss Elizabeth didn't have anything to do with it except show up, and she damn near didn't do that, she was so mad. She was also mad because Ruby hired Millard Cline, Nettie's second husband, to do the flowers. Arthur didn't give a damn. He only had eyes for Alta, who came down the aisle on Forrest's arm looking like an angel in her long white dress. Alta had the kind of looks a wedding dress is made for. The ex-Hot Licks stood up with Arthur. Alta's bridesmaids were her two first cousins from Marion and her friend Johnette Flowers from high school who cried out loud the whole time and tried to steal the show from Alta, everybody said. All born-agains are emotional.

Right after the wedding, Forrest Wood came up to Arthur outside the church and put his arm around him and said, "You take good care of my baby, you son-of-a-bitch" in his ear. The church itself looked like a gas station, which it used to be. Arthur didn't give a damn. He took Alta to the Fairystone Motel in Gatlinburg for a honeymoon and it was the finest four days of his life.

Everything about Alta just killed him. She had a little travel iron, she used to iron his shirts. She taped a Kotex across her forehead when she washed her hair, to make her bangs do right. She'd tape them down over the Kotex, with Scotch tape. It turned out that breakfast was her favorite meal. She used to eat two fried eggs. She put bubblebath in the tub. There's things you can't know about anybody unless you marry them, or live with them. And Alta would do anything in bed, she loved all that. But whatever they did, Alta would jump right up after it and put her nightgown on in case the motel burned down, she said. She had a long white nightgown, with buttons. Every day of the honeymoon, they rode the Sky-Tram up to the top of the mountain and looked out across three states.

After that they came back and moved into a little house they'd rented out on the highway, from old man Lewis, and Arthur quit the tire business and went into the A&P where he was the produce man and had more of a chance for advancement. For a while, it was fine. Alta went back to work for her uncle at the plumbing supply so they could save some money back, and get ahead some. She used to cook him dinner every night, real nice little balanced meals she had learned about in home ec, with a green vegetable. Arthur brought the vegetables home from the produce counter. He was a management trainee. It was like playing house, all of it, Arthur can see that now. She was just a girl. They had Verner

Hess and Miss Elizabeth over for dinner, and even Miss Elizabeth was impressed. She wrote Alta a note and said she was charmed. But they didn't see Arthur's family a lot, except for sometimes Candy, or Nettie and Fay. Alta said the rest of them made her nervous. Anyway they didn't see anybody much, when they were newlyweds. They used to watch TV after dinner just waiting to go to bed.

Somehow, this got old. It got old real fast before Arthur was ready for that or had thought what to do if it happened, it just snuck up on him. It was not Alta's fault. Alta was making curtains by hand and then she was pregnant. Arthur used to lie with his head on her belly and go to sleep, he loved her so much. But somehow in that time he started stopping off for a beer at the Liquid Lunch on his way home, and then for one or two. Then one time he went by the Liquid and Fuzzy was in there with his girlfriend and her cousin from Spartanburg, South Carolina, and he said, "Let's go over to the dam." Well, Arthur went. And they were drinking and one thing led to another and in the end, it was after midnight when Arthur got home. He had to hand it to Alta, that night. She was playing it cool. She had not called her mama. She had not been crying either, or if she had, he couldn't tell it. Which was the first time Arthur got a real notion of how tough she was.

"I don't want to know where you've been or what you've been doing, Arthur," she said. "That is between you and God. But I have been praying for you." Then she unbuttoned that nightgown and welcomed him home.

Then she had Brenda and Arthur had to admit he never thought he'd be as taken with anything as he was with that baby. He wasn't expecting it. He was worse than a woman about it. He used to get up in the night and look at Brenda, she was the cutest thing he ever saw, he couldn't believe it. But he was drinking. He got tired of produce and quit. Alta went off to work, and Arthur stayed home with the baby. He didn't drink then, in the daytime when he was home with Brenda, it was nights that he drank.

Forrest Wood came over and told Arthur that if he ever heard about him embarrassing his daughter or hurting her feelings, he'd break every bone in his body. But Alta cried—she loved him. She loved him then. And it was like she didn't care what he did, or how long he stayed gone, if he came home. "As long as you don't love anybody else but me ever," she said. She said she was praying for him.

Arthur worked selling cars with Owens Mooney for a while but it was slow going and Owens was a hard man to get on with, so he quit that too. He wasn't making enough to pay the baby-sitter. So he stayed home and took care of Brenda while Alta worked.

Verner Hess came out to see him one afternoon. Arthur was changing Brenda's diaper when he came in.

"This is no way for a man to live, Arthur," said Verner Hess.

Brenda was grinning and kicking her legs in the air. Over at the plumbing supply, Alta was pregnant again.

"You've got to get a hold on yourself, Arthur," said Verner Hess. "Your mother is worried sick."

"Did she tell you to come over here?" Arthur asked him. He picked Brenda up.

"No, she didn't," said Verner Hess. He sat down on the couch and looked at him. "She don't say a word about you. You know how she is."

Arthur knew all right.

"But she's worried, I can tell. And I've been worrying too."

Arthur sat down in the rocker and looked at Verner Hess. He was a country man, it was hard for him to come right out with whatever it was.

"Why don't you come on down and work at the dimestore," said Verner Hess, looking out the window so he wouldn't have to look straight at Arthur's face. "I'm at a point where I could use some good help, I'm getting on up to retirement age, you know. Think about it." He was a little old stooped-over man, real sweet.

"I don't know," Arthur said. Verner Hess was not his own daddy, and he was thinking about that. Arthur wished he was. But he was not, and somehow that had made some difference in his life, he'd be hard put to say just how. Arthur looked for his daddy for years and years and never found him, all he found was a string of women who said they'd known him, years ago. All he got from his daddy was the gun he had as a boy, which Nettie saved for him, and two records he cut in Bristol. They say he cut a third one, too, but Arthur doesn't have that.

"Well." Verner Hess lit a cigarette and smoked it all the way down without saying a thing. "You get a hold on yourself," he said. "Do you need any money?" and Arthur said, "Yes," and Verner gave him a folded-over hundred-dollar bill.

"That offer's still open," he said right before he left. Arthur sat there rocking Brenda and watched him walk out and get in his Buick and drive away. It was early April, everything blooming. Alta had planted tulips and daffodils all over the yard.

Now, Arthur can't see how it happened. God knows

he loved her. He loved those girls. But things went from bad to worse. He sold air conditioners, he worked as a lineman for Appalachian Power. He joined the church and quit drinking, but it didn't take. He sold insurance. He was a tree surgeon. Alta used to leave him and take the girls, and then come back. They'd make up like crazy. Arthur really loved her, and she loved him. He managed the Holiday Inn for a while. He got drafted, then not. He has a bad heart. Alta moved out, then back. They had a mobile home not far from the One Stop, for a while. In the prettiest little stand of pines. He and Alta used to take a blanket out there at night, in the summer, after the girls were asleep, and listen to the wind through the pines. Sometimes they'd listen to the radio. Disco was big, then. Saturday-night fever. Alta got softer, sweeter, as time passed.

Brenda started to nursery school, she used to bring Arthur these pictures of houses she drew, with smoke coming out of the chimney, and things like blue cats in the yard. One time he was gone for three days. Forrest Wood came over and said, "Arthur, I'm either going to kill you, or move to Florida," and Alta said "Don't kill him, Daddy," so Forrest and Ruby moved.

Then one time Arthur really got into it with some boys, and Verner had to come and bail him out of jail in Whitesburg, Kentucky, a sorry town. He couldn't remember how he got over there. Verner drove him home.

"This is your last chance, Arthur," Alta said. She wore her hair in a pageboy then, right below her ears. She looked so pretty. He could tell by something new in the tone of her voice that she meant it.

"All right, Alta," Arthur said. He went to working for Verner Hess, after all those years.

And he had to hand it to Verner. Verner didn't even seem surprised when he went over there and went up to the office to ask for the job. "I'd be pleased to have you, Arthur," was all he said. Arthur started off on the floor, as the assistant manager, and things went along just fine for a while. Arthur liked the job. He was good at it, too. He got Verner to put in an arts-and-crafts section, which went over big. They started carrying a bigger line of ready-to-wear.

Then they hired Rena Clark. Arthur didn't hire her, himself. Verner did. She was a little girl from out in the valley with nothing to recommend her. Dressed in jeans just like a boy. Slight, looked almost sickly. Rena Clark couldn't hold a candle to big, pretty Alta. Rena had frizzy, sandy hair and freckles, thin sandy eyebrows and eyelashes, she was kind of popeyed. Arthur doesn't know, to this day, how it happened. One day he was showing her the ropes—they started her off in records, tapes, and posters since she was so young—and then the next thing he knew, they were taking off their clothes. This started one Friday night, late, in the coatroom, when they had been taking inventory. Rena Clark was so thin that her shoulder bones showed white beneath her skin, like wings. It was foolish. They used to lock the Ladies and do it in there. Finally they were caught by Lorene Swift, who worked in housewares and called up Alta. "That's it, Arthur," Alta said. She packed up and moved to Florida, to live with her folks. Took his girls.

Arthur got good and drunk then. He was in the detox place at Princeton for a long time after that, and it was while he was in there sitting on those vinyl chairs and sweating it out that he formulated a plan.

Verner said he could have his old job back, he

thought he'd have a promising future if he'd lay off the ladies and the booze, but Arthur said no. No, he was going to make amends. He was going to make amends to Alta, and this is how he came to give up the only sure thing he ever had and move to Florida. By the time he got back, it was gone. Verner Hess had died, and the rest of them had gotten together and sold the store. Not that he blamed them either. Arthur took what he got out of it and bought a Sun Box. He put a Sun Box in the mall. This is a tanning franchise. You pay so much per hour, you can get a tan all winter long. Arthur thought it would go over big, especially with the college girls. Wrong. He went bust on that one, and then Inez Nation, who was his employee in the Sun Box at that time, took what was left and ran off with the driving instructor. Arthur can't stand to think about Inez Nation. She was tan all over, and left him in total despair.

But first, he went down to Florida with high hopes of making amends.

He went down there to be near his daughters and court his own wife.

But this was easier said than done. Alta was living with her parents, who hated him, and vice versa, in a bright pink house on a corner in Vero Beach, with palm trees and a chain-link fence around everything. Ruby had bought a Chihuahua and named it Baby. Baby was barking behind the fence. Alta was a secretary in an insurance agency. She had cut off all her hair in a pixie, and refused to give him the time of day. Brenda and Susie were in school down there, where their classes were half in Spanish. Arthur did first one thing, then another. He worked in a men's shop, he was a maître d'. Every week, he got the girls for two days, he and Alta worked out the details on the phone. Alta wanted them to see him, she said. Over her parents' objections. Alta said she knew the father was important, she'd read books.

Alta wanted *them* to see Arthur, but *she* didn't want to. She talked to him exactly like he was some guy who came up to her door selling encyclopedias, like he was a total stranger. They had come to that point, and passed beyond it, where she didn't care what he thought. Nothing he said could move her. She just didn't give a damn. Anybody else would have given up then, and come on back, but Arthur stuck it out for a while. Once you become determined to make amends, you can't believe that you're not going to get to do it. He kept thinking she'd change her mind, that she'd remember all those good times, that she'd come back. Arthur still thought she loved him, you see. He believed it. He was banking everything on that. He banked it all. He wore Bermuda shorts and kept his apartment as neat as a pin, for his daughters. Women he had in there, he got them out when it was time for Brenda and Susie to come. He took them to the beach a lot. He took them to Disney World. But they were growing up, they got some eyeshadow, they didn't want him to kiss them goodnight.

Then Alta announced, all of a sudden, she's getting married.

This almost killed Arthur.

He knew Alta had been seeing a guy, he was really a jerk. Worked for the post office, wore glasses, looked like Woody Allen. Arthur knew she was seeing this guy but he had continued to hang around, waiting for her to come to her senses.

So then Alta said she was getting married. She's taking a civil-service exam, she's going to work for the post office too, they're going to sort the mail together. Wearing uniforms.

Arthur went a little crazy at that time. He stayed up all night drinking and bought a gun. The day of the wedding, he went over to the pink house in the morning to kill the guy, or himself, or somebody. He had the gun in his pocket. Baby started barking behind the fence. Arthur thought he'd kill Baby, at least. But then here came Brenda and Susie running out, all dressed up alike in little pink dresses with bows. For the wedding. "Daddy! Daddy!" they said. They were always so glad to see him. "You all look real pretty," Arthur said. He never fired a shot, he stood there holding on to the fence and crying until Ruby Wood came out in a big awful purple hat. "Arthur, get lost," she said. So he did.

Arthur came home, and got all mixed up with the Sun Box and Inez Nation, and went flat bust and ended up house sitting for his old buddy Fred Bright who has found it a good idea to leave town.

Arthur needs to get back on the track again, get settled. The girls are coming for a visit this summer, he can't have them out at Fred's.

A lot of people have told him, "Arthur, you ought to swear out a warrant, you ought to be reimbursed." But he just hasn't got the heart for it. He is in despair. He imagines bloodhounds, chasing them through a swamp. He can see Inez Nation right now, tripping along through mud in her high heels. He hasn't got the heart. Also, Arthur has to say, fuck it. If his own wife Alta prefers to look for cocaine all day long with her new husband in Vero Beach, Florida, then fuck it. That's what he says. His girls are close to his heart. If Alta or any of them ever try to keep him from seeing his girls, he will kill them, they know that. His girls and him are in it together for life. But as for the rest of it, just fuck it, Arthur says.

In his state of total despair, Miss Elizabeth dying is one more thing. He couldn't get his mind around it, for a fact. She'd been a thorn in his side for years. "Arthur, how *could* you?" is all she said. He remembers her falling asleep in the glider on the side porch, waiting up for him to come home. After a while he used to stay at Nettie's. Nettie pulled into the hospital parking lot about the same time Dr. Don came sliding in, in his new yellow BMW. Dr. Don looked grave. He put his hands on Arthur's shoulders and squeezed. "*Arthur,*" he said. Don has been in seminars, you can tell. How to touch other men. Arthur didn't give a damn anymore, his Mother was dying. Candy told them when they got off the elevator. Candy's a toucher, too. She ran her hands over Arthur's hair, his collar, straightening. Candy always makes you feel better. "The preacher is here," she says. "The young one, that Mother liked."

Miss Elizabeth was in Intensive Care. They couldn't go in. Not that Arthur would want to, either. He'd just as soon let the dying go alone. He's got a bad heart, himself. Arthur looked around the waiting room, outside of Intensive Care: Nettie, Lacy, Dr. Don, Myrtle, Candy, Sybill, and his niece Theresa, Myrtle and Don's daughter. Lacy winked at him, he's always liked Lacy, a pretty little thing with troubles of her own now. Sybill and Nettie were smoking. The preacher was a young thin guy who looked intellectual, like he was in some kind of pain. Everybody was sitting in molded aqua chairs beneath the fluorescent lights. Arthur didn't care for the lights, himself. It seemed to him after a while that they were humming, and then that they were humming louder. He hated it the way they hummed.

"Does anybody want anything from the machines?" Lacy asked. "Coffee or anything?" She winked at Arthur again.

"No, honey," Candy said, and Sybill said, "No, thank you," in a hard tight voice like a goddamn queen. Arthur remembered how they all used to have to mind her, when they were kids. Later she told on them. Lacy went off down the hall, looking like a girl herself. The lights were hurting Arthur's ears and he couldn't figure out how any of them had grown so old. All these old children. He could see them again on the hillside, having apple wars. He could close his eyes right now and see Verner Hess. Who he loved. Who was not his daddy, that he never knew. Candy was crying. Candy's old too, Arthur realized, soft and wrinkled, kind of like me, we were the two who refused to amount to a hill of beans. Lacy ate a Hershey bar. Myrtle was crying too, her makeup running around her eyes. Dr. Don gestured, talking to the preacher. Who was Episcopal, maybe you call them a priest. Mother had nothing to do with born-agains. The last time Arthur saw his mother, she said he needed a haircut and that he had been for her a source of constant pain. Two of Mother's old lady friends, Miss Elva Pope and Miss Lucy Dee, came in crying. The jig was up. Some of Myrtle and Don's friends, these fancy young marrieds from Argonne Hills, showed up. The lights got louder. Sybill was walking back and forth, she was grinding her teeth. Arthur thought of his girls, raising their hands to answer questions in Spanish. They'll pierce their ears, like Spanish girls. The lights were killing him. Sybill walked back and forth, grinding her teeth. A big pretty nurse with her gray hair pulled back in a bun ducked in and out, in and out of Intensive Care, closing the door behind her. Although in total despair, Arthur enjoyed her looks. Her hips moved smoothly beneath her uniform, like the movement of horses across a field. Her big white shoes squeaked slightly. Another nurse and several more doctors went in and out. Lacy was crying and Candy was patting her. It's funny how it's clear when it's all over, you know it even though nobody's said. "Can we turn off some of these lights please?" Arthur asked then but nobody said.

"You'd better come in now." The taller, gray-faced doctor threw open the door. They jostled each other, crowding into the room. Arthur wouldn't go in, he couldn't stand to see it, he's got a bad heart. He would remember his mother dressed up for church, standing at the end of the walk waiting for Verner Hess to come around in the car. The lights hurt his head too bad. He should have been here when Verner Hess died but he was not. He should have gone to work for Verner right away and left the help alone and stayed married to his own sweet Alta and raised his girls. It's too late to make amends. Too late to make amends to Alta or Mother, or Verner either. People will die on you. Arthur wondered where his own father lay, if he was buried, or where he lived. Arthur wondered if his father ever thought of him.

"Don't you want to go in there?" the big nurse asked. "She's breathing her last." The nurse had a gap between her front teeth.

"I can't stand to see it," Arthur told her, "and I wish you would cut off the goddamn lights." Which she laughed at. And then went over and cut off some of them. This was not such a bad-looking big old nurse.

Then there came a big commotion from Intensive Care and everybody was screaming and crying and Arthur knew it was over at last. Her two doctors bent from the waist in the hall right outside the door, like penguins. Sybill was screaming the loudest. "She can't die," Sybill screamed. "She can't die, she has to tell me, I have to know. She has to wake up and tell me, I've been waiting," and Candy was patting *her*.

"Know what, honey?" Candy asked.

"I have to know if she killed him," Sybill was screaming. "I have to know. She has to tell me," Sybill screamed. "She can't just die." Everybody stared at Sybill, Candy and Myrtle still crying while Sybill screamed. "She's got to tell me! She's got to tell me!" Sybill kept screaming this stuff. Arthur couldn't believe it. Sybill, who would be a pretty middle-aged woman if she'd keep her mouth shut and act right, looked terrible. Eyes all bloodshot, her whole face blotchy and red.

Two little girls, candy-stripe volunteers, started to giggle, up the hall. They thought Sybill had lost her marbles. Maybe she had. People will lose their marbles, in the instance of death. People will shit in their pants. It's awful. Some young nurses got Sybill by the arms although she was trying to fight them off and get back in the room, beating at the nurse with her fists. In times of crisis, people will go off their heads. Arthur's been off his own head for years now. It's been one crisis after another. Sybill was screaming. "She killed him and put him down there. In the well. I saw him, I saw his face."

"For God's sake," Myrtle said. Myrtle leaned back against the green tile wall and then her head dropped

over to one side and she slid down the wall real slow
in the most ladylike faint you could ever imagine.

"Hey, hey!" cried her husband, Dr. Don. "Hey,
hey! Right here!"

"Mama, Mama," said pretty Theresa, who for once
had lost her cool, and a little old white-haired nurse
came running right over to Myrtle.

Death is a desperate hour.

Sybill had really lost her marbles this time.

"Elevate her feet," said the little nurse. Somebody
turned on the rest of the goddamn lights. Lacy started
crying real loud, like a kid, Myrtle was lying flat on
her back on the floor with her feet propped up on a
stack of towels. "She can't do this to me," Sybill
wailed. "She can-NOT do THIS to ME!" Candy looked
at Sybill and then slapped her once, hard. "Ooh!
Ooh!" squeaked Miss Elva Pope and Miss Lucy Dee,
scurrying out. They carried, for some reason, umbrel-
las. Arthur realized he was laughing.

He looked for the big pretty nurse. Mother is dead,
he tried to think, but so far this meant nothing. "I
have to know," moaned Sybill, sitting at last in a
chair. Arthur looked around for Nettie, old buddy old
compadre, to see if she was also getting a kick out of
Sybill's fit, but what he saw then brought him up
short.

Nettie was out of the whole thing, over by the far
window smoking, looking out toward the hills. Arthur
went over there and touched her shoulder. She whirled
around. Arthur had his face fixed to grin, he was
thinking *Get a load of Sybill*. You could hear her all
over the place. People were coming to stand in the
doors of the rooms, to hear her. It was awful. Just
then the big nurse came walking down the hall wearing a red sweater, you could tell she was going off

duty. "Excuse me, ma'am, but I wonder if you'd care to take a little spin with me, go out for a drink perhaps? I am in shock, as you can see." Arthur said this to the nurse. A person in despair has got nothing to lose, and he was never the kind of man to let a woman just walk on by. "Goddamn it, Arthur, you ought to be ashamed of yourself. You haven't even got a car," Nettie said. "I'm not myself," Arthur said to the nurse, "as you can see. Perhaps some other time." The nurse was laughing. "For future reference," she said, "the name is Mrs. Palucci." Sybill yelled, "How can we find out now? How can we ever know?" "How do you spell that?" Arthur asked. The lights were real loud. Mrs. Palucci passed on by. Arthur looked over at Nettie thinking she might be amused in the end by Sybill, Nettie's a tough old bird, but Nettie's little black eyes were as sharp and as bright as cinders, as glowing coals. Nettie's eyes were terrible. She said, *"Elizabeth is lost."* Nettie looked past Arthur, past Sybill, down the crowded hall, beyond the hills. *"Oh Jesus,"* Nettie said.

*I*T must have been a hundred degrees that afternoon. Her own beauty shop swam, for a second, in her eyes as she came out, turned back, and locked the door. Her mind was a jumble, her mother was dead. But it calmed Candy, coming back from the hospital to her shop, closing up, it always did. She dropped the key in her pocket and looked up to see Don waiting for her, his BMW parked at the curb. Don looked exhausted, the way she felt.

"Listen, Candy, are you sure you want to do this?" he asked abruptly, and Candy looked him in the eye and said, "Yes."

"I've done it before," she said.

Don stood sweating on the sidewalk, looking at her. "That was different," he said.

"It's okay," Candy said. But she appreciated him coming down here, when he had so many other people and things to tend to—he had gotten Myrtle home, and in bed, and had seen to all the rest of them too, she reckoned, and made all the arrangements—after all of this, he had come to see her. After he'd gotten Dr. Grey to give Sybill a shot for her nerves and told her to hold her tongue. In those words, that's what he'd said, "Hold your tongue!" Candy had heard him. Candy had slapped her, earlier, and told her to shut her mouth, and got noplace at all. But an old maid will mind a man. And Sybill wanted somebody to shut her up anyway, you could see that. Sybill in her whole life had never acted the way she did that afternoon. She never had. Candy remembered Sybill sitting inside with Mother while all the rest of them went out to play in the snow. Sybill didn't want to get wet, or cold, or dirty. She wouldn't eat snow cream either. She thought it might have germs. Later, she wouldn't learn to jitterbug. So Sybill couldn't be happy, screaming the way she was screaming that afternoon.

She had gone somewhat crazy, if you asked Candy. Now this is okay, and natural. Candy has heard it, and seen it, before. Sybill is not any better than anybody else when push comes to shove. If you're not crazy sooner, you'll be later, is the way Candy looks at it. Little kids who are so wild will make Phi Beta Kappa and grow up to be brain surgeons. Tony was this way. He used to smoke cigarettes when he was eleven, now he's in law school. She can't take any credit. That's the way things are. People who have done it right all their lives will go off their heads in their thirties and forties. A man might go out for a pack of Winstons and never come back, for instance, or go out in the woods to live in a solar teepee. Candy's seen it all. The line of work she's in, she's seen it and heard it all. Life is long and wild and there is usually a point where it makes you crazy. That's natural.

So Candy for one was glad to see Sybill act like a

real person for a change. It was funny, though, slapping her—funny in the sense of weird. It made Candy realize that it's been years since she touched Sybill, years. She does everybody else's hair, even Miss Elizabeth's. But Sybill left, and now she gets hers cut up in Roanoke, so that's that. That's fine. Only if it was Candy, she'd feather it around the face, to soften her, and layer the back and sides. She'd give Sybill a Spun Sand rinse to blend in the gray. Sybill's face felt funny to her hand. She shouldn't have slapped her. The trouble with Candy is, she's always done exactly what she feels like, that's just the way she is.

She's never *not* done anything. But she should have let Don handle Sybill. Leave it up to a man. This reminds her of when the kids were little and she was raising them herself, sometimes she felt like some man could walk in off the street, any man at all, the garbage man or a guy from the water company, and tell them to do something or other, anything, and they'd say "Oh sure" and do it. Right away. They'd just say "Oh sure" and do it, when she'd been telling them to do it for half an hour. Not that she told them much. But that's not what she means, that's not the point. A man's the point. Any man at all. It used to make her so mad, but there it is.

And there was Don on the sidewalk to ask her, taking care of it. Taking care of business. Like Elvis. Elvis pitched a fit at his own mother's death. In fact he used to keep chickens at Graceland because his mother liked to throw them corn. Candy can see that. And Don, if she told him, could see that too. Elvis had a sense of family. Don does too, which is funny, since it's not even his family. Not his own blood kin. Or maybe it isn't funny. Arthur can't do it, he's too delicate and too drunk, he's got a bad heart, and

Nettie's old now, with her own hands full. Somebody has got to do things. When a hole comes in a family, somebody has got to come forward and fill it. Somebody has to get on the telephone, make arrangements. Don is the orphan, the one from no family, and yet he's the one with more of a sense of it than anyone else.

"We'll keep this in the family," he said to Sybill at the hospital, said to all of them. "You can hold your tongue now," he said, and Sybill did. She was probably glad to. It's a terrible thing the way most women—well, most people, really—want to be told what to do. Candy runs into that. Sometimes she tells them. They ask her, and she tells them and sometimes they do it, or not. She's not a person who likes to tell them, but they ask. They like to be told. It's all in her line of work. Or it might be that they just want somebody to listen, and that's all. Because there's nobody at home to listen to them, so often that's all. That's finally what shut up Sybill. "We hear you, Sybill," said Don. Sybill put on some lipstick then and drove herself back to the motel. Maybe that's all she wanted.

So Don took Myrtle and Theresa home, and took Lacy up to Miss Elizabeth's, and Nettie took Arthur. Candy came on home by herself, which is the way she likes it. You get spoiled, after a while. You need your time.

Candy came back, and Doris was straightening up, and she told her to go on home and said she'd close up herself. Doris left. Doris said she was sorry about Miss Elizabeth. Doris is a sweet heavy girl from out in the valley, saving up to go to beauty school, with the prettiest, whitest teeth. She sweeps up and shampoos. Candy hopes she will keep on saving, and actually go, and rise up in the world. A woman needs something to do. But Doris has a boyfriend, so you can't tell. Kids around here get married so fast, they can't see beyond the back seat of a car. They can't see the trap. Well, it doesn't look like a trap, then. Candy couldn't see it either, nobody can. And you can't tell them.

Doris finished and left. The phone was ringing. Candy let it ring. She knew it was about Mother, everybody in town wanting to know. Two people had already come over, she saw, and left food on the counter, all wrapped up. People in Booker Creek are real thoughtful and sweet. It was a macaroni salad, with English peas and pimientos in it, and a sour-cream pound cake. "From the Kitchen of Holly Sue McCready" said a little sticker on the foil around the pound cake. Candy couldn't see how people already knew. Doris had known already, too. Candy wasn't sure who the macaroni salad was from. She has done Holly Sue McCready's hair for fifteen years, she remembers when it got so thin after she had the twins. They ordered her a partial wig then, from California. Candy remembers everything. You have to.

Well. She put the macaroni salad and the pound cake in the refrigerator she keeps there, in back of the shop. She put the pound cake next to Lydia's bean sprouts and cottage cheese. Lydia is real skinny and real young. She talks a mile a minute. Lydia's all ready for the punk look, she can't wait for it to hit Booker Creek. She can't wait for somebody to come in and tell her to give them a Mohawk and dye it green. Fat chance! Candy tells her. She's got ladies that still want a bubble, or a French twist. Lydia isn't long for Booker Creek. She's read too many magazines—and Candy straightened the magazines. *Redbook, McCalls, Family Circle, Good Housekeeping,*

Vogue, Cosmopolitan, Harper's, Town and Country, Gourmet, Ladies' Home Journal, you name it, she's got it. Candy's ladies save them and bring them in.

It calms her, closing up. You're one step nearer the grave when your mother dies. Nobody standing in between you and the great beyond, as Miss Elizabeth herself would have said. Candy used to get so mad because her mother always had another word, a fancier word, for whatever it was. Not Candy. She calls a spade a spade. But the older she gets, the more she understands that about her mother. She'll make her look real pretty too, the way she would have wanted it. Candy's got taste. She's not morbid, either. She can do it. Dying doesn't scare her, but all she's got time for's the here and now, which is plenty enough, and more than enough, for her. She straightened the magazines, checked the dryers, put all the brushes in the solution, put the towels in the bag for the laundry. She has a pale-pink-and-gray décor. She loves the way it smells, in a shop. That was the first thing that got her about it, in fact, in addition to the fact that she has always liked hair. The smell calms her, now. It's perfume, and shampoo, and formaldehyde. After she gives a permanent, she sprays pine Lysol in the air, so there's that, too. It's sweet, but there's an edge to it. Candy likes that. She went around with a bag and got what she needed, and closed up. She has rose-pink shag carpet on the floor. It took her a long time to get her own shop. She had it planned right down to the carpet by then.

"Are you sure you want to do it?" Don asked again.

They stood outside on the sidewalk in the sticky heat. People were passing by. "Hey, Dr. Don, hey, Candy," they said. The mercury vapor streetlight on the corner came on then, soft and sort of slow the way it does, magical. Growing up, Tammy always said it was magical. Tammy's real artistic. The light is lavender. Don looked old.

"I've done it before," Candy said.

Mrs. Vance Bristol came up and grabbed her elbow. "Honey, I'm just so sorry," she said, "if there's anything I can do—" Candy said no, but thanks, and watched her click off down the street in her spike heels. Fashion takes a long time to get to Booker Creek, in spite of influences such as magazines and little Lydia Nicewander. Suetta Bristol has worn shoes like that for twenty years, and she used to look good in them. She'd bring a ham, Candy knew, probably take it up to Mother's or over to Myrtle's. Suetta Bristol is famous for her baked hams which she always takes to the family when somebody dies. She bastes them with Coke and orange juice.

"I'm just going up to change first," Candy told Don. She lives over her shop, where she's lived for years. After a while, it's hard to move or change. Your habits set in. It might have been that some time back, she might have—but you can't tell. Time passes. There's some things you'll never know.

He looked so tired. "Can I come up there, Candy?" he asked.

She looked both ways on the street. They'd been at this for twenty years. "Well," she said.

Candy went up the stairs and after a few minutes, he came too. She poured him some gin in a jelly glass and he stood by the window, looking down on the street, to drink it. He wore khaki pants and a navy linen jacket, with a striped tie. White shoes. Candy always gets a kick out of the way Don looks here, in her apartment. Probably she ought to straighten up. But she keeps her shop straight, so she likes to let things go at home. Don doesn't fit, he looks funny in her apartment, he's never said one word about it. Maybe by now he likes it. Don sipped his drink and looked out the window.

You can see everything. Right across the street is Hardison's Hardware, and then the Family Shop in what used to be Millard Cline's Florist, years ago, and the bank on the corner, and the dimestore's next on the corner across from the bank. It's gone down, since Verner Hess died. In front of the hardware is a wooden stand that has tomato plants on it, and marigolds, and rosebushes, and a high-school boy out watering them with the hose. On down the street is the jewelry store and Bickman's furniture store and an office supply, and you can see the steeple on the Episcopal church beyond that, and then the old houses that have been made over into lawyers' and doctors' offices, like the old Harrison house, which is OB-GYN. The Smith house is now the Cardinal Tearoom, put in by Lou Durgin's son who was an alcoholic in New York and came back home. At the far end of the street is Miss Elizabeth's up on the hill. Candy lives right here. The streetlight makes a lavender pool on the sidewalk that's magical, Tammy said.

Don said, "Do you remember that time when we were all up at Miss Elizabeth's for Thanksgiving dinner and Karen and Tammy got under the dining-room table and nobody could find them? Remember how we sent all the other kids out in the yard, looking? We really thought they were lost," he said.

Candy said, "The corn pudding burned."

Don said, "I remember." Their girls when they were little looked alike, with yellow hair. She used to French braid it. It's funny. She's known Don a long, long time, since high school. It's been infrequent.

There was a time when she was married, and a time when she thought Gray Justice would marry her. She's known other men, off and on. Don has never said a word, or minded. Well, how could he? But you know, deep down, he could. You know what men expect. Except for Don, who is different, who is a genuinely good man. He loves his wife and family, he works on it. He is a man who does right. Sometimes Candy thinks he works on it too hard.

And as for her, Don says she's the wild card in his deck. He never meant for it to happen, or to continue. Candy believes this. Often, they'll go months, or years, between. It's up to him. She's here. And it has suited her, too, since she doesn't want a regular man—Candy likes men, but she doesn't want one. She's beyond making plans, or fixing up the house, or asking somebody what they think about something in the paper. She knows that's what most people want. But not her. She knows what it can be, after all. And she and Don are like an old pair of shoes, real comfortable, back in the closet. Don's different here. Here, he says, he lets down his hair. He doesn't have to get ahead in the world, or figure anything out.

"Candy, Candy," he said.

She had her slip on. She came back up behind him and put her arm around his stomach. Don used to be real skinny, in high school. Then he got sort of heavy. Now he's real trim, he runs three miles a day. Myrtle goes to Total Woman health spa, but Candy doesn't do a thing. She's too busy working, that's a fact. Plus she really doesn't care.

"Every time somebody dies, I feel like they're dying twice," Don said. "When Verner died, it almost killed me, because it made me miss my own father. I guess because I never knew him. It was like two deaths. And now it's the same way with Miss Elizabeth. It makes me miss what I didn't have, kind of like the way they say a leg still aches when it's been cut off."

"Hush, Don," Candy said. She has yet to meet a man who didn't try to talk too much. And Don is into this—relating, he calls it. Expressing his feelings.

Her own feelings went like this—in about ten minutes she had to go over to the funeral home and fix her mother's hair and makeup so she could lie in her coffin looking good until they buried her, the next day. The coffin cost fourteen hundred dollars, paid for by Dr. Don. Candy planned to put a White Mink rinse on Miss Elizabeth's hair, to tone down the yellow. And hugging Don from behind, she thought, I wouldn't mind it, you know, right now. There's a link between somebody dying and this. But we both know better, we know what's right. Don finished his drink and straightened his tie, and kissed her. It was businesslike. He was on his way home, and nervous.

Candy was a little nervous too. She kept trying things on, deciding what to wear. This was not like her. I'll have to see people at the funeral home, she was thinking. She couldn't just wear what she usually did, a smock and slacks, or a uniform. Finally she put on a pale blue pants suit.

She parked between two hearses in the back, and Mr. Gurney Fletcher let her in. Gurney Fletcher is a big man, maybe two fifty, two sixty, with fat red cheeks. Every Christmas, he's Santa in the Shriners parade. The children in town all say he looks like a pig, and he does. Gurney Fletcher, Jr., Little Gurney, who is Tony's age and played on the junior-high football team with him, is just as bad. He used to sit at Candy's kitchen table, eating peanut-butter-and-marshmallow-creme sandwiches. Little Gurney stood right behind his daddy, both of them sweating, wearing suits.

"Hello, Mrs. Snipes," Little Gurney said. He's already losing his hair.

"Come in, Candy honey," said Gurney Fletcher.

Candy had been there, before. She had fixed up old Tyler Balsam, and Mrs. Clarence Wampler, and Janette Little who died in a wreck by the Chicken Bridge. The boy who was driving, Hugh Roberts, never got over it. Janette Little was real hard to do, but it meant a lot to her mother, who has been one of Candy's ladies for years. The saddest one she ever did was Juanita and Ted Sizemore's little girl who was born with a hole in her heart. Why does this stuff happen? you ask yourself. The answer is, you don't know.

Miss Elizabeth was wearing her gray voile dress with the white lace collar and cuffs, which Lacy and Myrtle had picked out. The dress had a spray of silk violets at the collar. Her hands were folded on the little white Bible she kept by her bed. That was a real nice touch, Candy thought, but she'd have to work on her nails. They had asked the Fletchers to put stockings and shoes on her too, even though she'd be covered from the waist on down. It didn't seem right not to, although Gurney had told them that most people don't have it done. Somebody was singing "Mister Sandman" on Gurney Fletcher's FM radio.

"Well, what do you think?" Gurney said.

Candy reached over and took off her mother's glasses. She looked funny without them, blank and soft, old. After a woman reaches a certain age, you can tell what she's like by the lines on her face. Miss Elizabeth's face looked sad in death, and sweet. Not angry, or mean—Candy has seen that, too. Just soft and sad and kind of worn out. It's hard to be a good woman. "You all have done a real good job, Gurney," she said.

And it was neat as a pin in that back room where they worked. He had her coffin on a kind of a little cart, wheeled over to a table where Candy could spread out her stuff, which she did. Gurney and Little Gurney and their assistant, Ralph Joiner, stood back and talked about fishing while she worked, to put her at her ease. Candy had known what to bring, but she hadn't known what to expect. About her mother, that is. The main thing was the thing which is always true and which you always tend to forget. Miss Elizabeth was dead. Her spirit was gone. Her flesh was flesh, like it all is, only a little bit more like modeling clay. You could make, and Candy did, a bit of a smile, the way for instance Miss Elizabeth might have smiled to glance down and see a flower in her yard.

Candy covered up her face and got to work. She used the dry shampoo, then a little White Mink to dull out the yellow, then she sprayed on Redken Airset and blew it dry. Then she set her magnetic rollers, as usual, thinking that hair is a funny thing—it's not like flesh. It doesn't change in death. It's the most vital organ of the body by a long shot. It's the most responsive. You can damage hair any way you want and it will still come back as healthy as it ever was. It will grow after death. It's one of the great mysteries. Along with death. Candy has always been good with hair. And sometimes she thinks she was born knowing all about death, too, which might be why she's lived like she has. She took the rollers out, took the towel off, and combed her out around the face and at the crown and the sides, where people could see, and then sprayed her. She did her nails, Dusty Mauve, and cleaned her glasses, and did her makeup. She put her glasses back on. The radio was playing Willie Nelson, "Georgia on My Mind." By then Candy's hands were shaking. Gurney was telling Ralph Joiner about a sand shark he caught one time at Myrtle Beach. Candy was glad they were in there.

Then Gurney came over and did a better job of folding her hands on the Bible, intertwining her fingers. The Dusty Mauve looked real pretty. He said he'd take off her rings right before he closed the coffin, and give them to the family. He said he always did that.

"She looks real nice," he said. "Most people put too much blush on. They think it makes them look more alive but it don't," he said.

Candy said, "No."

She could hear people already coming in the front. They had switched the radio to religious. She could smell the flowers. Miss Elizabeth was a lady, and she looked like a lady in death. She had lived, Candy reckoned. She had had children, she had felt things, thought things, she had died. She had loved one man, and another man had loved her. It's hard to say which of those conditions is better, or worse. Sometimes, neither one of them happens. That's probably the worst. Candy knows—she's heard it all. But Mother had had a life. And as for God, what she believed in, Candy couldn't tell you. She's not the type to say a word about God. Mother looked peaceful, at rest, the way you're supposed to. Not all of them do. While she was alive, she was worried so much of the time—about money, about what people would think, about her children. Miss Elizabeth and Candy never saw eye to eye. They were natural strangers. They couldn't help it. Candy has turned out different from what her mother hoped. There was a time when Candy had to get out, to get away, or she would have died. *Died.* There were other times, too. Well. Candy thinks back on those times now and it seems crazy how upset she was, it seems like another person. But it was her. Candy used to get so upset, she used to hate Miss Elizabeth. She took off her mother's glasses and put a little silver liner right along the lashline. She was certainly a lady, you know she couldn't have killed Jewell Rife, no matter what Sybill thinks she saw. Sybill is crazy anyway, it's just like her to try and spoil everything. Don told Sybill he would deal with it in due time. Then he made her promise to shut up about it.

Candy put her mother's glasses back on her just as Lacy, all trembly, came in. Candy touched up Mother's lipstick. She was crying.

"There," she said. She stood back. She felt good, but she was crying. "Isn't she pretty?" Candy said.

*E*LIZABETH is dead and Nettie has got to go to the funeral. You have to dress up for a trip to town, you have to dress up for a funeral. *But you stay here.* Elizabeth has died of heart failure which comes to us all in the end except for a few like Cary Grant who is more in demand than ever or Douglas Fairbanks Jr. still suave and handsome he hits the big seventy-five mark on December ninth he has been on *Love Boat* a couple of times recently. He said we would take a trip, well why not go on the Love Boat? *I just want a good time girl,* he used to tell me that. Lively Ann-Margret grew up in a funeral parlor which is where Elizabeth is now. Imagine that. He used to pick up the mandolin and sing. *You have to walk that lonesome valley you have to walk it by yourself, nobody else will walk it for you, you have to walk it by yourself.* That midget's sick he's got an incurable disease he can't walk he's not long for this world he'll have to walk it by himself. It's a long valley between here and town. Before that of course he'd like to set the story straight about his painful divorce and his departure from Fantasy Island, now that's a trip. It's important to have insurance which Ed McMahon will give you if you will respond before March twelfth. Of course you can't buy insurance for failure of heart. Jackie Onassis will not marry again. Instead, she'll travel. She's had it! Ha ha and me too! *I'm getting out of this one-horse town* he said *honey, I'll take you too. We'll take us a big long trip, we'll go to Florida you'll like it there you can get you a suntan, honey, there's flowers blooming all the time.* A lady from California drove through and told Nettie they get All My Children faster out there, a month ahead of us, and Erica has already died in a wreck. Which must not be true as she's not even planning a trip although currently she is estranged from all. Erica's such a bitch. The Wacky Way I Met My Mate was that my next-door neighbor asked me to take care of his dog while he went to Reno, Nevada, for a divorce. I could tell he was a nice man since he fed his dog chicken livers, a high liver, ha ha! Well the dog bit me! And he came back and took me out to dinner we fell in love by candlelight. It's a heart-shaped scar and now every time I see it, I think about the Wacky Way I Met My Man. Love leaves scars. Love hurts, and love is blind. In Ogdensburg, New York, they've got a state order to keep Dr. L. D. Bogdanovitch from operating on patients because he's blind. I do it by touch, he says. But doctors can't save Elizabeth now she has to walk it by herself. *At Daytona Beach the sand is so wide you can walk for hours you can see for miles I'll take you there, you'll have to wear dark glasses.*

*I*LLUMINATED by rosy light from Jesus's robe, they stood together to recite the anthem. Afternoon sun fell through the stained-glass window onto the printed program in Lacy's hands. Jesus himself stood holding his shepherd's crook amid a circle of fluffy white lambs and little children. The children, wildly out of proportion, came up to about his knees. In the middle window, he was kicking the moneylenders out of the temple; sun came in through the shimmering gold as it spilled down the left-hand side of the window, out of the moneylenders' grasp. Saint Catherine stood in the last window on Lacy's side, head bowed, against a royal-blue background. The golden spokes of her wheel formed a shining halo about her head.

This, too, had been Lacy's ambition: to be a saint. She used to fast—at least she skipped meals—and pray. Odd that she never noticed how weird the children look in the first window, like Munchkins. The Shepherd of Oz. Her mother lay in her coffin, banked by flowers, at the front of the church. The smell of the flowers was heady, almost overpowering up at the front where the family had to sit. Like the junior prom, which Lucy attended with Louie Scuggs. Like the scent in Millard Cline's florist shop, all those years ago; she can barely remember. If only she could sit at the back.

George Llewellyn, the pale young rector, looked splendid in all those robes. Those vestments—that purple cloak. No wonder she wanted to be a saint. Yet he was nervous, too; perspiration, in spite of the air conditioning, beaded his upper lip. No wonder: right before the service, outside the church, Arthur addressed him as "Your Honor." Arthur said, "Your Honor, I know you'll pardon me if I just stay out here, I have a bad heart. I'll be with you in spirit, Your Honor." Sybill had been furious. Now Lacy envisioned Arthur outside in his car, hand over his heart. It won't do to get tickled now. Arthur's car was long, yellow, dented, and made a terrible noise. If only she could sit at the back—not seeing them, she could feel even more somehow the weight of all the people they had grown up with, the full weight of the past, behind her in these pews, pressing her up against all the flowers. Lacy has never really liked hothouse flowers. She wanted, desperately, to be a saint. But now the anthem:

I am the resurrection and the life, saith the Lord;
he that believeth in me though he were dead, yet shall
  he live;
and whosoever liveth and believeth in me shall never die.

I know that my Redeemer liveth,
and that he shall stand at the latter day upon the
  earth;

and though this body be destroyed, yet shall I see God;
whom I shall see for myself and mine eyes shall
    behold,
and not as a stranger.

For none of us liveth to himself,
and no man dieth to himself.
For if we live, we live unto the Lord;
and if we die, we die unto the Lord.
Whether we live, therefore, or die, we are the Lord's.

Blessed are the dead who die in the Lord;
even so saith the Spirit, for they rest from their labors.

Lacy sank back gratefully onto the cushioned pew.
There was some comfort to be found in language,
after all. Her mother was right about that. Miss Elizabeth had left the Methodist church of her youth to
become an Episcopalian because she found the service more lovely, she said. She said it was "sheer
poetry," and adamantly opposed the new *Book of
Common Prayer*. She signed petitions, which came
in the mail. And the language was still lovely. She
was still right. But it seemed strange to Lacy, after so
long, to feel the phrases rolling on her tongue, to
taste their familiarity. The thin gold cross on the altar
was the same gold cross. Lacy felt sure that she was
the only one who had come to church with Mother
out of desire. Sybill came because she thought it was
her duty, which seemed to be why she did everything. Verner Hess came on Easter because she made
him. A country man, he was uncomfortable with
exactly what she loved, this ritual, what he called "all
the whoop-dee-doo." Arthur wouldn't come, nor would
Candy, after a time. Myrtle switched to the Methodist
church because it had a more active youth group—
the Episcopal church, at that time, being attended

mostly by old ladies and Lacy, the congregation numbering under thirty on any given morning. Myrtle's MYF used to have Sweetheart Dinners, and make field trips to Myrtle Beach. There was a way in which Lacy wanted to go to the MYF, like Myrtle. She wanted to go to Myrtle Beach. But she was afraid she wouldn't have anybody except Louie Scuggs to ask to the Sweetheart Dinner, and besides, she loved to kneel on the velvet kneepads, and see the candles glowing on Christmas Eve. Kneeling, and standing, and sitting: it was a comfort having something to do, in a church. Knowing that no one would have a chance to say anything out of order, or—as Mother would say—anything in bad taste. Lacy could see how she felt, kneeling and standing, and sitting, and kneeling, making the right responses that in the end we shall all ascend into light.

When was it, how was it, that Lacy ceased to believe? She remembers the way it was, believing, the rush of emotion, the way her head felt light. It seems that one moment she was a saint, and then she was a student, and then somehow she was married. All with a fearful intensity, with a total disregard for the facts. She makes no excuses. That's how it was. She transferred all that belief straight from God straight to her professors straight to Jack. Who was also one of her professors. Unfair to everybody concerned, including herself. But she can still remember the way she felt. *I sing a song of the saints of God, patient and brave and true, who lived and fought and loved and died for the Lord they loved and knew. And one was a doctor and one was a queen, and one was a shepherdess on the green, they were all of them saints of God and I mean, God helping, to be one, too.* The service continues. Lacy is a whiz at the right responses. Her mother is dead. This is what she hates, this coldness she sees in herself. She wonders if it's new, or if she's always had it. She could kill Jack. They had such good intentions, she and Jack. She loved him. But when a man leaves you, you hate him, too. Lacy hated her mother sometimes, too, in a way. It strikes her how the two are similar, death and divorce. In divorce, one person dies to another just as surely as if a physical death has occurred. Only it's a lot harder because the corpse is still there to be dealt with, still up and walking around. Still *talking*. Impossible, then, any coming to terms: she will never come to terms with her mother either, of course.

Those questions which she never asked in real life will continue endless in her head: *Why did she go, why did she leave me? Why did she let Sybill be the mother, so often, to me?* Sybill, almost ten years old when Lacy was born, took care of her until she was eight, until Sybill went off to school. They never write letters, now. Lacy buys Sybill a nice sweater every Christmas. Was Mother just tired of it, of raising children, by then? Were Candy and Arthur too much for her? Or was it some particular thing, or the lack of something, in Lacy? Especially since she tried so hard, she was so good—Candy, for instance, was *bad*. Bad when she flunked Spanish, when she got kicked out of band, when she ran away from home, when she got pregnant, when she got married. Candy took up attention, and tears, and time. Mother lay on the fleur-de-lis loveseat before the bay window and wept: "Why does she do this to me?" And somehow, everybody seemed to feel, you couldn't expect much from a boy. Boys will be boys, especially Arthur. Sybill made straight A's, and did the laundry. Myrtle was Miss Everything. Perhaps by the time Lacy came along, everyone was simply exhausted, except for Verner Hess. A sweet and limited man. It felt so good to cry. Lacy loved him, she did. How has she grown angry, and old, and cold? She did have good intentions. Now she will not be a saint, even though she kneels, after so many years, in prayer.

O God, whose mercies cannot be numbered: Accept our prayers on behalf of your servant Elizabeth, and grant her an entrance into the land of light and joy, in the fellowship of your saints, through Jesus Christ our Lord, who lives and reigns with you and the Holy Spirit, one God, now and for ever. Amen.

Amen. Into the land of light and joy. At Cape Canaveral this morning the shuttle *Challenger* took off at 7:30 a.m. and rocketed Sally Ride into space. "Sally, have a ball," her husband said. Somehow Lacy always knew she'd never have a ball. But maybe she's coming to some glimmer of understanding. At this age, growing up—or is that ever possible? Her niece Theresa, at the funeral home last night, reminded Lacy of herself as they all stood together greeting those who came, and everyone came, discussing gardens and baseball and how many babies they or their children had had and where everyone went to school. Theresa, pale and confused, asked, "Is the conversation at something like this always so *trivial?*" That's Theresa, who used to be a cheerleader and now wants to be a writer and says "shit" a lot, and sees everything as ironic. Which is only partially true in Lacy's opinion and has long been grasped by her own tough Kate. In the newspaper photograph this morning, for instance, the shuttle's launch was pictured from across a lake, so that its ascent, that phallic thrust, those clouds of smoke, also appeared in reverse, as it seemed to be burrowing into the depths of the lake, into the lake's reflection. Trick photography: up or down? That's the problem with irony, someone should tell Theresa. It can go either way. The lake reminded Lacy of the silent tarn in the beginning paragraph of "The Fall of the House of Usher." Her head is so full of ridiculous things. Small wonder that she couldn't finish, didn't want to teach: Lacy feels she has nothing to say, and a lot to learn. Still there came that glimmer, in the parking lot of the Piggly Wiggly, how ironic: Yet why not, why not there as well as anywhere else, as well as here? Lacy finds it ironic that her mother and Sally Ride have ascended into light together. While the rest of the world bats around in the dark—

"Let go," Lacy said, and they stood, Sybill clutching at her sleeve. Even now, Lacy realized, even now Sybill thinks I have to mind her. Of course she's crazy, hysterical. Maybe she's always been crazy. *"We'll get to the bottom of this,"* said Don. In a clear still lake in Florida, the missile roared, descending. Lacy wants to get to the bottom of this, too. She wants to know. Is it because they are the two outsiders, Lacy and Sybill, that they need to know? Is it because they are cold? Even when Sybill first explained it there at the hospital, Lacy had a chill, a premonition, a notion. *There might be something to this, after all.* She could kill Jack. And in some terrible, ancient, resentful part of her brain, she began to feel, irrationally, that Sybill may be somehow right. Except Lacy has also begun to feel that it is her own body under discussion, her own body there at the bottom of the well. Lacy is terrified.

And the only person she wanted to talk to was Jack. Dressed for the funeral home last night, she stared at the old black phone in Mother's house for the longest time; she nearly dialed. She imagined Jack and Susan having dinner, *coq au vin*. Jack is a pretty good cook. It was pathetic. Jack was the only person Lacy wanted to talk to about this, about how scared it made her. Susan has long black hair. She is very young. Lacy was pathetic. Reminding herself of one of Pavlov's dogs—or that horrible thing she read in the paper about abused children, who always want to return to the abusive parent, it seems, always, if given a choice. Jack said, "Lacy, I don't love you. I'm sorry, but there it is. I am in love with someone else. I'm telling you this to avoid misunderstanding and false hopes. I will always think very highly of you, of course." *Of course.* She's so scared. Now she thinks she stopped being a saint because it was too scary. Now she feels open, bloody, exposed—like a wound. Not a pretty image. And the image ladies are all here at the funeral: the Poetry Society. Slim pastel volumes privately printed. Chicken-salad sandwiches and sonnets, on summer afternoons. This strikes Lacy as lovely. And Miss Elva Pope herself was to read "'Tis the Last Rose of Summer" beside the grave, at Mother's request. God knows what else Mother requested, in those letters left in the safety deposit box, inscribed with her spidery hand. "Concerning My Last Rites." "Concerning My Worldly Possessions." "My Last Will and Testament." They hadn't opened the other two. God knows what else she wanted, what any one of us really wants. *Not to die.* The Poetry Society had appeared in force, and the Garden Club. At the end of the Rites for the Burial of the Dead, printed on the program, Lacy found:

FLOWER IN THE CRANNIED WALL

Flower in the crannied wall,
I pluck you out of the crannies,
I hold you here, root and all, in my hand,
Little flower—but if I could understand
What you are, root and all, and all in all,
I should know what God and man is.

The sun, reflected through Jesus's robe, glowed
crimson on the page. It was lovely. Almost in a trance,
Lacy knelt, and prayed, and rose, and sang. Mrs.
Luther Crouse, who used to teach all of them piano,
was pounding the organ to death. "I Know That My
Redeemer Liveth": not an irony, a lie. They filed out,
one by one. Candy, sobbing loudly and leaning against
her grown son Tony whom Lacy hasn't seen for years
and wouldn't have recognized; Myrtle, also crying,
but more tastefully, supported on one side by Dr. Don
and on the other by Sean, glowering, all dressed up;
Theresa, pale and ethereal, trying to give the impression of having nothing to do with Don's sister Louise,
the down-to-earth Louise who walks out beside her;
Sybill, perfectly in control; and Kate, and Nettie, and
Lacy. Nettie wore a shiny black dress which buttoned up the front, the buttons made of something
like mica, catching the light. Kate, who had nothing
but jeans, wore the navy-blue skirt Lacy had bought
her this morning at J. C. Penney. Lacy wondered
what Nettie thought of all this, Nettie who went to
the primitive log church in the old days, when they
were girls, and then not at all. Nettie wore a man's
black workshoes. Lacy kept noticing details she'd
point out to Jack. Candy and Myrtle were both crying.
Lacy felt closer to them than she had in years. She
remembers Mother planting daffodils in autumn, she
remembers holding the little basket with the bulbs. It

was hard to imagine then that spring would come. Everything in childhood took such a long time.

The sun was enormously hot, they had to shake hands with the rector. Arthur's car was gone and there was no sign of Arthur, either, he was probably drunk by now, or dead too. It was just so hot. So hot, and all the blazing light. So many people, and where is Kate? Myrtle said, "Lacy, I tried to catch you. Jack called just before we left the house. He said to tell you he's coming, he'll be here tomorrow." Myrtle's mascara was running, her pretty blue eyes were red. "I don't want to see him," Lacy said, whispered, but Myrtle was gone. Nobody heard. The stones of the church burn her arm, her shoulder, but she's all right. Shit. She was doing just fine, let's get to the bottom of this. Lacy leaned against the stone wall of the church with her heart doing some absurd little two-step as if she were twenty again and Jack were coming courting as if they were still in love; for a minute she couldn't even move, oppressed by the weight of the sun.

*A*FTER a while it got him real nervous, looking at the church, and thinking what all was going on in there, and frankly he was hot as hell too. His car didn't have any air. So he thought, Well, I'll go out to the One Stop, and see what Clinus and them are doing, so he did. The first thing he noticed was Clinus's billboard, which said REST IN PEACE. Clinus never missed a trick, even if he never set foot hardly away from the One Stop. Candy said Dr. Don said Clinus has got that disease where you won't leave home. But they call everything a disease these days. What Arthur's got is nerves and despair.

Roy Looney was out in front pumping gas for Mrs. Brown who used to teach third grade. Since her husband died, she's been spending all his money, she's got a new black Buick Regal. Roy gave Arthur a big wave and a big grin, he looked like a Texaco ad. Happy motoring! He was a nice kid, though, like Nettie said he's got him a scholarship to East Tennessee State. Roy has good prospects and high hopes.

"Hello, Mr. Hess!" Roy said. Mrs. Brown had small black beady eyes.

"Well, I'm so surprised to see you're not at your own mother's funeral, Arthur," she said.

"Well, Mrs. Brown, fuck it," Arthur said. Then he could hear her hollering behind him as he climbed up the One Stop steps. He could hear Roy talking real smooth to her, trying to calm her down. Arthur didn't give a damn, either. The world is too full of sorrow and real despair to worry over ex-third-grade teachers who are mean as a snake. Arthur felt bad enough as it was. He would have been at the funeral, he would have been right there in the front row, if he could have. "Clinus?" he yelled. No Clinus. He got a beer from the cooler and went on back.

It takes a while to adjust your eyes to Fay. She keeps it so dark in there. It's like walking into the movies when the movie's already going. And then once you *can* see, you'll wish you couldn't—the way Fay has gained weight in these last years, she has put it on equal all over. She looks like the Pillsbury dough girl. You can't see her eyes over the top of her puffy cheeks. Her wrists pooch down over her hands now, those ankles as big as a child's waist, she keeps both feet stretched flat out in front of her on this round orange stool. Wears white bobby socks and shiny gold house shoes. It's hard to see a thing like that.

Arthur kept looking, though. Something was different and he was damned if he could figure out what it was. Fay was mumbling, kind of, and shifting inside her dress. This was a flowered dress which looked like it was made out of a curtain, probably it was. She'd had it on for about a month. She kept switching the channels around on her little box, and mum-

bling. So she was agitated all right, but that wasn't it.
That wasn't what was different.

Then it struck him.

Fay was wearing a hat.

It was a green felt hat like a turban, with a feather
on the side. Naturally, it looked terrible.

"Clinus!" he hollered, and Clinus said, "Come on
back." Clinus was in the kitchen.

"Where'd she get the hat?"

"Had it, I reckon." Clinus was wearing an apron,
standing by the stove. "She's got a whole closetful of
stuff, if she'd wear it. Some of it not bad."

Arthur sat down in the chair. Clinus's apron, which
had net ruffles on it, used to belong to Miss Elizabeth.

"You look real cute," Arthur said.

Dress-up day at the One Stop.

Clinus grinned. Clinus never says much, which
might be why you talk to him. Sometimes Arthur will
catch himself going on and on. Everybody does. It's
like since you know he's retarded, it doesn't matter
what you say, the way you might spill it all to somebody you happen to sit next to on a bus, because you
know you'll never see them again. That's how it is
with Clinus, too. It's like you're not really telling
anybody but he pays you just enough mind to where
you will go on talking. Doesn't say much back, though.
Clinus just looks at you while you're talking. He's got
eyes like the eyes of animals in kids' books. Bright
blue and completely round. Hair like Harpo Marx,
and wears a hat. He was wearing a Red Sox cap that
afternoon. He was mixing stuff up in a bowl. Arthur
got himself another beer out of the refrigerator and
started to talk. Arthur told him all about what Sybill
had said at the hospital and about that attractive
woman, Mrs. Palucci. He was sure Clinus had al-

ready heard about Sybill and what she was saying, but Clinus never let on if he had or hadn't. He just stared. Arthur told him all about having a nosebleed the night before and about Mother leaving the envelopes in the safety deposit box. Clinus was mixing cornmeal and buttermilk together in a yellow striped bowl. He looked down and measured some soda and sugar. Arthur went on talking. Clinus looked right at him, mixing with a big wooden spoon. You can't ever tell if he's taking it in, or not. But you *think* he is.

"What the hell are you making?" Arthur finally asked.

Clinus grinned. "Hushpuppies."

Now that beat all, making hushpuppies in the middle of the afternoon. It's a zoo out there at the One Stop. No use asking him why he's making them, either, you know why—because he wants to. Because he's got a taste for them right now. All right. Arthur started feeling better. He got himself another beer and watched Clinus get out Nettie's heavy old black iron skillet and pour in the grease. His little net ruffles swishing, it was comical. Mother used to wear that apron in front of company. Arthur could hear Fay out in the other room, over the TV, it sounded like she said "Unh-unh."

"Seems like Fay is up to something," he said to Clinus. "What's going on?"

Clinus said, "Beats me." He put a little dab of batter down in the grease, to test it, and it spattered, so he put in more. He threw those dabs down in the grease like an expert. All these years Arthur has known Clinus, he's never shown a sign of making hushpuppies. Maybe he only feels like it when it's a hundred degrees in the shade and there's a funeral going on.

"Trip," Clinus looked up from his frying and said. "She thinks she's taking a trip."

Arthur realized he meant Fay. Well, why not, why shouldn't she take a notion as well as the rest of us? Probably thought she was going to the funeral, since Nettie went.

"Done it before," Clinus said. Now this was saying a lot, for him.

Arthur said, "I tell you what gets to me more than Sybill if you want to know, it's Candy fixing Mother up, you know what I mean?"

Clinus was turning the hushpuppies over in the pan. His eyes were like round blue marbles.

Arthur said, "I mean fixing up her own mother that way. It's not right, it's not natural. But it don't seem to bother nobody else, Candy included."

Clinus said, "It ain't her mother."

"What?" Arthur had been drinking but he thought he heard Clinus right.

Clinus laid paper towels up and down the counter, for his hushpuppies. "Candy's a love child," he said. "I thought you knew."

"What are you talking about?" Arthur stood up and grabbed Clinus by the ruffles but he just ducked his head and grinned, and wouldn't say anything else. He was through talking. He had said more than Arthur ever heard him say before, and maybe more than he meant to. What the hell did Clinus know about a love child, anyway? A love child! You can't tell what Clinus knows. He might be crazy, or he might be crazy like a fox. You can't tell. Clinus wouldn't say anything else.

Then the kitchen door slammed shut and in came Roy. He stood there looking at them. *I guess we look like we're nuts*, Arthur thought, *or else like we're dancing. Two grown men, dancing.* Alta used to love to slow dance. Her favorite tune was "Mister Blue." Arthur let go of Clinus and sat back down. Roy was sweating and looking real puzzled at Arthur.

"I wish you hadn't of done that, Mr. Hess," he said all respectful and reproachful. He meant old Mrs. Brown. He's going places, that kid, you can tell.

"I wish I hadn't of too," Arthur told him, "but son, it's too late now."

Roy stood there sweating and looking at them. Clinus started taking the hushpuppies out with a spatula, one by one, laying them out on the paper towels. "Get you a beer there, Roy," Arthur said, "and pull up a chair." So Roy did, and Clinus threw some more dabs of batter into the pan, and they laid into the ones that were done, and that turned out to be some of the best eating Arthur ever did. Clinus puts a little bit of onion in them, that's the trick. It was nice in Nettie's kitchen, too. It was hot as hell outside, but in Nettie's kitchen it was cool, with the air conditioner going, and the grease sizzling, and Clinus cooking, and Roy and Arthur and Clinus eating the hushpuppies as fast as they came up out of the pan.

*M*y dad said it one time and like every other faggy thing he ever said it's kind of true, which is why he pisses me off so bad. He said, "Son, you don't appreciate things. You don't know how good you've got it. How soft it is." Then he punched me in the stomach to show he's a good guy after all, he's one of the boys. It hurt. He's not one of the boys. I'm not either, I guess, whatever that means. Mom used to say Why don't you have some friends over to play, honey? Get that, to play. She wants me to ask her friend Mary's little asshole son over here, the one that wears the Izods all the time. Izod everything, all those faggy little lizards. I bet his underwear is Izod underwear, probably they've got Izod toilet paper in every faggy bathroom in their big faggy house. Another time she said Honey, why don't you have a party? I could just see it, she'd put all these glasses out just alike, she'd have them on some kind of tray.

But what I was saying is, Dad was right. It used to be bad around here, okay, but now it's the pits. It got so bad right before the funeral I almost said, "Hey Mom, I think I *will* have a party," just to blow her right out of the water. She's sweet, though, Mom. Aunt Sybill's the bitch, or I thought she was until this thing that happened yesterday. The thing is, you don't ever know. You just don't ever fucking *know*.

So okay it got real zooey around here after Grandmother died. Everybody's all upset and crying, and Aunt Sybill comes up with all this shit and they're trying to shut her up. They don't want anybody to *know*, right? Big deal. Somebody in the tennis club might find out. Lucy Hillsborough's faggy son might find out and then he wouldn't want to play.

Mom says to me, "Oh of course there's nothing to it all but don't you tell a soul, I don't want *one word* of this to ever get out of this house," and Dad says, "Well now, first things first. We'll settle the estate and then we'll solve this little mystery. It may not be such a bad thing after all, to look into it, for all of you to get these feelings out in the open and come to terms with them. Growth is painful."

Dad said this to Mom and Aunt Sybill the morning after the funeral, in the kitchen, while he was putting on his ankle weights to go running. Mom sat at the kitchen table and cried. Aunt Sybill stood in the middle of everything hugging herself and shivering like it was winter instead of probably the hottest damn day of the year which later it turned out to be. "Well I just had these *headaches*," she said. "It was unbearable. Surely you see my point." Now all this is happening in the *morning*, right? So I just got up and I come in the kitchen for some orange juice and what do you know? Mom's crying, Sybill's crying, Dad's putting on his ankle weights all dressed up in a little white outfit, the king of clean. "Where's breakfast?" I say. Mom starts crying harder, and Dad says, "Son, can't you fix yourself some cereal at least? Is that too much to ask?" "Just fuck it," I tell them all. "See you later," and I leave. "Son, get back in here," Dad is yelling. "I'll be back in a little while," I yell back. "I'm just going out for a while," and grab my bike which is right outside the door, and I'm gone. *Gone*. I can hear Dad back there yelling. Adiós to the zoo.

It's nice, a morning like that, all the grass has still got dew on it so it looks like these little jewels, all shiny, but the sun is hot already and it smells real nice, strong and sweet and funky. I ride all over the place. I went miles, and since I didn't get any breakfast, I started feeling, I don't know, kind of *rare* or something, like I was having a mystical experience. It was like, while I was riding my bike, I was *watching myself* ride my bike, up and down those streets, past all those houses. All over Argonne Hills. Blue shutters, green shutters, picture windows, old houses with lots of little panes. I know who lives in most of them. Who the hell knows whatever goes on inside? I rode downtown and saw Candy in her shop there, doing hair. I stopped and she gave me a Coke free out of her machine. Then I rode up on Grandmother's hill but nobody was awake in her house yet, you could tell Kate was still asleep. Kate's flaky, she's cool, Lacy's cool too, for a grown-up. The thing about Mom and Dad is, they *act* so super-grown-up all the time, they're always so sure about everything. Even when they're fucked up, they act like that. You can't ever tell what's happening.

I got off my bike up there and sat under a tree by the side of the house for a while and once I thought I saw my dad, running along down at the other end of Main Street. I could barely see him. Somebody was running. I had to put my hand up to my eyes to see him at all, even then I wasn't sure. All that green and then the street and then a flash of white. In the summer sometimes you can't be sure, it all starts to wave in the sun. Heat rises, you learn that in school. I sat on the hill waiting for Kate to get up but she didn't, and then I got to thinking about Grandmother and about that kind of chocolate cake she used to make, that had mayonnaise in it, and then I got to thinking about how she used to cut things out of paper for me when I was little. She could take a plain old piece of paper and make a bird, a little man, a hat, a boat. Sometimes after it rained I'd go up there and get her to make me a bunch of little boats and then I'd sail them down the creek that ran off down the hill then, after a rain. Grandmother had blue hands. She used to take a piece of paper and fold it, and fold it, and fold it some more, and then she'd cut out a little boy, and then she'd call me and say, "Here, Sean, take his hand." So I'd hold one of the little boy's hands and she'd hold the other and move back, sort of, and all of a sudden we'd have ten little boys, all holding hands. This kind of made me cry, thinking about it, on the hill at her house that morning.

But then also she used to correct what I said all the time, and tell Mom about my manners. Fuck manners. But then it was like I could see a whole line of pale little boys all holding hands and running down the long green hill through the rising heat. I thought I'd better go downtown and get a doughnut, Mr. Fowler at the Rexall will usually spring for one. It felt like my bike was wobbling, I wasn't feeling so good by then.

So I go in the Rexall, and I'm getting this dough-nut, which is when old Aunt Sybill shows up. She saw me before I saw her, I would of left if I'd seen her first. Sybill looks all funny and her skin is pulled too tight across her face. She's buying some kind of pills. She gets the little bag, and pays Mr. Fowler, and I'm kind of hiding out by the video machines so she won't see me, over behind the cosmetics, but she sees me anyway. I act like I'm playing Ms. Pac-Man.

"Why Sean!" Sybill says, like we're at some kind of faggy tea, like she hadn't just been crying in my mom's kitchen two hours before.

"Yes ma'am." Everybody in there is looking at me now, including John Greenwood's sister who's in high school, with the big tits. She's over by the makeup, looking at me.

"Here...here..." Crazy Aunt Sybill goes fishing in her purse then and comes up with some quarters. Which she starts trying to give me, and I start trying to back off, only there's noplace to go. "Don't you want to play some games?" Aunt Sybill has a big shrill voice like that woman on "The Jeffersons."

"No ma'am, not right now," I tell her.

"Here—" she keeps saying, "here." Then I catch on that she really *wants* to give me something, any-thing, it's like a real big deal with her and I'll never get out of there if I don't do it, so I *do* it, I take the quarters and put one of them in Universe Zero, which lights up of course, so I start playing it. Sybill stays right beside me. She won't go away. She keeps trying to make conversation, you can tell, and I'm playing this game called Universe Zero. This is a game where you do okay if you come in from the left all the time and get the red asteroids first. Aunt Sybill is holding the back of my T-shirt saying stupid things. She says

"What does that mean?" when I go into the second stage and the screen turns yellow. Then she says, "How do you know which one you are?" and I say, "What?" and she repeats it, with kind of a catch in her throat. "How do you know which one you are?" she wants to know, which is so stupid I can't stand to answer so I just act like I can't hear her, over the sound of the game. I'm the one in the green starship. I move through the second stage and the third stage, I destroy the goblins and the giant mind behind the moon. I move through stars in the Nether World, I get zapped finally by a goonybird in from the right, what the hell. One hundred eighteen thousand isn't bad, at least it doesn't suck or anything, and when I turned back around, crazy Aunt Sybill was gone.

Now here's the thing I meant when I said you don't ever know, because what I felt like then was real weird. I felt sad, kind of, about Aunt Sybill, like she might not be so much of a bitch after all, for some reason having to do with how much she wanted to give me something and the way she kept asking me things. Aunt Sybill never had any kids and she won't either, you can tell. The best she'll ever get is a mercy fuck, I thought, but that made me feel mean, and real sad. *I don't want to be like them but I don't want to be like anybody else either.* I put the other quarter in and when the game starts I'm so hot I'm awesome. I move through all the stages like it was nothing, the screen goes blue, and yellow, and green, and blue again. I destroy the goblins and the mind behind the moon and this dude I've never even gotten far enough to see before, man, who comes out in the ninth stage. I move through space and time. The screen goes purple, red. I'm the one in the green starship, making tracks. I fly alone through Stellar

Space. One hundred forty-eight thousand, finally. I get to put my initials, SBD, in the machine. The B stands for Bird, my grandmother's maiden name. One hundred forty-eight thousand. SBD. It was awesome.

SYBILL sits in the striped armchair in her mother's parlor, having a hot flash. Or something. Something *like* a hot flash, not that she'd mention it to anybody in her family since they're treating her so mean. Well, they'll see! When the contractor comes to grade the hillside, then they'll see. But Sybill sighs. She doesn't really believe it any longer herself. She stares out the window, down the hill toward the town which lies flickering in a haze of heat and then she remembers, unbidden, playing hopscotch in summer, so many summers ago, and how the heat would rise that way, above the concrete in the schoolyard. She was not good at hopscotch, or any other games. She disliked them. And now she dislikes this game, too, the one they are assembled here to play, and can't imagine what in the world her mother was thinking of, to leave such instructions in that envelope.

In these four days since the funeral, Sybill has come to think of Miss Elizabeth in two completely different ways: as the overly careful, sensitive, sweet mother of her childhood, leaning down to kiss her goodnight, smelling always of lilac—and also as that mythic figure in the streaming rain, with ax upraised. Actually this second mother is more like an oil painting done in thick brilliant strokes by some crazy foreign artist, and doesn't have a thing to do with the first one. It just pops up from time to time. The space between these images is filled with hot flashes, with upset stomachs, chronic now, with sudden heavy poundings of the heart, with palpable doubt that rises to Sybill's tongue and tastes metallic, the way it used to taste when you licked a scab.

Ugh! These horrible things from childhood keep coming to mind now, she can't stop them—but worst of all are the dreams, which Sybill can't control at all, obviously, and which often feature Mr. Edward Bing in a variety of postures she'd never consider in real life. Nor would he, she's sure! These sexy, seedy dreams leave Sybill exhausted. Sometimes she wakes up weeping in her room at the Holiday Inn, and can't even remember who she is, Ms. Sybill Hess the head of Language Arts at the Roanoke Technical Institute, manager of The Oaks, and not some lowdown hussy running from the law, some woman who lives in motels and washes out her underwear in countless bathroom sinks. She longs for her true self, her own life. She longs to watch "Dialing for Dollars" with Betty again, and to fill out the little condominium order forms calling for more gravel, or woodwork repair. She'd rather, on balance, have headaches. The pursuit of truth is worse than headaches in the long run, being more painful, and bringing its bearer no sympathy whatsoever, none. Period!

You'd think they'd feel sorry for her, and appreciate what she's had to go through, but oh no. "I'm all for leaving the skeletons in the closet—" Myrtle actually said that. "You mean in the *well*," said Sybill. "Now Sybill—" Don had the nerve to grin at her, just grin at her, exactly like she was a small child they were humoring. It's humiliating. Nobody believes her, and Sybill isn't even sure that she believes herself. What she remembered wasn't clear anyway, not even the first time when she told it to Bob, and now the more she thinks about it, the more confusing it seems. Maybe she *did* make it up, after all. Maybe it was just a dream.

Sybill cranes her neck to look out the side window now, past the cedars and up at the pretty hillside with the lilac and hollyhocks by the fence, at the smooth green waving grass where the well used to be. Certainly, there's no well now. It seems crazy to imagine that a well was ever there, that *anything* was ever there at all except what she sees now—the long soft grass, the apple trees, the mountain, sky. Family legend goes that Verner Hess had the well cemented over when Candy started to walk, since she was such a "lively baby," as Mother said. *They liked Candy better than me*. But Mother hadn't liked Candy finally, in the end. Candy was too wild, and Mother had loved Sybill more. And now Sybill is only trying to be responsible, but it's so confusing. Her whole family just ignores her whenever she brings up anything about Mother and Jewell Rife, or the well . . . Sybill wishes she'd never gone to the hypnotist at all, period.

In fact Sybill has tried to call Bob several times, long distance, to give him a piece of her mind. It seems like it's all his fault. But what she gets is Bob's machine, and his soft recorded voice which says, "This telephone is being answered by a recording device. I am out of town at the moment. At the sound of the tone, please leave your name and number so that I may return your call. Thank you." Thank you, my foot! Sybill left her name and number, all right. You'd better believe it. She also called his home number, where she talked to some man—or some nearly grown boy, sometimes it's hard to tell—who said that Mr. Diamond and Mrs. Diamond have gone to Hawaii for a ten-day vacation. Hawaii! Sybill could have screamed. "Thank you very much," she said, hanging up. It was heaping insult upon injury, for Bob to go to Hawaii. What business did he have there, that pudgy little man, on those wide white beaches, under palm trees? She could just see him, surrounded by big pink shells and dancing girls with fat brown bellies, wearing a tacky purple Hawaiian shirt and an orchid lei. What a ridiculous person! Sybill can't believe that she has allowed such a figure of fun to go down in her subconscious. She has left her name and number with the houseboy, or houseman, or son—whatever he is. She said it was an emergency. And it *is* an emergency, too, of a sort which Sybill even now can't quite grasp—she feels this literally—there's nothing for her to hold on to, sleeping out at the Holiday Inn, and slipping each day into this murky messy space which opened up when her headaches left.

At least no one can tell. She's careful to dress appropriately, and do her nails. Sybill looks at her nails. Sybill looks around her mother's parlor, at them all. They have all dressed appropriately, in fact, or as appropriately as they ever will, even Lacy, although her skirt is a jeans skirt, and Candy, who wears a spanking-white uniform, and even Arthur, whose short-sleeved wash-'n'-wear shirt is more worn than washed. They all sit quietly, all dressed up. It's ten o'clock in the morning. *But this is an emergency!* Sybill wants to scream. On the other hand, she wants to say, Oh, don't mind me, let's just forget the whole thing, I must have made a mistake, and let them all come to her then, and hug her. Which they would never do, of course; and Sybill probably couldn't stand it if they did, in fact. The only one who ever really hugged her, Sybill thinks suddenly, was Daddy. But Mother always approved of her, and would approve of her now, of the way she's dressed and the way she sits in this striped wing chair, caddycorner to the window, wearing stockings and Nine West heels, her feet crossed demurely at the ankle. Mother would never ignore her, the way the rest of them do.

Well, that's not *quite* accurate. Actually they're perfectly pleasant to Sybill except when she brings up what they don't want to hear. Then they just turn a deaf ear, and change the subject. Maybe they're right. Maybe she *is* crazy, nutty as a fruitcake, after all. At any rate, they'll all see before long. They'll see for sure as soon as the contractor comes to grade the hillside, but nobody except Sybill herself (and undoubtedly, Don) seems to have grasped the significance of it. Secretly Sybill is sure that Don is having all this remodeling done in a rush to satisfy *her,* to shut her up, to solve the mystery once and for all, and Sybill would like to share a significant glance with him right now to let him know that she appreciates it. But she can't catch his eye.

Myrtle and Don sit like figurines, on the loveseat. Mr. and Mrs. Wonderful. Myrtle wears a green linen suit, and pearls which are probably real. She doesn't look a day over thirty-five, although Sybill hates to admit it. Don, on the other hand, could easily be fifty. He looks older every day, on purpose; he's decided to be the one in charge here, and looks that way. Don wears a tan summer suit. It's irritating the way they just sit there, on Mother's fleur-de-lis loveseat—but fitting, too. Even Sybill has to admit it.

Because Miss Elizabeth, in that second envelope, left the house to *Myrtle!* It came as a huge shock to everyone except Dr. Don. It seems like he was all ready for it. But here's what Miss Elizabeth did: she left her money to be divided up among them all, as they expected, and there's a lot less of it than they thought. And then she left the house to Myrtle, Myrtle of all people, who has a perfectly lovely home of her own in Argonne Hills, with wall-to-wall carpeting. What could Miss Elizabeth have been thinking of? Here's poor Candy, who's raised two kids in three rooms over her beauty shop and never complained, and Lacy, who'll have to sell her own house in Chapel Hill any day now, and go homeless in the world, and Arthur, although anybody with any sense would never leave Arthur a thing. Not to mention Sybill—Sybill who's been the good one, all these years. When the will was read, Sybill was most astonished, and most hurt. But then they all assumed that Myrtle and Don would sell the house.

Imagine their shock—right then, yesterday, in Mr. Constantine's downtown office, when Dr. Don announced firmly, with no hesitation, in a calm voice like Dan Rather, that he and Myrtle planned to move into Miss Elizabeth's house right away, as soon as they finished remodeling it, and that they would start remodeling it immediately. *"Immediately,"* he said in a very significant tone. Myrtle's head had swiveled on her neck like a face on ball bearings, her eyelids fluttering. But she didn't say a word. She isn't saying a word now, either, as she sits on the loveseat, and waits for Mr. Constantine to get on with it.

Mr. Constantine fumbles with the third envelope, which reads, "Instructions for the Disposal of all my Worldly Goods: to be read to my assembled Offspring, following my Demise." Actually they already know what the instructions are, Mr. Constantine having briefed them on it yesterday, and his reading them today being merely a necessary matter of form. So why does he have to act like Bert Parks announcing the first runner-up in the Miss America contest, why does he have to fumble and clear his throat and create suspense? A further question is where in the world Miss Elizabeth ever found Mr. Constantine anyway, since not even Dr. Don appears to know him. Mr. Constantine has recently moved to this area, he says, from God knows where. Sybill thinks it must be Miami, or at the very least Atlanta, he's such a sleazeball. Look at his shiny, light gray suit, and the way his jowls drip over the collar. The only thing that makes sense—the only way to connect him to Miss Elizabeth at all—is Candy's theory, which is that Mr. Constantine's office is in the same spot, the same building, where old Eben Leaf's office was, so many years ago, and he was first their father's lawyer, and then Verner Hess's. Years back. That's probably it. But Mr. Eben Leaf wore fine dark suits and carried a pocket watch. Upon his death, his law firm, Leaf, Leaf and Manning, moved its offices to the mall. Probably Miss Elizabeth never realized this. Probably that's why she went to Mr. Constantine, never knowing the difference. . . . Mr. Constantine is a damp largish young man who reminds Sybill of the singing pigs in those Valleydale ads.

". . . so that there may be complete accord among

my children," he's reading now, "and no bickering."
Mr. Constantine clears his throat. Any division of
property is to take place right now, right here, with
all living children present. Anything left in the house
after today may be dealt with by Myrtle as she sees
fit.

This is not fair, Sybill thinks, because Myrtle has
always had *everything*. Still, maybe there won't be so
much left, for Myrtle to deal with. Sybill will try to
see to it that there's not. The last line is " . . .that my
children and their children may long enjoy whatever
it is in my power to give them." Candy starts crying
softly into a Kleenex. Sybill sits up straight and takes
a list out of her pocketbook. She made this list so she
wouldn't forget about some of the things that might
come in most handy, such as sheets, you never remember sheets. And she fully intends to keep her
mind on her business today, this business of dividing
up Mother's worldly goods, and not even act like
she's listening for the bulldozer down at the bottom
of the hill, and not even act like this is such an
emergency which it is. If Don Dotson wants to act
like nothing is happening here, then that's just fine.
That's just fine with Sybill, who can hold her tongue
with the best of them, who can be as cool as a
cucumber, as cool as Don. Sybill concentrates hard
on the list in her hand, which is shaking. Some
things that she wants but doesn't really need, like for
instance a set of bedroom furniture, especially the
spool set, she can just store in a self-storage until the
time comes. What this time will be, exactly, she's not
too sure about. In fact she feels so bad she wouldn't
mind putting herself in self-storage too, until all this
is over with.

Mr. Constantine is folding up the instructions slowly,

in eighths, placing them back in the envelope. He really does have a sense of drama, to be such a big lumpy person. He wipes his whole face with his white handkerchief. The air conditioner in the side window isn't doing too well; Sybill wonders if Myrtle and Don will have central air put in now. Probably. If they're putting in a pool and a patio and a wrap-around driveway, they'll have central air at the very least. Sybill runs her finger down the list in her hand, unobtrusively, she thinks, and looks up to see Arthur watching her. He doesn't even bother to look away. Arthur is just a ne'er-do-well, Sybill thinks, a living example of somebody who hasn't lived up to his potential. Arthur makes Sybill so nervous, though, staring at her like this, like there's something wrong with *her* instead of him, like she's got a terrible disease instead of a memory, like she's got herpes or AIDS.

A disease which has been, of late, on Arthur's mind. It's just hit the news, 1,641 victims as of last week, 644 deaths since it was first identified. Even Arthur has got to admit it is worse than despair, more quickly terminal, even though everything is terminal these days, finally. It makes him glad he's not gay. Arthur used to wish he was gay, sometimes, anything to be delivered from total enthrallment to women, from following his cock to hell and back, a trip he's often made. But he couldn't stand the idea of fag clothes or going to antique shows, not to mention what else they do. Still, it's serious. It's a serious time in this country when sex will make you sick, AIDS or herpes, gay or straight, take your pick, both incurable.

Arthur is sure that Mrs. Palucci does not have AIDS, and doubts that she has herpes. He has not called her yet, not wishing to act with unseemly haste. But he has driven by her house five or six times, and approves of it. Mrs. Palucci's house is neat but not too neat, a plain small brick house not far from his mother's, in fact, in the old Pines subdivision off to the right at the bottom of the hill here, where the big pines used to be. Three times when he's driven by, there's been a five- or six-year-old kid out in the front yard, playing with the hose. Several times the kid has been standing in the driveway shooting the hose straight down into the gravelly dirt at his feet and making the water spew back enormously, a wonderful filthy fountain all over himself. Arthur likes his looks. He thinks it's good that Mrs. Palucci has such a kid. Arthur's assuming that Mrs. Palucci is a single woman, based on this instinct he has. Still, he's happy that no Mr. Palucci has appeared in an undershirt on a lawn chair. Mrs. Palucci has a daughter too, or apparently; a pretty young thing with a low black ponytail comes and goes, driven around in cars by boys. Mrs. Palucci herself drives a big blue Buick convertible, proving her to be—as if Arthur ever doubted it—a woman of discernment and spunk. The only fly in this ointment at all is the presence of an apparent mother in the house, or at least Arthur thinks she's a mother. He figures that Mrs. Palucci needs all the help she can get, taking care of her wild little son while she goes to work, but this mother is ridiculous, Arthur's only seen her twice, and both times she was wearing a shower cap. The first time, she was standing in the front door wearing the shower cap, and a bathrobe, and yelling at her grandson in the driveway with the hose. The second time, she was sitting on the front steps wearing a different bathrobe, but the same shower cap, and eating a piece of pie. This was red pie, and looked like it might be strawberry pie from Shoney's, one of Arthur's favorites. Still, Arthur wishes he would be interested in a single woman with no children and no mother, a woman who lives in a little loft someplace with skylight, who eats breakfast at all hours of the day, exotic egg dishes, and wants to fuck at the drop of a hat. There are bound to be some women around like that, like the women in the Paco Rabanne ads. In fact, Arthur used to know some women like that, in Florida. But he has probably aged out of this group. And don't forget they've all got herpes now, anyway.

Mrs. Palucci's house is far too well-kept for her to have herpes, and besides, she's a nurse. Nurses keep Lysol in every room, Arthur thinks, plus pretty little containers of it in their purses. Arthur is waiting until the time is ripe, to call upon Mrs. Palucci. Women like Sybill, he's thinking, such women with no children and no boyfriends often have a gleam in their eye which means trouble, indicating an immense interest in being right. Sybill has such a gleam. Better to have mothers in shower caps and little boys with hoses than an immense interest in being right. Arthur stares at Sybill. As far as he's concerned, she might as well be from Mars, he understands so little of what makes her tick. Still, she's a lot like Mother. She's starting to *look* a lot like Mother, too. Again he remembers Miss Elizabeth standing at the door in the pearly spring dawn, saying, "Arthur, where have you been?" She was so tired-looking, so pale, that her face in retrospect appears pale blue. Where *had* he been, anyway? Probably out with the Hot Licks, chasing girls.

"Come on, Arthur," says Dr. Don. Apparently he's been standing there a while, by Arthur's chair.

"I guess I've been in what you might call a reverie, Doc," says Arthur.

"I guess you have," says Don. "Let's go upstairs, why don't we, and see if there's not something you can use."

"Such as what?" Arthur does not want to participate in this grabbing of objects, not a bit, this greedy ghoulish parceling out of his mother's things. He's only here at all because Don and Mr. Constantine told him he had to be, or the others wouldn't be able to do it, and claim what they wanted.

"The stuff I want is ephemeral, Doc," Arthur says.

"Well that's true for most of us," Dr. Don says, steering Arthur toward the stairs. "But a sports coat is not a bad thing."

Myrtle, looking distracted, flies down the stairs as they go up. "Sybill wants the flat silver!" she announces in obvious exasperation.

"Draw straws," says Arthur. "Play hot potato."

"Ooh!" Myrtle rushes on, then halts on the landing. "You know that's not such a bad idea," she says, looking back at them. "I *do* want that cranberry glass globe," she adds then, noticing the hanging fixture in the stairwell as if for the first time. Arthur and Don are laughing. A strange kind of giddiness seems to be taking over. It's the *strain*, Myrtle thinks, distracted, we've all been under such a *strain*—what with Mother dying, and then Sybill's accusations. . . . Myrtle refuses to think about Sybill's accusations at all, or about this bulldozer which has just started up down there at the bottom of the hill. She will put the bulldozer right out of her head and not mention it once. Nobody will mention it, and then they can gently say to Sybill, "Okay, look, honey. There's nothing there," and Sybill can seek appropriate treatment, as Don said. Oh, he's right, he's right. He's always right. It's best to resolve it once and for all, to leave no stone unturned, no questions unanswered, while the family is still together. Besides, it really will be nice to have a pool. Don says pools are easy now, all you do is dig a hole and then the people come and pour something in it. Don says we'll be swimming in two weeks. The phone starts to ring. "Oooh!" Myrtle says, pulling a stepladder over so she can reach the dangling rose globe to affix a sticker to it. "Can you get the phone, honey?" she calls up to Don, who picks it up at the top of the stairs.

It's Jack, again.

"Lacy," Don calls.

Lacy gets up from the dresser in the bedroom where she's going through Miss Elizabeth's jewelry, which turns out to be all fake anyway, lots of it probably from the dimestore although you couldn't tell it, she looked so elegant always—Lacy comes to stand in the bedroom door, eyebrows raised in a question.

"Yes," Don says to her.

Lacy shakes her head, moving toward the telephone. Don and Arthur are grinning at her.

"Jack, we're all real busy over here," she says into the receiver. "I told you not to call anymore."

Jack has been at the Ramada Inn since Tuesday, the day after the funeral, having left Bill with his girlfriend Susan. He says he'd just like to talk things over with Lacy, who would not like to do this at all.

"It must be exhausting," Jack says to her brightly, over the wire. "How about dinner later? You call me when you're through there—and then maybe a movie? *Flashdance* is on in Buncoe."

"Oh honestly, Jack! Go home!" Lacy slams down the receiver.

"What'd he say this time?" Dr. Don is amused. He never liked Jack particularly anyway, finding him supercilious, so far above the concerns of the skin.

"He wants me to go see *Flashdance*." Lacy makes a face, and Arthur begins to laugh.

"I hear it's not bad," Don says.

Behind Lacy, in the bedroom, Kate and Theresa start singing "What a Feeling," and Lacy swats at Kate. "That's your father you're making fun of," Lacy says, and Kate says, "So?" Kate and Theresa hold on to each other's shoulders and try out some cancan kicks, still giggling, but Lacy turns from her daughter and goes to stand for a moment at the window, staring out at the patches of phlox like brilliant blue scatter-rugs drying in the long grass which stops at the treeline.

Now Sybill and Candy are flipping for the spool bedroom suite, which Sybill wants very badly although she'll have to store it, and which Candy does not want at all but thinks might be nice for Tammy Lee to have, or Tony if he ever marries. "Heads," Candy says. "It's *tails!*" shrieks Sybill. "I get it!" Sybill thinks this is a lot like "The Price Is Right."

"Then you take the pineapple bed," Myrtle says to Candy.

Candy nods, biting her lip. Tammy Lee, who is artistic, would like the pineapple bed.

"Well, I want the cedar chest," Sybill says, consulting, again, her list.

"What cedar chest?" Candy asks.

"The one in the guest bedroom, it's mine anyway. Mother said to me one time, I distinctly remember, she said, 'Sybill, you can have that for your hope chest.' "

"I find that ironic," Theresa says pointedly, to nobody in particular, as she goes to answer the phone.

Which is for Lacy again. It's Jack, asking if she'd like to go see *Trading Places*. "Eddie Murphy's in it, playing a stockbroker," he says. "It's like an update of *The Prince and the Pauper*. Come on, it might relax you."

"I *know* Eddie Murphy is in it," Lacy says. "Dan Ackroyd's in it, too, and I don't need to relax. Now leave me alone, Jack."

Kate and Theresa link arms, singing "Every breath you take, every step you make, I'll be watching you."

"You really ought to be more serious about all of this," Lacy says to them severely. "You'll probably want some of these things in years to come, when you have children and houses of your own."

"Not me," Theresa says. "I'm never going to get married or keep house. I'm going to raise all my own vegetables and have lots and lots of lovers." Theresa's pale blond hair swings back and forth as she and Kate continue to kick, one-two-*three!* like chorus girls.

"Whoa now," says Arthur. He and Dr. Don stand in the hall laughing.

"Every breath you *take*, every step you *make*, I'll be *watching* you!" the girls sing, kicking. They've changed the tune. Everything's changing, Arthur thinks. Boy George wears makeup and Mother is dead.

"Go on now, all of you," Lacy says. Lacy looks harassed.

"I'll be watching *you!* I'll be watching *you!*" The girls kick and sing, out on the landing. Down below, Myrtle descends from her stepladder to deal with Sybill.

"I don't think we should break up the set." Sybill refers to the dining-room chairs.

The phone rings, and rings again, but nobody answers. Everyone knows who it is.

"Have you seen *Star Wars?*" asks Kate. This cracks them up.

"I wish you all would just *hush!*" Myrtle throws this up the stairwell to the girls.

"Have you seen *Gone With the Wind?*" giggles Kate.

Lacy shoos them down the steps and shuts the door. Through the wall she can hear, or almost hear, Don and Arthur, going through the men's clothes in the closet where her mother put them—Jewell Rife's from long ago, her daddy's from ten years back. If any clothes are left there now—Lacy remembers her mother trying to press them on Jack, and then of course there's the PTA thrift box—somehow, the thought of poor people all over town wearing her father's clothes makes Lacy infinitely sad. As does the thought of her husband Jack, who is behaving so badly—or strangely, at least. As does her mother's jewelry—only the rings were real. The thing of it is, Mother never appeared in public without being thoroughly turned out: the blue curls in place, the stockings, heels, the earrings and matching necklace. These ensembles were so impressive that everyone assumed the jewels were real, or at the very least, good costume jewelry. Lacy locks the door. Then she seats herself at the dressing table. She affixes large pearl earrings to her ears, a pearl brooch at the center of her T-shirt. She picks up vial after vial of perfume, sniffing. There was a particular way her mother smelled in later years, first it was lilacs, but later, it was something else, something—she can't quite get it, but that's close: Estée Lauder and loose powder, old age. Lacy narrows her eyes and looks at herself in the pier glass mirror. Who's getting the pier glass mirror? Lacy can see her mother in herself already, the way the flesh droops a bit at the sides of the mouth, the mouth itself, a perfectly symmetrical bow, the wide forehead with the vertical frown mark, just there, between the eyebrows, from reading. Reading too much will age you and make you crazy, just see what it's done to Jack. Lacy will look exactly like her mother, in thirty years. And then will she be able to remember the way she feels right now, or how she felt at the funeral or at the Piggly Wiggly, or how she felt the first time her lover took her to bed in his basement apartment on Stinson Street in Chapel Hill, will she remember Kate doing a cancan on the day they split up her mother's things, Kate wearing a slouch hat? What will she recall?

Lacy removes her mother's earrings and the brooch, and stands up. She walks to the dresser and pulls out a drawer at random and finds to her surprise a lavender beaded purse, lovely, which Kate will want. She sighs. It's like a puzzle, all this going through the house. It's like those search-and-find pictures they gave you in school, the forest with the animals hidden in the trees. Can you find (1) the elephant, (2) the boa constrictor, (3) the monkey? Can you go through this house and find the family that lived here once? Can you ever know how it worked, or what it was really like? Lacy concentrates, remembering, listening to the voices below, on the first floor, Candy and Sybill and Myrtle, the kids, Dr. Don and Arthur in the guest room, and this new sound, the racket of the bulldozer out on the hill where Dr. Don is going to put in the swimming pool. Can you find the secret here, at the heart of the house?

Lacy concentrates, remembering Sunday dinner and her mother in flowered voile at the head of the table, wearing these pearl earrings, this brooch: it seems to be summer then, too, it's so hot, but not one of the men has removed his coat and tie. There's molded Jell-O salad, a ham, fried chicken. Arthur does something bad and is sent from the room, he pulls Lacy's hair on the way out. Lacy has long curly hair. "Arthur!" she cries. "Hush, dear," her mother says. Everyone listens to the Episcopal rector who's come for Sunday lunch, who talks about visiting England. Lacy thinks she'll die, and imagines her death in great detail, exactly what will happen, who will cry. For dessert they eat ambrosia and angel food cake. As soon as he can, Daddy escapes out the back where he smokes Camels—she won't let him smoke in the house—and takes a nip or two of bourbon. This is the time when the children come to him, one by one, with problems, while Mother sleeps, fully dressed and perfectly rigid, flat on her back on the lacy white spread on this very bed.

But you took your problems to Verner Hess, who dealt with them one by one and often by saying nothing, just listening until you were finished talking. Sometimes he gave you money, or talked to a man on the phone. Often he said, "If I were you, I wouldn't bother your mother with that," or, "Don't tell your mother, it's no sense bothering her," and they didn't, either, so that eventually they all had isolated, or insulated, Miss Elizabeth from whole sides of their lives. Daddy's aim seemed to be to keep her completely pure, unsullied by any consideration of reality. He worshiped her. Even now, Lacy can't quite understand it, although she knows there doesn't really have to be a reason, you worship what you worship, you love what you love, and can't help it . . . but it seems to Lacy that this is the secret, the hidden beast in the forest, around which that household revolved: Verner Hess's total, obsessive worship of his wife. How odd that such a small red-headed man should be the possessor of such a love! How different from Lacy's own marriage to Jack, all that good will and the mutual interests and ideals that seemed to be so important, and seem to her now to be inconsequential. Better a blind obsession, better a fascination with the nape of somebody's neck.

Lacy takes out all the dresser drawers and arranges them one by one on the bed, so that everybody can get at their contents. As she does this, she glances out the window at the yellow bulldozer, backing up and pushing dirt into a huge, pointless pile which Sean keeps riding up and down on his bike. Don says they're going to extend the driveway all the way around the house, and put in a pool, a patio, and a gazebo. In some way, Lacy realizes, her mother knew what she was doing when she left Myrtle and Don the house, assuming—as Lacy assumes—that she wanted the house to stay in the family. Despite Miss Elizabeth's dreamy distance from the world, despite her regal austerity, she knew what she was doing, she always knew what she was doing; and for this reason, Lacy believes, she could never have killed Jewell Rife. Sybill's having a nervous breakdown, that's all. It's not uncommon. In fact, Lacy may choose to have one, too. She places all the drawers neatly on the white lace spread and rifles through the fragrant sacheted contents idly with her hand, surprised to feel, at the bottom of the last drawer, something hard—a book? She pulls it out. It's a composition book in the old style, with a mottled black-and-white cover, the little white space for the title, which reads, in her mother's elegant, spidery handwriting: *Days of Light and Darkness:—Memoirs by Elizabeth Bird, 1928.* Heart thumping wildly, a strange lightness in her head, Lacy clutches the composition book to her and opens the door and starts rapidly down the stairs.

"Look!" she cries. "Look what I've found," but her voice is nearly drowned out by the bulldozer's drone, louder here, and by the ringing doorbell. Sybill and Myrtle are arguing in the kitchen. Arthur, Kate, Theresa, and Mr. Constantine are watching something on TV in the parlor. Who'll get the color TV? "Look!" Lacy cries, waving the journal. Dr. Don goes to answer the door. At first it crosses Lacy's mind that this must be Jack, again, but it's not, it's somebody wearing something like white pajamas, and a kind of helmet. Who is it? Nobody knows. Dr. Don talks to this personage briefly, shaking his head, gesturing. There must be some mistake. You can't hear a thing because of the bulldozer. Dr. Don cups his hands around his mouth, finally, and calls to his wife, "Myrtle! You didn't call for an exterminator, did you?" and Myrtle looks up from the kitchen table where she's counting silver teaspoons with Sybill, and cries, "No!" Her mouth remains wide open, a perfect O. The front door shuts, the noise diminishes, and Lacy says, "Just look . . ."

Days of Light and Darkness: —Memoirs

BY ELIZABETH BIRD

1928

I approach the Past as a young maiden, bearing a candle, might approach a deserted mansion deep within the Enchanted woods. The path I take is overgrown with briars. The dangling limbs of blackened trees, the thriving thistly tangle of underbrush, the slick, wet, slimy stones conspire to thwart me. Above, the Moon herself is but dimly visible, and that at intermittent intervals through the limbs of the Trees which reach like ancient fingers toward the gray, low-racing clouds. The wind, surprisingly, is warm. It carries the sickly sweet scent of decaying flowers, it whips my frail Skirt to and fro, wrapping it about my legs as if to impede my Quest. This wind is my anxiety manifest. I shield the candle with my trembling hand, and if I reach the mansion, will its paltry light be sufficient to illuminate That which lies therein?

After what seems an eternity I approach the gate, which gives inward easily with a sorrowful, groaning sound. Heartsick, I proceed. The huge old door is overgrown with hoary Lichens, crisscrossed by vines, and yet:—I see by my flickering Light—it, too, stands ajar. "Deliver me," I pray, and setting my shoulder to it, and gathering whatever Courage the Almighty has to give, I push with all my might. An odor of must, as of the grave, assails me. The pool of Light cast by this ridiculous candle falls about my feet:—the light too weak to reach the recesses of this hall; the high imagined ceiling; the other doors to other, further rooms. And an antic wind from the open door is playing tricks:—casting monstrous shadows at the edges of this light, creating flitting shadows in the deeper dark above, shadows like wings:—

But I am here. Hand on Heart, I rest awhile. This mansion is no place for the faint of heart, no place for the unprepared. And so I have come armed with what I have:—with Honesty, with Courage, and with Love. Though the wind do its best, my candle shall not be extinguished. Though I walk these wide Halls with fear and trembling, I shall enter every room.

My Father seemed always on horseback, I know this was not So. And yet, how many evenings did we wait at the lower gate, in our pinafores, little hearts thumping wildly, to see him coming in the distance, up the long hill? First a speck we saw, and then the rising dust, and then at length, his gallant Form. When he saw us there, his girls, he would set spur to flank and gallop wildly that last stretch between the glowering pines; "Hi, Jennie!" he'd cry to his spotted horse; he knew we loved it So. Winter and Summer, he wore a wide black Hat. And oh, then how we'd squeal, and tumble from the gate, and race up that long walk to our happy home, skirting the side front porch, and running around to the side where Johnny would be waiting to take the horse, and Mama, fresh from the kitchen, all ruddy-faced, was wiping her hands on her apron and pushing back the escaping tendrils of her curly auburn hair.

Jennie was reined to a stomping halt, and dust flew in all directions. "Ladies, good evening!" my Father bellowed. Dismounting with a Flourish then, he'd sweep up my Mother in his strong arms and spin her about the yard. Faster and faster they would go, her petticoats billowing. "Lem, Lem, let me go! Stop it this instant!" she shrieked. "Put me down!"

My Father roared with laughter. "Not until you give me a Kiss," he'd vow, and she said, "Oh not now, why here are the girls, I tell you, put me *down*!"

We jumped up and down, clinging together, Nettie and Fay and I. "A kiss! A kiss!" we shrilled. "Give him a kiss, Mama!" Invariably I was sure that something terrible would happen if she did not, that he would spin her right off this earth into the blue Empyrean and we would never see either of them again. For me, this homecoming ritual was frightening, thrilling, and deeply satisfying all at once.

For at length she gave him the kiss, and he put her down, and they stood stock still on the whirling ground for a second to get their bearings, both of them panting, out of breath, Mother shamefaced and beautifully blushing, hand to her heart, and Father grinning devilishly behind his flamboyant Moustache. "Oh, Lem!" Mother cried. "Lem, for Heaven's sake!"

"And now I'm hungry!" he shouted then:—oh, we knew it was coming; already we'd begun to scatter. "I want a tasty bite of a little girl!" How we squealed, how we ran, even Fay who could barely toddle—all in vain, to be caught at last, tossed high in the summer air, and feel Father catch us and hold us close and "bite" the back of our necks, beneath the ribbons.

"Yum, yum," he'd roar, licking his Lips, setting us back on our feet at last.

"These girls are not quite sufficient—too small and bony!" he announced. "Miss Mary, what's for dinner?" To which question, my Mother made a murmuring reply, still disconcerted, attempting to pin up her unruly hair, and then Father gallantly offered her his Arm, and she took it; they entered the house.

Although we were busy from dawn to dusk, Nettie and Fay and I, nothing else that happened could quite compare to Father's returning home Thus, at the dinner hour.

Thomas Lemuel Bird, our Father—to grant him his proper appellation—was an imposing red-faced Giant of a man with riotous hair that sprang into curly black ringlets when he entered the house and removed the ubiquitous black hat. And when he shed the black frock-coat, I was ever thrilled to see the pearl-handled Revolver in his shoulder holster, to watch him remove this too, and place it in the hidden drawer in the breakfront in the dining room, the breakfront which his brother, a master craftsman, had made for their marriage in 1906. He needed the gun, Father said, "at the mill," where we were given to understand that rough men worked, and terrible things might happen at any time. Fistfights and dismemberments were rumored. I likened this distant World of men with the way my father smelled when he swept us up to "bite" us, or when he leaned down, as he did each night, to kiss us into sleep:—a mingled scent of tobacco and fresh-cut wood. In fact I never smell fresh pine that I do not still think of these days. (It saddens me to think thus: my candle flame wavers and dims. It will not Do. For I intend to go ahead here, through all the perilous chambers of my Heart.)

My Father in his prime weighed well over 250

pounds. Large of Frame and Feature, he moved always with an air of authority, of command. He was a man of his word. He was feared, among men, for his temper. He was known to carry a grudge, and even then, upon occasion, to drink intemperately. As a child, I was not aware of these traits. It's possible that my mother was not aware of them either, or that her awareness of them was slight. For oh, how Father loved his Ladies! Every roughness of manner, every masculine Vice, was left at the foot of the hill.

He never tired of watching Mother, of asking her details about her Day, nor of praising her handiwork. I remember when she was making the needlepoint cushions which yet adorn the dining room chairs, how pleased he was, how astonished each day by the appearance of still another rose, another vine, created with her tiny, perfect stitches.

But he adored us all. Nothing made him happier, it seemed, than the time he Spent with us, questioning Fay endlessly about her imaginary playmates, roaring with laughter at her droll answers; reading aloud with me the books which Mother had brought from the Eastern Shore or which we borrowed from Grace Harrison; or Exploring with Nettie in the woods on the mountain behind the garden. If men came to our house to see him on Business, he met with them outside where they stood solemnly on the side lawn by the hitching rail, smoking, and squinting off at the Horizon.

Obviously, he adored Mother. The fact that he had won her hand only after great difficulty seemed to make him prize her all the more. The story went that he had been hired to drive old Mr. Harrison, a retired minister, to a retreat at Lake Junaluska, North Carolina, a Methodist Summer Encampment. He was to spend the night, rest the Horses, and then return. But there he had encountered Mary Davenport and all her family from the Eastern Shore of Virginia, who had come to escape the unhealthy Vapors which summer brought to the low-lying swampy area where they resided. This whole family was in mourning for a beloved Brother, who had recently succumbed to Influenza. Mother, with her flaming hair, her simple black linen shift, and her air of pious grief, made quite an impression upon the uncouth young giant from the mountains. One of four rough-and-tumble Boys orphaned early on, Father was a "wild young buck" at that time, uncertain of which Path in Life to take. Although he had learned to read and write, his early schooling had been sketchy. Mother and her sisters had had a Governness, they knew French. Deeply smitten, Father did not return with the Horses as planned. He courted Mary for two weeks by the deep, still waters of Lake Junaluska, among the solemn Mountains, between the inevitable lectures, prayers, and meetings. Dr. Harrison, abetting the Young Lovers, bought him a Suit of new clothes so that he could properly attend these functions. How difficult it is for me to imagine Father, rosy-cheeked above his stiff white collar, sitting in a straightbacked chair absorbing Culture:—surely it must have seemed to him that he had entered a different world, as indeed he had. Mother, as she later reported, was Charmed. What a complexity of emotion must be encompassed in this simple description of their feelings! He was Smitten; she was Charmed. At length Father was "run off" upon the arrival of Mother's father, a prosperous oysterman, and told to present himself when he had some Prospects.

By the time he reappeared, at the end of the Summer, to fetch old Dr. Harrison, he had made a start. He and his brothers had leased some land; Sam, the next-oldest, had won a band-saw in a poker game; the lumber Business was in its infancy. Father had given up his gambling and drinking, or swore he had, and had indeed put his Shoulder to the wheel. He bade Mary another Farewell, and brought Dr. Harrison home. They were separated by all the distance of Virginia for eighteen months.

The lumber Business was thriving when he appeared in Accomac to claim her; his Prospects seemed handsome indeed. He visited with her family for three weeks. At the time of his departure, they were officially affianced. But the Marriage was to take place, her father had stipulated, only after Father had arranged a proper Home for his bride. Perhaps her father hoped in this way to forestall the union, giving his daughter time to come to her Senses. Perhaps he simply felt that a further test of Father's good intentions was necessary. At any rate, the land was purchased. Only the prettiest spot would do, this hill, at that time just outside the tiny town. Plans were drawn up, and the Work was begun. It was to be a House as large, as stately, as pretty as any in town, a home fit for a Lady. Dr. Harrison corresponded with Mother's father, to assure him that all would be as promised, that Father's accounts were not mere mountain Tomfoolery. At last, Father and Mother were married in the First Methodist Church at Accomac in June 1906. Following a Wedding Trip to Old Point Comfort, he brought her all across Virginia, "home." This wedding trip must have occasioned, for her, a heady mixture of emotion, of joy in her handsome young Husband combined with the sadness of leaving her own Family and the Landscape of her youth. She must have felt as if she were moving to Madagascar.

What she found was a teeming Lumber camp, a raw boom Town, and her fiery young Husband deeply engaged in a brilliant career, with his lively brothers: —our Uncles:—trooping in and out of the house. Draperies and furniture were ordered from Richmond. Her mother sent flower seeds. One by one, we were born:—myself, Catherine Elizabeth Bird, in 1908; Nettie Davenport Bird in 1913; and Constance Fay Bird in 1915. I was then seven, I recall Fay's difficult Birth all too well. Mother labored for two days, and many months had passed after this Birth before she regained her sprightliness. Father for his part lavished her with attention and sweet solicitous Care. He bore well the disappointing fact that their union had failed to produce, once again, a Son. The busy Time passed. There were Dancing Parties. Oh, we lived well, in those days! Johnny worked about the place, Aunt Suse kept up the house. And yet, although she was as busy and happy as a young Wife could be, a certain sadness seemed at times to overtake our Mother. Letters flew back and forth between the mountains and the Eastern Shore, but visits were seldom. Although I am told that I visited the Davenports when I was small, at perhaps two or three years of age, I do not recall this trip. When Mother's own father died, she was prevented from making the arduous Journey due to the confinement necessitated by Nettie's imminent birth.

How often, in later years, I came upon Mother unawares, gazing at her father's photograph:—an immense man looking at a great gold watch, standing just to the left of a tremendous pile of Oyster shells, before a wide expanse of water. The Chesapeake Bay? I never fully comprehended the import of this Picture. Why did he thus regard his watch? Was it a

Gift, perhaps, or the token of some Recognition? For me, in recent years, this photograph has come to possess the symbolic overtones of "Ozymandias," with its solemn theme. For how soon indeed does glory fade and how little our material Possessions—that great pile of Oyster shells at his feet which tell of countless ships, and men, and voyages into the briny deep—how little such things can withstand the silent, stately feet of tramping Time! Mother's Sisters and the one remaining Brother married, and produced families of their own, babies were born and died, life was too complicated to allow for much Visiting. But ah yes, she missed them. Sometimes there was a sadness in her.

At other times, these memories brought her Joy, as when she'd tell us how to go clamming. One wore a bathing costume, she said, and old, worn-out shoes, and a Hat against the sun, and waded into waist-high water with a certain kind of Rake. A raft, attached to one's waist by a rope, floated along beside. One waded carefully, feeling along the slimy bottom for the hard, round Shells. And then the raking, the scooping up, and flinging mud and shell and all upon the raft until, piled high with bounty, it was guided into shore. Mother described the ensuing Clambakes on the lawn, she told us how to make Clam Fritters.

She was never more elated than that moment when, near Christmastime, the enormous hoary barrel of oysters in the shell, ice-packed, arrived by train. This was Father's special Gift for his Eastern bride. And then we had oyster Stew, and oyster Fritters, and Fried oysters, inviting all the neighbors in to taste these delicacies.

Mother was famous also for her baking. I recall how she tested the oven, Suse in attendance, with a piece of fine white stationery. The oven was ready for a cake when the stationery browned evenly in just one minute. Then, in the Cakes would go! Lady Baltimore, a white cake with raisins and nut custard between the layers and a boiled white icing on top, was my favorite. No wonder Father grew so huge!

At Christmas, the whole house smelled of Pine, with garlands up and down the staircase, and on the mantels. Father's men had brought the fragrant greenery from the mill. Nettie went out with Father, to Shoot down the mistletoe which then hung from the rose-glass lamp in the hall. On Christmas morning, we were always awakened by the Shots which rang out all across these snowy mountains, an old custom. At breakfast, we ate the fresh Oranges which arrived each year from Mother's parents, and after the opening of the Presents came the huge Christmas dinner, with turkey and roast and ham, sometimes venison, where we often had sixteen or more at table, and three or four women in the kitchen, helping out. In the afternoon, we all took Naps. Later, my uncles would play their Banjos, and often there would be Dancing, far into the night. Often I fell asleep to the banjo's breezy twang and the rhythmic patter of Dancing feet.

These days did not last. In retrospect, I see Harbingers of our decline, although, in a sense, I doubt their validity:—One always knows that the lovely Rose of summer will brown about the edges, will lose its Petals and will fall, does one not? After the fall, moments of prescience may be easily imagined. But I do recall two such moments particularly.

I was about eleven. We had a pony named Old Joe, as phlegmatic a pony as one would ever hope to see. My father judged him Safe for us to ride. One windy afternoon, I believe it was in late March, I had Johnny to saddle Old Joe for me and I rode down the long hill between the murmuring pines, through the town, and out the valley road to Father's Mill. I intended to Surprise him. I also intended to gather up the little scraps of wood which I used to fashion furniture for my Dolls. My sidebags held a paper sack filled with ham Biscuits and apple fritters, which provender Mother had urged me to share with my Father when I arrived. This Lunch did not transpire.

I tramped through the sawdust in the yard, speaking to Father's men, I bolted through the outer office with its desk and leather chair, calling "Father! Father!" carrying my saddlebags. Receiving no reply, I barged right through the inner door, shouting, "Hello!" For the first time, he did not come to me. He did not rush over to sweep me up in a Hug. Instead, he and two of my Uncles were deep in conversation with two large—very large, as large as my father—Men in black suits, Men I had never seen before. They sat around the big Table which our Uncle Lewis had made for the Office when he left it to move to Roanoke and open his Carpentry shop. They were smoking cigars. My father looked up at me as if he were unsure of who I might be, his broad face creased into unfamiliar lines of concern. "Run along now, Elizabeth," he said.

That was all. He was not Rude. These men were Money men, I learned that later. The family lumber business had fallen, already, upon Hard Times. Father had extended Credit where none should have been extended; he and his brother James had disagreed. His brother Sam, on the other hand, presented another sort of problem; he had become uninterested in the business, inattentive. He was not

Pulling his Weight. I recall that I ate no lunch on that particular day, the day of my unlucky Visit to the mill, angrily slapping the long reins against Old Joe's neck, trying to urge him past the gentle Trot which was his fastest gait. I did not mention Father's conduct to anyone.

The second premonition was occasioned by my Mother, who always spent a great deal of time in her Garden. She had the prettiest Flowers in town, and if she was a vain woman in any sense, it was in her flowers that her vanity resided, and justly so. Of course we had a vegetable garden too, up on the hillside near the well, but it was worked by Suse and Johnny under Mother's supervision. The Flower beds were a different story. Here, Mother wielded Trowel and Rake herself, planting, separating, weeding, edging:—there were tasks enough to keep her busy all Spring and Summer long. The Moment which I now recall occurred in that same Year as my noon-time visit to the mill, but later, when the Spring was more advanced.

I was in the house, Reading voraciously as was my wont. She was in the garden. "Elizabeth!" she called. I know she called; I know I heard her. I laid down my Book and went. She sat there by her pansy bed, on the brilliant emerald grass, the gardening gloves cast down beside her, staring down the hill at the double row of tiny new Boxwoods which Johnny had just planted along the walk. "Mother?" I said, coming to stand beside her. She did not reply, except to brush her hand across her breast, and place it at her thickening waist. She was With Child at this time. Had the Pain started then, already? Butterflies fluttered everywhere. "Mother?" I asked. But I could not understand her reply; she had responded in French!

"What, Mother?" I inquired. She blushed, and smiled, and drew me to her, and gave me a squeeze. "I'm sorry," she said simply. "I have forgot why I called." I laughed merrily, thinking it funny to see an Adult so befuddled, but yet I felt an inward Shudder, what it is called when someone Walks across your Grave.

She died in October of a ruptured Appendix. In the morning she was quite well, by afternoon she was Deathly Ill; that evening, being carried in a wagon toward the closest Hospital, in Roanoke, old Dr. Greer having diagnosed the complaint but refusing to perform Surgery due to her delicate Condition, she died. My father was with her, holding her hand. He said later that she seemed to be staring beyond him, and that a Shadow fell across her face, followed by a light as if of Love, or recognition. She did not Speak. How much better it might have been for him had she bade him a final Farewell, had she not thus left him so mysteriously!

For oh, how he Mourned! We all thought that he would die, too. He was Heartbroken. He roared and moaned and beat his breast, he kicked in the barn door, he wandered the house all night sobbing. He shot her horse. He drank continuously, Suse fled. Our Uncles had to come, and Stay in the house with us. We were terrified. I was twelve then, Nettie seven, and Fay, five. We cried too, for our sweet Mother who had gone to be with God, and Women from the town came, and comforted us. Especially our Mother's Friend, Miss Grace Harrison, was attentive to us in these Dark days. But he raged! And would not be comforted. Our Grief paled, appeared so puny as to be insignificant beside his magnificent mourning. Now I see, as I look back, that this time so Difficult for us all may perhaps have taken its Toll most drastically upon Fay. I remember searching for her all one Evening, and finding her at last in the bottom of Mama's Wardrobe, all hunched into a ball, sucking her thumb. She alone did not cry, not then, nor Later, I believe, unless her little tears were shed in private. Mother was buried in the graveyard of the Methodist Church which she had Loved. We sang "Shall We Gather at the River," I recall, yet almost no one sang, as all were weeping So.

It was the last time Father ever set foot in a house of Worship, so far as I know, for the rest of his life. He lost his Faith that October, when he lost her. Or perhaps he never had it, the True Faith, perhaps he only believed in her, and accompanied her to Church because she wished it. Certainly, our Uncles were not noted church-goers! And yet my own Faith is ever strong, growing through all Adversity, and ever Strengthening me. God has given me the Courage to bear the considerable disappointments which have come my way, and to lead a good life, and to appreciate Beauty in all her guises.

What a Horrible:—what a frightening Beauty there was in that Awful scene:—Mother returning to the Earth, her coffin lowered into the wet black ground, while all around, the gay brilliant leaves of autumn swirled. My Father would have jumped into her Grave. Indeed he tried to do so, and had to be forcibly restrained; our Uncles took him away then, and did not bring him back for three days. He returned somewhat chastened, and happily, more subdued.

Miss Grace Harrison stayed with us during this time. Of her, a few Words will be necessary. The oldest daughter of the Harrisons, who had taken an interest in my parents ever since old Dr. Harrison bought Father the Suit of clothes at Lake Junaluska during their Courtship, she was a Maiden lady who, though well-educated, chose to reside at home. We could not precisely tell her age. Although older than Mother or Father, she was not yet really Old; she had the sort of pale, Artistic visage which does not fall prey to Time. She was wan, ethereal, elongated:—what a strange turn of phrase I here employ! and yet it springs to mind—willowy, and graceful in all her movements. Although she possessed a Degree from a College in the North, she preferred not to teach at the little Methodist School which we and all the other children in town attended until it closed and a fee was got up and Another school begun.

At any rate, Grace Harrison preferred a life of leisure:—the state of her Nerves, it was whispered, precluding any more active existence. She rose at Noon, she walked through the town, shopping sometimes for her aging Mother, her Father having passed to his Reward, she read book after book, seated in the wicker swing on their front porch. Her Dresses were gauzy, wispy, pastel. I had never seen such Dresses in my life. She spent hours and hours lying on a chaise longue in the Parlor, all this because she had been, as Mother explained to us, "disappointed in a Married Man."

Grace Harrison loved my mother, who was her only true friend in town, and whose vitality, I presume, enlivened her Days, and because of this friendship, Miss Grace early undertook the task of supplementing the simple Education offered us at the Methodist School. Miss Grace was to talk to us about Ideas and Literature, Mother was to instruct us in French, but she died before these lessons were yet begun, so busy had she been with the Cares of our household. And as for the Literature and Ideas, I was the only One, among the three of us, who gave a fig for Such. But ah, through all the golden days of my childhood, until that Catastrophe which struck us when I was twelve: —ah, how we read together, Grace Harrison and I, often in the Harrisons' parlor with Grace stretched out full length upon the chaise, a pillow beneath her feet and another beneath her head, her Book illuminated by the shell lamp on its stand, with its pink translucent shade. We read Lord Byron. We read Shelley and Keats and Dickens and Tennyson, and William Shakespeare. We read novels, such as *The Castle of Otranto*. I did not understand three-quarters of what we read. I would give anything to have this Chance again, to read with Grace Harrison. But alas she is Gone, estranged from me by a gulf as wide as all the Oceans of the world. The gifts she left with me are invaluable, a love of language, of Nature and its Beauty, of the Finer Things of Life. She did not much care, I should hazard to guess now, after the passing of so many years, for People. Most people she found, as she had found the married man, Disappointing. To my regret, this harsh Category came to include, at length, my Father.

For he was suffering, and suffering also a Change in his manner and bearing and habits, a change which was grievous for him and us. Without the softening influence of my Mother, and due perhaps in part to the Business problems which we at that time knew Nothing of, he was reverting to the harsh ways of his youth. His delightful ebulliency turned to brashness. He grew loud, abrupt. His dress became imperceptibly more sloven, more like those about him. He was often silent, moody, and short with us, except for Nettie, who was his Favorite. More and more often, he was not at Home; he hunted; he gambled, I think; he spent more time in the company of men, he had become again a "man's man," and our fine House and all the appurtenances of his life occasioned by our Mother began to assume the guise of encumbrances.

And yet, of course, he Loved us. He did not abandon us, far from it, and these difficult days of change were made easier by the ministrations of Grace Harrison, who arose from her bed to become the softening Spirit of our household, urged forth by feelings of Duty, of Loyalty for our sainted Mother, of concern for us, and by some vague motive as yet unclear even to her. Grace Harrison came to us nearly every day for a year, and supervised the reassembling of our distraught household. It would never be, again, as it had Been. Mother's joyful energy, which had seemed effortless, could not be replaced. But Suse was at length induced to return to us, and to live in the room above the kitchen, assuring us at least of regular if simple Meals, and a second girl was found, Suse being old by this time, to come and clean. Boys from the mill appeared to do the heavier chores.

Grace Harrison continued to Read with us as she often had; from time to time she appeared to supervise our lessons after supper. She came to our house then, and sat with us while my Father, glass in hand, stared moodily into the fire, and after these Occasions, he donned his black hat and frock-coat, and walked her home. Aside from the fact that she was admittedly more ambulatory than in former days, her Behavior was much the same. She was ever calm, quiet, and gentle to the point of listlessness. A spot of Rose had come to either cheek, though, perhaps the result of the unwonted exercise, and her pale fine hair appeared to spring up even more angelically around her face, floating, it seemed, as she moved. She was quite Lovely; I say that now, after the passage of so many Years. "Lovely" would not have occurred to me then. I do believe it occurred to my Father.

I never knew, nor Wished to know, exactly what transpired between them. Suffice it to relate that these events caused me yet another irreparable Loss, following close upon the heels of the first. There came a summer evening when Grace had been with us at dinner, my Uncle Sam was there also, and upon his departure, Grace Harrison rose to take her leave as well.

"I'll walk with you, Grace," my father said abruptly.

"That shan't be necessary, Lemuel," she said, as she always said, but he insisted, and gallantly returned to the parlor to fetch her shawl. This was a lovely fringed and printed shawl from India, which I admired.

"Now here," he said in the deep voice which was less hearty than before. "The wind is chill." He insisted upon placing the shawl about her shoulders, and was it my Imagination, or did his great hands linger there? At any rate they departed, the two of them, down the long front path along the paving-stones, between the boxwoods. He did not return before our bedtime.

Grace Harrison never appeared in our house again. At first I inquired, as the oldest and closest to her, where she might be. Was she ill?

"She does not concern you," Father said abruptly, in a deep and Final tone. That was all.

After a week had passed, I went alone to the Harrison home, where I had whiled away so many delightful hours in her company, under her tutelage, to inquire for myself into the State of affairs. I was then fourteen. I found Grace Harrison upon the familiar chaise, her cheeks flaming, eyes hollow and sunken. Upon my approach, she stiffened and clutched the delicate Afghan more tightly to her.

"Leave me," she said.

"Oh, let me stay!" I implored. "Let me do something for you. We did not realize that you were ill."

"Ill," she mused, as if to herself, in that way she had of turning Inward even while addressing her conversation to one directly. "Ah yes, I am quite ill. I have never been quite well, you know. And now I'm afraid my illness is such that it may necessitate a rest cure. I shall miss you, Elizabeth," she said with sudden Emotion. She reached forth her pale, trembling hand.

I grasped it. I was weeping.

"*Do not cry,*" she said quite forcefully, so that I ceased, and took in each Word she uttered. I have never forgot her message. She lay ethereal there in the rosy glow of the shell-shaded lamp, beneath the scalloped afghan. "You are the Lady of your house now, Elizabeth," she said. "Remember your Mother. Remember me."

I kissed her hand. It was indeed quite warm, she was feverish. She closed her eyes.

"Perhaps it would be best if you left now, my dear," came the quavering suggestion of her mother, a lady so small and ancient that all of us actually feared her. I had not noticed her in the parlor. Now I perceived her dark shrunken form by the door, in shadow.

"Yes," I said. I departed abruptly.

Grace Harrison spent the next year and a half in a sanitarium in Baltimore. When she returned, she was quite Different. Even her Appearance had changed, she had grown stouter, more stolid, her pale complexion appearing pasty, like dough rather than like French porcelain, the image which had ever sprung to mind as I considered her visage.

She returned to nurse first her Aunt, and then her Mother, through the last Ravages of old age, and to Bury them next to her Father, in the Methodist church-yard. Then she lived alone in her house for many years, a determined Recluse. When Visitors came, as they often did, as people in a small town feel it their duty to "look in" upon one another, she entertained them nicely, serving iced Tea with mint on the side porch in summer, coffee in winter, in the parlor. She answered their questions, but asked none in return. She was perfectly pleasant, yet unfailingly Distant, seeming neither glad nor sorry when her visitor or visitors departed. Sometimes I went in those years, with a question about a poem or a novel or a play. She would answer that question, if she knew the answer, and volunteer no More. Books still lined the walls of her parlor, and of her Father's library. I have no notion that she ever read them.

As far as I know, Grace Harrison and my father never spoke to each other again. I continued to visit her infrequently, but all our true communication had ceased upon that fateful Day in my fourteenth year. Perhaps it was just as well. For I took her Words to Heart, and have endeavored since to model my Life upon the precepts she suggested. "Remember your Mother, remember me!" Ah, Fateful words! Words which form the hinge of this last, yet this most rusty and difficult Door to open in the deserted mansion of my heart. I push. I shove, yet not with the full weight of all my Being, for I dread the Pain which must accompany my perusal of this dark chamber.

And yet, I know that God resides here also, for in

the years which followed Mother's death and then Grace Harrison's departure from my life, I came to know the stern joys which the proper exercise of Duty brings to those who are Duty's handmaidens.

"Remember your Mother":—I endeavored to manage our Household as she would have done. It became my task therefore to beat out the rugs if they needed beating, to see that the cut Glass shone with crystal fire through due application of water and vinegar, to have the mahogany rubbed with lemon and oil, the silver polished, to sew buttons where buttons were needed. Despite the time taken up with these chores, I continued my schooling, as I was uncommonly Bright. I finished with it in my sixteenth year, having lost a year during our severest time of Crisis. Dr. Harker, who was the Principal then, paid a call upon my Father at this time, offering me a partial Position then at the new town school, helping with the youngest students, which I declined, or alternatively, suggesting that I should be sent to the Normal School for Girls, at Radford, to continue my Education in the following Fall.

All knew that this was what my Mother would have wished. Father acceded, but by the knitting of his brows, I knew he did so with a Heavy heart. And I was torn. How I wished to go, to pursue that Learning which has brought me all the Joy of my Days! And yet, I could not, I felt, leave Father to manage alone. We compromised in the end, deciding that I should leave in my eighteenth year, by which time Nettie should be able to take over for a time the tasks which I had mastered:—alas, too Well!

For that Day never dawned. Several events conspired to push it off into a distant future which became, at length, Oblivion. Father's affairs did not prosper, although I am not sure, to this day, of the particulars of it. I know that the lumber Business had declined everywhere in this section, the best timber having long since been harvested. And without Mother's calming Influence, I suspect, Father's decisions were often hasty, rash, unwise. He quarreled seriously, over these and other matters, with Uncle James. Another personal Tragedy befell our family also at this time, when Uncle Sam, whose affairs of the Heart had ever been dubious, was murdered, shot in the back on the Long Valley road under cover of Night. No one seemed to know why he was out on horseback at such an Hour, but rumors flew. I remember curious Nettie asking question after question, to no Avail.

But in some way, this horrendous Event appeared to trigger a final, tragic Quarrel between Father and Uncle James. It was the evening of the funeral, with Uncle Sam not even cold in the grave, when tempers flared to such a Point that Uncle James declared his intention of leaving the firm, and Father in his anger was driven to brandish a Poker at him. Then Father dropped the poker, sank down by the Fire, and sobbed heartily into his hands. "Go, then," he told his younger Brother. "I'll buy you out fair and square." He did so, and James, newly Rich, left for St. Louis, where he married well and has resided ever since. Father, short of ready cash, was forced to borrow, and borrow again, paying exorbitant rates of interest, he was too proud a man ever to ask for help from James or from Mother's people who had become, at any rate, strangers to us since her death. Father and I were quite close during this Period, although I could not approve of his gaming nor of some of his Questionable companions, yet he confided in me some of the details of his Business and I attempted to economize at Home as best I could. Father depended upon me, I had become indeed the Lady of the House. We both knew, although we did not discuss it, that Normal School was out of the question, at that precarious time.

It might have been Thus, at any rate, for I had my hands Full in those years, as I still have, attempting to deal with Nettie and Fay. For my Sisters have ever been sources of Care and frustration for me, I pray Constantly in their behalf. During this Time, as Always, they disobeyed my commands, and preoccupied with the Business, Father gave them None. He refused entirely to set his foot down, and to Control them as he ought.

Fay, for her part, was merely silly, and refused to pay attention to me or to anyone else, and refused to do her Lessons. I saw to it that she should attend Church, but often as not she'd slip away, to be found an hour after the Service, happily wandering by the stream that runs by the Methodist Church. I saw to it that she attended School too, as she would not learn her Lessons with me, but at length I received a visit from the new Headmaster, a Mr. Peterson, who stated in the gentlest possible Terms that he felt Fay could not benefit from further education. "But she can read!" I cried, quite taken aback. "Ah, but she *will not*," he enjoined.

I should mention that Fay, always a hearty child, had grown almost overnight, it seemed, into a very large girl indeed with burgeoning womanly attributes. Mr. Peterson further hinted that her wandering about the town should be curbed, and I assured him that I should attempt to do so. To that end, I assigned Fay more little tasks about the house, tasks which she performed willingly, and even with Delight. Though she spoke seldom, she seemed Happy, and I trust, she was So. Her sweet presence thus became a clear delight to my Father, and also to me. It was not the case with Nettie:—alas, that Bitterness can grow, all unawares, between two Sisters! For I could not condone her conduct.

Always the tomboy, Nettie careered about the countryside on horseback and refused entirely to become the Lady she was born to be. Father gave in to her every whim, having bought for her, before our severest financial reverses, several Spirited Riding Horses which she entered in Horse Shows, actually riding them herself! It was a great expense, was Folly in fact, and yet Father seemed truly proud of the silly Ribbons she carried home. She traveled alone about the county, about the state. It was unheard of. And yet, he would not intercede in my behalf. Nettie also had friends from town of whom I could not Approve, both male and female, with whom she went dancing at Roadhouses, and Fishing, I know not what Else, as freely as if she were a Boy. I attempted to reason with her. I prayed aloud for her, in her Presence, but all for naught. The differences between us were a source of vast sorrow for me. So I was concerned about Fay, and about Nettie, and about our Father's fortunes, and spent my teen years Thus.

And yet, in this back room, I find something Lovely as well:—or Lovely at least in initiation, though Dreadful in aftermath. For it was at precisely this time that I was courted and won by Ransom McClain. Ransom McClain and I could not have been more like had we been poured from the selfsame mold! The son of Hudson McClain, our Commonwealth's Attorney, Ransom had been delicate as a Boy, and had been sent away to Boarding School at an early age. So I had never known him, growing up. We met for the first time at the Episcopal Church, which I was attending one Sunday in early June of my Nineteenth year, as the guest of my former school-friend, Rosalie Gates.

He sat two rows before us. I noticed him right away. With his lofty brow, his springing pale hair, he seemed the masculine counterpart of Grace Harrison, this initial Impression proved to be so true in many ways. We were saying the Lord's Prayer. I confess I could not help but lift my eyes, stealing glances in his direction. At the conclusion of the services, I eagerly questioned Rosalie about him.

"Oh, that's Ransom McClain," she said idly, fingers playing with the satin ribbons at her waist. "I'll introduce you if you like." Her Attitude conveyed indifference. Rosalie could not be bothered much, as she was engaged that summer, and would be married the following Fall. Encouraged by her, and by my other Friends, I, too, from time to time had attended Dances and Concerts and Church Suppers, when the press of Duty allowed it, but I confess I had found none among the town lads to interest me. My Sensibilities were too refined perhaps, or their Merits too few. But now I said, "If you will, please, Rosalie," holding my breath.

Ransom McClain bowed from the waist, a Gesture which both pleased and embarrassed me, as I feared others in the church-yard that day might be Amused, and declared it his pleasure to meet me.

"I have not seen you here before," he remarked as we fell into easy step together, strolling up Main Street, with Rosalie lackadaisically following behind.

"I'm a Methodist," I said, "but I'm thinking of changing over." The sudden Truth sprang from my lips all unawares.

"Why so?" Ransom asked as if it were important, his large pale Eyes intent upon my visage.

"For the beauty of the Language," I said then, to my surprise, and thus it has remained.

"Oh, *really*," responded Ransom McClain, as if my words were significant, eying me keenly. I believe he viewed me at that moment with New Eyes, in a New Light, perceiving those spiritual Qualities which had been suppressed in me by Duty and Tragedy for so long, following my estrangement from Grace Harrison. I blushed a bit, I think, and swung my beaded purse, and that was all. We parted at the Corner, he to the Left alone, and I to the Right down Main Street, with Rosalie. I could scarcely Breathe.

He appeared upon the front porch at four o'clock, and shook hands with Father, and escorted me down to Lowe's Emporium for an ice cream Soda. I stammered and blushed, I think, and yet how I did enjoy It. How sweet and young we seem, the two of us, in Memory! How lovely the Afternoon! Others were present, too:—Rosalie and her fiancé, Todd Bell Sims, and the Clinton boys, home from the University of Virginia where they studied Law, Elva Pope whose family had recently moved to town, and yet Others. Many of These were the friends of my Schooldays whom I had known, and had by and large Lost track of since, as they had continued their education while I had assumed my Cares. Everyone laughed and engaged in silly conversations. Perhaps more Grave by nature, I was nevertheless Enchanted. It was the first time I had ever felt myself to be, in fact, what I truly was—a marriageable young lady, a member of the town's Smart Set, despite the foibles of my Family. Elva Pope had studied literature at Sweetbriar College, we conversed about Poetry, joined by Ransom McClain who knew little of it but liked the idea, and liked, furthermore, his companion, *me!* It was a delicious, luscious, languorous Afternoon. He touched my hand in parting, I knew he would return. I ran up the stairs and fell upon my counterpane half swooning, and recalling, strangely enough, how Grace Harrison had once said, "Remember me!" I felt as if the Emotions invoked in me by all my hours with her had been imprisoned in a cellar until this moment, and that now they ventured forth cautiously into the sun. The tastes which she had fostered came back to me in full—there was no controlling my voracious Appetite then, and no slaking my Thirst! I had lived a life of Sacrifice for far too long. For one of my tender years I had worked too hard. I am nearly ashamed to admit that I fell into a summer of sun-drenched Abandon and the Purest form of Love, all concentrated in the person of Ransom McClain. Yes, it is understandable, but ah, how it is painful to remember and relate! For Ransom reciprocated my love in full, and more than full. Even after all these years, pain and joy return to me in equal measure as I recall those halcyon Afternoons.

He read to me by the river, or I to him, we sat on a quilt beneath the huge soughing Pines, half-dead from longing, from Love. Ransom McClain possessed a slight congenital deformity of the foot, which occasioned an elevated shoe and caused him to have a Limp, noticeable only if he became fatigued. I used to consider this Condition, when alone, and fairly Weep with love. Nettie laughed at me for it, I hated her. Father held his tongue. Ransom and I Kissed, it seems, all August, long rapturous Kisses, hotly chaste, quite spiritual, Kisses which are framed in my mind yet, as photographs:—and when he left, by train, for

Charlottesville to study Medicine, how I tripped along beside the puffing vehicle, blowing kisses, I wore my pearl gray Gloves. Father had come down too, to see him off, and Nettie, and Fay, who seemed more interested in the Train. His parents, too, were there, his Mother kissed me, and urged me to be Brave. For we were to be Married in a Year.

He wrote me lovely letters, one, two, three, and then these ceased. They ceased as abruptly as if they had never been, I received no explanation. Ah, how I wept! How ill I fell, how I neglected both Chores and Appearance, and walked the misty mountain in my grief. At length, Father paid a call upon the McClains, returning with stormy demeanor. "It is over," he said. "Young Ransom did not know his own mind, it appears, and he is embarrassed to communicate with you. You must endeavor to Forget him." And even Nettie was sorry, and urged me to come with her on her rides and jaunts about the countryside, but I declined. I felt embarrassed to face again the new friends with whom I'd whiled away those lovely summer days, save for Rosalie and Lucy Dee and Elva Pope, who were then, as they are now, true Friends, as staunch in adversity as in Fair Weather, particularly Elva. We read together. We walked, and I began to take instruction in the Episcopal Faith, and my Lord was with me, and comforted me during this trying Time.

I have attempted to analyze, in my own Mind, my Change of Faith. Of course God is ever our Father, and looks over All even as He does the Sparrows, as we are told, and resides in every House of Worship, whatever the denomination, and in every Heart where faith lives. But I had come to feel that the Methodist Church of my Youth was that indeed: the Church of

my Youth. It did not fully feed my Swelling Soul.
Furthermore I could not stand the Pastor, a Mr.
Boomer, who was afflicted by partial paralysis of the
Face, so that occasionally, when he was caught up in
one of his interminable dour sermons, the spittle
drooled from the slack corner of his mouth, down to
his chin. Mr. Boomer's clothing, furthermore, carried
a faint, rancid Odor. His knowledge was slight, his
vision simple and gloomy, concentrating as he did
upon the fires of Hell and the joys of Heaven, the
latter considerably more difficult to attain than
the former, dwelling often at unseemly length upon the
sufferings of Jesus on the Cross. He gave me headaches. Also my friends Rosalie, and Lucy, and Elva
were Episcopalians. I found I loved the Prayer Book,
and the rituals, and the old Priest, Mr. Holloway, a
person of refinement who had come originally from
Lynchburg. Sometimes, in his sermon, he interspersed
his Bible messages with bits from Shakespeare!—And
all the Leading families of the town attended the
Episcopal Church. I fancy that my own sainted Mother
would have switched over in time, had she lived until
the unfortunate advent of Mr. Boomer, and so I made
this Change, and saw nothing Wrong with it, and
began to learn my Catechisms, and to take instruction in the Faith.

It was *in no wise True,* as Nettie asserted, that I
made the change in the vain pathetic hope of seeing
Ransom McClain when he came home from the University of Virginia. I would not have resumed a romance with Ransom had he been the last man on
earth! His nose, in fact, struck me as decidedly too
long, when he returned for the Christmas holidays,
and his pallor appeared unhealthy, his Manner ef-
feminate. I remarked for the first time how his full

lips indicated Peevishness, and Weakness, and moral Flabbiness, and a tendency toward Dissipation, which tendency I am sure he has given in to, during his venture into Academe. I base this opinion upon the day he toyed so, until properly reprimanded, with my Sash. I have nothing but Pity and Scorn for him. I refuse even to give him the satisfaction of snubbing him, thus acknowledging that there was ever any Accord between us two. Instead, I speak coolly, and cast down my eyes. He is a Weakling of Body and Mind. I was, quite simply, Deluded. Nettie's assertion was, therefore, wholly untrue and Ridiculous, and when the news came two years ago that he had become officially affianced to a girl from Norfolk, I could not have been less interested. I have joined the Episcopal Church because I love it, because I love the Prayers and the Collects, and I love the way Mr. Holloway does not make so much of the unrefined elements of Christianity such as the Blood and the Cross, and there is real Wine at Communion, and I love the way the Light falls through the stained glass Windows.

But in truth, since the events of this Sad Chronicle, I confess I have been able to muster no interest in the members of the Opposite sex. Though opportunities have arisen during the several years which have followed these occurrences, I have brushed them aside with a firmness which I now, in retrospect, sometimes Regret. One of Rosalie's Cousins from Kentucky, who came here to attend her Wedding, fell prey to my charm, and questioned Todd Bell Sims in private concerning his Prospects. I let him know, in short order, that he had None! Uncouth young men from the town, boys with whom I had never associated, such as Roy Eustace, Luther Dill, and Verner

Hess, appeared at our door bent upon trumped-up errands. Of those three, Verner Hess was the most persistent. I sent them all packing! For I well knew that they would never have Dared approach, had I not been so Shamed.

Thus did I, in my grief, upon impulse, terminate my Possibilities, closing all gates that might open upon the fair avenue of Marriage. It was during this time that Elva became engaged to Lawrence Dooley, who had long cared for her, and I wept with her, and was Pleased and Sad, at One. Father, deep in the throes of financial Distress, and but a Shadow of the man he once had been, seemed oblivious to all my sorrow, and to Nettie's wild adventuring, and did not even attempt to curb her behavior. For Nettie had begun to spend her time with low companions, she wore Trousers, and worked in Father's mill. Father did not lift a Finger to stop it, seeming, rather, pleased with her Efforts! I could not reason with him. He had no innate sense of responsibility, I realized then, having merely appropriated my Mother's for a while. Fay became ever more my main Companion and responsibility, being easy to amuse, however, as she is now, taking delights in the Flower gardens which I have maintained in Mother's memory, and working like a Trojan at whatever task I proposed. I myself was accepted into the Holy Fellowship of Saints. And Elva was married to Lawrence, with myself as Maid of Honor, I wore a Rose silk dress.

But I progress too Rapidly here, attempting to quit this last room before I must face the final dark corner of it, my Father's Death. He went as he had lived and that, I suppose, is the Best that can be said of it. His mighty heart ceased suddenly one Noon while he helped his men unload a wagon in the lumber yard.

Nettie was called directly to his side, but by the time she reached him, he was Gone. It was so sudden. We buried him from the Methodist Church, in deference to our Mother, with the drooling Mr. Boomer officiating. It was necessary to ask assistance of two additional Pallbearers, to take his weight. The two graves now lie side by side in the little church-yard behind the church, not far from the rippling stream. I have planted pink alyssum like a carpet over All, and wine-dark roses by the headstones. It is so Sad.

When I reflect upon my parents, and upon their love, how often am I moved to Tears! My Mother died in her prime, yet full of joy and hope, plucked like a rose at her Very peak. My father fell more slowly, as an old tree in the forest, buffeted by winter after winter, by the increasing severity of the Storm. It is my fondest hope that his Soul, too, is with the Lord, although I can but doubt It. For he lost his faith when he lost her. Perhaps, I hope it fervently, his love for Mother has tipped the Heavenly scales in his favor, and they are together now in death. But who can say? Though a rough man by Nature, he loved her Fondly, and found No One in those ensuing years who might replace Her, and I am moved, in reading this sonnet by Elizabeth Barrett Browning, to copy down these words which speak the thoughts he would ever have been too mute to frame:—

> I love thee with a love I seemed to lose
> With my lost saints,—I love thee with the breath
> Smiles, tears, of all my life!—and, if God choose,
> I shall but love thee better after death.

So thus do I quit this last, this final chamber, full of darkness shot through yet by the occasional ray of

Love. Gently do I close the Door. I hold my guttering candle aloft as I tiptoe gently back down this wide hall, down the tottering stair, and take my leave of this Mansion of memory, pulling the creaking door to, as best I can, behind me. It will not fully close, the lock is gone, the keys are long since Lost. It rests ajar. I turn to face the world, but ah, the Night outside is dark and wild, though dawn must now by rights be fast approaching. The moon is scarcely visible behind those low black Clouds. I cross the weed-choked Garden, I open and close the rusty gate. The antic wind in a frenzy whips my skirt about my ankles. It blows my candle out.

February 10, 1928

1933, ADDENDUM

Alas! And let me quit that dreary house, and abandon Symbol. Let me abandon indeed all symbol and sign, the world has quite Enough, nay more than enough, of Pain to offer me. Wild winds and dark nights and creaking mansions will not be necessary. The Mansion I most hope for is Above, and yet I shall not shirk my duties here upon this desolate Earth.

In the years which have passed since I penned those last sad lines, I have felt the walls of this real house, my own, close in around me, I have grown older, sadder, wiser. Let me elaborate, but let me yet be Brief, for these dire Facts speak for themselves.

Upon Father's demise, we were astonished to find that he had accumulated Debt upon Debt, so that, in short, we lost the Business, and not only that, but in the aftermath, I lost my sister Nettie as well. For Nettie conceived a wild scheme, and felt that if we sold this House, we could recoup our losses, *she* could manage the lumber Business, converting it into a construction firm or some such, and all would be well. I could not in good conscience condone such speculation. Nor could I stand to see us sink so Low. I remembered our Mother, and the manner in which we had lived during our Childhood, and my heart was grieved past bearing it. She would not have wished us, ever, to leave this House, this situation. Nor, I felt, would *he*, this house built of timbers which he had felled, this home he had made for her. I could not but say "No." But ah, how Nettie fretted, and railed against me, and the terrible things she said!—At length I did prevail, as my signature also was required. The business was duly Sold, and we have now an Income slight but sufficient for Fay and myself to eke out our existence here.

For Nettie is gone! She has with unseemly suddenness married a man from out in the country, a hunting companion of our Father's many years older than she. He is a rough man of uncouth manner. It is not a suitable union, and we seldom see one another. Yet he has Land, and will, I suppose, provide for her, as she refused to take a penny of money from the sale of the mill, declaring that she had nothing to do with it. Ah, Nettie! Headstrong and willful, determined to live beneath your Class, what will become of you?

And even more to the point, what will become of us? Of poor Fay, and Myself? I have lost Mother, Father, Sister, Ransom McClain whom I would not have anyway if he were offered to me upon a silver Platter, and Grace Harrison as surely as if she were truly Dead. I suppose I should not Complain. I have my home, my flowers, my friends, I am busy from Dawn to Dusk with the Cares of the house, and of Fay, now fully grown but with a mind more like a Child's, and with my Duties such as the Altar Guild and Garden Club. The Lord is with me, as He has been always. Ransom McClain seems merely silly to me now, the merest nothing, dandelion fluff in the wind. A further sad note:—Elva's husband has lost everything, and Shot himself last April, and I am necessary to her too, as Comfort and Confidante, as well as to Fay. My cares keep me contained.

My Life is full of Duty, Work, and Love:—Love for the Lord, and for his handiwork. I persevere. Yet in some Way, I fail:—for how often, despite my efforts to keep busy, to do good, how often does a Cloud of blackness from I know not where descend upon my soul, and sit upon my brow, and rest there awhile. And at these times I can do Nothing, for I *am* nothing, a vessel of mere *gloom*.

It was thus, I recall, last evening. I sat here. I sat here upon the fleur-de-lis loveseat brought, I've heard, from France, by Mother's people. I sat here to rest awhile, having come into the house in the late afternoon for a drink of Water, as I had been out gardening, separating the Day Lily bulbs that they should bloom more profusely come the Spring. I had left my gardening gloves and shears upon the front porch steps. I wandered into the Parlor thus refreshed, admiring how the last long light of the autumn afternoon fell through the windowpanes to make a pattern, blocks of light and shade, upon the flowered carpet. It is a lovely room, this time of day. I sat here. The Chinese screen before the fireplace seemed to glow, strange birds with fiery plumage, dancing men, pagodas. The plump green cushions on the velvet sofa were fluffed, so, and the fine wood gleamed from the coffee table, the piano, the credenza; the mirrors shone. It is a room of shining surfaces and Comfort, this dark green velvet, the striped armchair, the needlepoint stool. I noted the pattern on the carpet, how it shifted as the Sun sank lower in the west.

And Gloom came then, to sit with me awhile. I could neither move, nor stand, nor lift a finger in any way to finish up my chores, although I willed it, I rested there immobile until the sunlight reached me. One corner of one yellow square fell at my feet. At last then all a-tremble I arose, and attained the porch, and gathered up my implements. It was that moment twixt day and dark when the mind Floats, that luminous time in that part of the year where the Seasons battle for ascendancy. Fleeting Summer had left mementos everywhere, like a Lady at a garden-party who drops a lacy glove, that a Gentleman may not forget her. Climbing roses bloom on the trellis yet, and purple asters nod along the walk. In the rock garden, mums bud jauntily.

But leaves fall here and there, and the breeze has a Chill to it. The dogwood leaves are already turning. Beneath the spreading oak at the side of the house I bent to my task, digging deep into the rich black loamy Earth with trowel and fork to find the round white Bulbs in clusters in their dark, secret Home. I broke them up, and spread them out, saving some in my little basket to put down by the road, at the end of the walk, to gladden the hearts of passers-by. The Flesh of the bulbs was soft and pale. I held them in my hand, then removed my gloves, to feel their coolness, their soft mysterious texture, as I mused upon this miracle of life:—that a frail form such as this can hold such sap within, so far beneath the soil, and

should spring forth so abundantly and with such
vigor, for these are the tiger lilies. And then, I know
not Why, I lifted them up to touch my own face,
smudging my dress, and then I dropped them, and
wept. I cannot now imagine what I was thinking of.
At length I rose, and fled to the house, and bathed,
and prepared our simple dinner, though I confess I
had but little appetite. All the circumstances of my
life are Calm, yet it seems I do not know my own
mind, neither can I arrest nor understand this Tor-
ment in my soul. I shall trust in the Lord and persevere, concluding thus:—

OVER ALL

God is good and God is light
In this faith I rest secure,
Evil can but serve the right,
Over all shall love endure.

John Greenleaf Whittier

ALONE on the loveseat in the bay window, Lacy closes her mother's journal. Then she stands up, stretches, and goes to put the journal in the front hall beneath her own purse. No one else seems interested. Myrtle and Don have said they'd like to read it later; Lacy doubts that this day will ever come, but she'll keep it for them, and for her own Kate. None of them would know what to make of it right now. Actually, the only person Lacy knows who would be able to appreciate this journal is Jack, her own wacky Jack: that fool. Lacy sighs, running her hands through her sandy hair. She can hear them all in the kitchen talking, eating lunch. But she's not hungry. She stands at the parlor door looking in at the stickers on everything. She sighs again and then thinks of something. She wipes her palms, suddenly damp, on her skirt as she hurries through the hall and into the dining room where the old breakfront stands, its door wide open, its contents spread about the room. They're still not through with the cut glass, or with the china. One problem is that no one knows how much anything is really worth. Sybill swears that this big blue platter, for instance, the willoware, is worth as much as two or three of the prettier ironstone platters, because the willoware was made in occupied Japan. Can this be true? Or is it merely that Sybill wants the ironstone? Clinus won't come to tell them, since he has agoraphobia. They have to consult him by phone. Lacy goes over to the breakfront and runs her fingers along the dark smooth wood, pressing. Nothing at the front, the sides—no, wait a second. That fretwork panel, around the bottom. . . . Lacy presses again, and the panel swings open. And there it is, her grandfather's silver-handled revolver after all, and after all these years.

Kate, passing through the dining room with a Coke, stops dead in her tracks. "Oh wow, Mom, let's see that," she says, and Lacy hands it to her very carefully.

"It might be still loaded," Lacy says, pointing the barrel down, and Kate grasps it gingerly.

"How'd you know it was going to be there?" she asks. "In that little place?"

"Your grandmother mentions it in her journal," Lacy says. "It belonged to her father."

"So that's my—"

"Great-grandfather," Lacy says.

"Oh wow!" Kate turns the revolver over in her hands and then goes running back into the kitchen and comes out with Sean, whose whole face lights up when he sees it.

"You mean this is *real?*" He picks it up too, and points it, sighting down his arm out the window. Lacy is amused that his first reaction is to point it, while Kate's is to examine.

"I'd like to have this," Sean says immediately.

Lacy laughs. "I'm sure you would, honey. But it's part of the estate, and so it has to be thrown into the pot along with everything else we're dividing. Besides, it's probably really valuable, I should imagine. It must be real old. We'll have to ask Clinus about it."

Sean whistles through his teeth, shaking his head. He wears cut-off jeans and an Ocean Pacific T-shirt, and checkered vans. "It sure is pretty," he says.

"Go show it to your daddy," Lacy tells him. "Nobody's seen it yet but us."

Sean and Kate leave the room and then, because it bothers her to see it standing open, after all those private years, Lacy closes the compartment door in the side of the breakfront, and goes into the kitchen for lunch.

Sean and Kate are not here, having gone to look for Don, presumably, but there's a kind of quiver in the air which lets Lacy know they just left. It's that energy they both have, that they carry with them everywhere, they're almost literally radiating with it, both of them. Bill doesn't have it, Lacy thinks, he's a calmer child, a more disciplined child, getting up at five to swim all those laps, making A's, staying right now with Susan, whom he probably likes just fine. Bill's an easygoing, adjustable child. He likes most people just fine. Susan's face is very dim in Lacy's memory right now, but Bill's face glows sharp and bright in her mind, like the face of some sweet young animal. Lacy balls her hands up into fists and fights back tears, Bill just kills her. She misses him. Kate and Sean, on the other hand, are children like Candy and Arthur were, the kind of kids that can walk in a room and chairs fall over for no apparent reason, kids who never clean up their rooms and give the substitute teachers hell, and don't get along with anyone's parents.

"Come on in here and have a sandwich, honey, you look all done in," Candy says from the round table, and Lacy comes and sits down in the chair.

"You know what I've got here." Candy's grinning, eating an enormous sandwich.

"What?" Then Lacy remembers. Candy always used to make sandwiches out of the leftover turkey and cold dressing, with mayonnaise. Her sandwich looks wonderful.

"I think I'll try one," Lacy says, pulling the turkey platter and the mayonnaise jar across the table.

"It's nothing but fat and cholesterol," Sybill warns. She's fixed herself a salad, and nibbles at it daintily. "Also I've read that if you don't take the dressing out of the turkey cavity right away it'll poison you. I wouldn't touch that dressing with a ten-foot pole," Sybill says. Mrs. Newsome, down the hill, brought the stuffed turkey up here two days ago. It's good, too.

Lacy spreads dressing flamboyantly, in lumpy swirls, across a piece of white bread, something she never has in her house in Chapel Hill, where she keeps only whole wheat and rye. Jack was a health nut. And Lacy's lover was a vegetarian whose idea of a really good meal was a baked potato with sprouts and cottage cheese on top of it. Lacy realizes that she's thinking of her lover in the past tense now. She smiles, putting more mayonnaise on top of the dressing, then slices of turkey. Dark meat, which has more flavor. She grins at Candy, then at Arthur, who opens three beers and brings them over.

"None for me, thanks," Sybill says too brightly, too

politely. She's right at the end of her rope, a place she recognizes, a place she's been before.

Lacy says, "And as for cholesterol, I just don't care. When you're going through a major trauma, you can eat anything, you never gain an ounce." In fact, she thinks she's *lost* weight since the funeral, in spite of all the wonderful food she's been eating.

And so has Myrtle, which is not surprising, since she never seems to sit down or eat a bite. Myrtle sails through the kitchen right now looking distracted, stopping only long enough to take a Diet Coke from the refrigerator. She lives on Diet Cokes, which just came out, and Merit menthols. Myrtle looks so worried—Candy and Lacy eat their turkey-and-dressing sandwiches and drink their beer, but Myrtle zooms on through the house to the parlor where she sinks down upon the old velvet sofa in some confusion. She doesn't understand herself, these days. Don doesn't understand her, either. Don has said they need to take the Couples Communication Course again, which is true, but there are a lot of things on her mind lately which Myrtle doesn't want to communicate to Don. Anyway, the Couples Communication Course won't be offered until September. A lot can happen between now and then. Myrtle's mind goes reeling, as she tries to imagine what these things might be. She almost had a heart attack and died on the spot, for instance, right in the middle of counting silver teaspoons, when Gary Vance showed up at the door this morning in his pest-control suit. It was entirely too much like mental telepathy—because to tell the truth, Myrtle had been thinking about him. She'd even gone out there, much to her own astonishment.

She could tell you exactly when it started, when Gary Vance burst back into her mind which he hadn't crossed in days and certainly not since her mother's death—it was in Mr. Constantine's office yesterday afternoon, at the precise moment Don announced that they would move into her mother's house right away. Well, to begin with, she was just amazed! Hasn't she spent the last three years decorating her own home in Argonne Hills until now it's nearly perfect? How could Don imagine that she'd even consider living in this old place which needs so many repairs—and just imagine the fuel bill, with these high ceilings! But Don, surprisingly, was adamant—when Myrtle buttonholed him outside Mr. Constantine's office, perfectly furious, to say what she really thought—which she couldn't do at the time, she'd never make a *scene* in front of everybody—well, Don was just adamant, that's all.

"Listen, honey," he said firmly, "that house has been in the family for almost a hundred years. We can't let it go. And I believe she knew we wouldn't— she trusted us to take care of it, and restore it, which we'll do. And modernize it too, of course, don't worry!" Here, Don pinched Myrtle's thin cheek. "We'll put in a whole new kitchen, a new washer and dryer, central air, whatever you want. You just name it. The sky's the limit, baby!" said Dr. Don.

And Myrtle simply didn't know what to do then. She loves to be married to a man who can say, "The sky's the limit, baby," and *mean* it. But Don has no idea at all of the work involved, the work *she'll* have to do while he's at his clinic curing acne and taking off warts. She'll be the one who has to deal with the contractor and call the electrician and drive to Roanoke for fixtures. "I'm just not up to it," Myrtle said. They stood on the blazing hot sidewalk downtown, outside Mr. Constantine's office.

Don looked at his wife carefully, lovingly, paying her that rapt attention which she never could resist. Then he put his arm around her. "You're just upset about her death," he said. "But don't worry, I'll make all the initial arrangements, you can pick up the slack in a week or so."

Don, always a go-getter, has become a man possessed. His graying blond hair seems to stand almost straight up and crinkle, giving off sparks. He looks ready for anything, like an astronaut. He looks like John Glenn, in fact, instead of George Peppard. . . .

"I'd like to get the pool put in right away so we can use it this summer," he said.

Myrtle wanted to tell him that their things, the things they have now, like the king-size bed and the wicker conversation set with its lime-green and pink cushions, these things will never do in her mother's house. It's not Myrtle's style, it's just not. She's entirely too young for such an old house. They'll have to have a garage sale. And how can he assume that she can handle a whole new house anyway, when she keeps locking herself out of her own? But Don doesn't know about that, Myrtle reminds herself.

"I want to take the driveway on around the back and down the other side, full circle," Don said, opening the car door for her, carefully closing it. "Like that house in Atlanta that I showed you in *Southern Living*."

And he talked on and on and on about her mother's house, as they drove home, but Myrtle just couldn't follow it, her mind skipping back, oddly, to Gary Vance. When Don detailed plans for a gazebo, she thought of the mole in the small of Gary's back. When Don mentioned a deck off the kitchen, then steps down to the patio, she remembered a little dark spot, a kind of a fleck, in Gary's left eye.

So she lied like a rug, as she said to herself triumphantly, she was so smooth, making up a grocery list and then telling Don that she just had to run out to the Piggly Wiggly. He didn't even seem to notice, sketching plans for the pool and the driveway on a tablet, figuring things on his pocket computer. Myrtle went into the downstairs bathroom and washed her face and put on new makeup. In spite of the strain she'd been under during these last few days, she thought she looked fine. She covered the shadows under her eyes with Germaine Monteil Hides Anything and then considered her face critically. Losing a few pounds had given her some *cheekbones*, at least. Myrtle put a little extra blush on her new cheekbones and left, swinging her purse, calling back to Don, who was too wrapped up in his own plans to answer.

Then she drove furiously, recklessly, out the interstate to Gary's house, past the One Stop, past the Cash 'N Carry and the Happy Times Day Care Center, careening into Gary's littered driveway in a cloud of dust. The ground out there was parched and hard, and no grass grew. The familiar termite car was gone. She'd missed him. Myrtle braked abruptly, turned off the ignition, put her head down on her steering wheel, and wept. He had said, "Come back if you want to," and she was here, but he was not. And his house was as awful as ever—more awful, in fact, the aqua cinderblocks glowing in the late afternoon sun, Clorox bottles and cat-food cans scattered in the weeds. Who had a cat? Probably some former tenant. Gary Vance might be a former tenant himself now, for all she knew. She felt no connection with this place.

But yet some force propelled her from her car, out into the heat, and across the yard to the door which she knew was always unlocked, and so she went, and opened it, and stood for a minute in Gary's living room. If you could call this living! There was the armchair with the saucepan under it, the TV on the floor, newspapers scattered about. There was the odd pale water stain on the far wall, where the roof leaked. Myrtle wanted him so bad she thought she couldn't stand it, she thought she would die at first, staring at that water stain, as waves of horrible longing came over her, leaving her all weak and washed out from desire. "*You're crazy*," Myrtle said to herself, which didn't help at all. Gary Vance himself seemed suddenly secondary to her love for him. In fact she couldn't really remember exactly what he looked like, just those odd bits of him, that speck in his eye, the mole on his back, his bony feet. All spring and summer, he went barefoot. If he had been there, he'd be barefoot. But he wasn't. Myrtle stood for a while in Gary Vance's living room looking out his picture window at trucks roaring by on the interstate. She felt as light and insubstantial as the dust that turned in the sunlight that came through the glass.

All the times she'd ever been here were impossible, all the chances she'd taken, the guilt she'd felt. The first four or five times, Myrtle had been quite sure she'd left her iron on, back in Argonne Hills, and that her whole house would be a blackened smoking pile of rubble when she returned. And yet she'd stayed, and yet it wasn't . . . *ladybug, ladybug, fly away home, your house is on fire, your children are gone.* This memory made Myrtle smile, but it all seemed so long ago. Well, she had no more business here. She knew it then as surely as she had known she'd marry Don, after their first date. Whatever it was, it was over. What had gotten into her? What was she doing, standing here in an empty house? Myrtle felt so thankful to have missed him that she blessed her lucky stars all the way home, and drove carefully, waving at Clinus when she passed the One Stop. His billboard said REST IN PEACE.

That's why it was so shocking for Gary Vance to show up this morning at Mother's. Did he know she'd gone out to his house yesterday? Had she left anything there, so he could tell? At least he'd had the sense to wear his pest-control suit. Does he want her back, or does he simply want to let her know he's *here*, if she wants him . . . maybe he just plans to show up forever, year after year, wherever she is. Then Myrtle decides, looking around her mother's parlor, that if she *does* need an exterminator, she'll just get Orkin to come over from Buncoe. A licensed firm is always best, and the sky's the limit, as Don says. But she can't imagine her big glass coffee table in this room.

"Myrtle, can you come here a minute?" It's Lacy in the door, looking harassed, and so Myrtle gets up and follows her sister into the dining room where Candy and Sybill are arguing over a pink glass pitcher.

"It's Depression glass," Sybill says. "It's worth a lot. A lot more than this whole dessert set, for instance, which is relatively new."

"You just want that dessert set," Candy says.

Wait a minute! "Actually, I think I ought to get the dessert set anyway," Myrtle says, "since Don and I gave it to Mother in the first place. We gave it to her for Christmas 1976."

"I didn't think we were going to do it that way."
Sybill's tone is very aggrieved. "If that's the case,
then I ought to get that blouse which you gave to
Elva Pope, to remember Mother by."

"It wouldn't fit you," Candy says.

"That's beside the point," says Sybill firmly.

"Do you really *want* the dessert set?" Candy asks
Myrtle.

The truth is, Myrtle doesn't know. She just doesn't
know. What she really wants is a cigarette, but they're
in the kitchen.

Lacy runs her hands through her hair. "Let's go
call Clinus," she suggests, "and ask him about Depression glass and occupied Japan."

"You can take my word for it," Sybill says firmly, to
nobody, as Candy and Lacy and Myrtle head for the
kitchen. Her words hang in the air like cartoon words.
Sybill puts a sticker on the dessert set and follows
them into the kitchen where Arthur sits at the round
table drinking and dreaming of his own blond Alta
who often merges in his mind these days with Mrs.
Palucci, and then Lacy is dialing, and the phone
rings and rings at the One Stop where Clinus can't
hear it, over the barking of his dog, and Nettie doesn't
even bother to answer, she's so busy helping Clinus
to look for Fay, who has, of all things, disappeared!

But she's not far. Fay in fact is finally ready for that
trip. Except she thinks they might try to stop her,
Nettie and Clinus, if they find out, so she's hiding,
sort of, or as much as she can, she's so big, stretched
out in the back seat of Clinus's car, *ha ha! It's all
over now, it's time to shake the dust off your feet
honey and hit the road. But Lord it's hot you can't
breathe in a closed-up car honey a Pekingese would*

*die on the spot who is also a dog, the one in the
schoolbook, but Bert had better shut up barking like
that, he's a bad, bad dog. Shut up, Bert. It's so bright
out here but we'll buy you some sunglasses honey,
you'll need them in all that sand. The beach itself is a
mile wide in places, imagine that. Imagine the beach
it will take us three days to get there nobody else will
go except you and me honey this is our secret honey
oh honey we'll go in the car. We will go in the car,
Lacy who looks like Princess Di says won't you come
in the car Fay to see them, all those flowers on the
hillside, and all that blue. Princess Di honey I've been
there. I've been there too, and laid among them, and
looked straight up over his back at the old blue sky.
The wacky way I met my mate was he took me for a
little spin or a little walk or perhaps it was in a
bowling alley, I forget, I forget. Luke and Laura
spent an unforgettable night in Wyndham's Depart-
ment Store. All my children live in Pine Valley including Greg and Jenny the starcrossed lovers destined
to spend their lives apart, you have to walk it for
yourself. Opal has never loved anybody else but Sam
the electrician and never will, she's leaving for NBC
now, bye bye. You have to have that spark and then
you have to fan the flames. We will all see greener
pastures in the sweet bye and bye, which Elizabeth
wouldn't let him sing at home, but he could have gone
places with so much talent. You never know. Why
Alan Ladd was a potato digger before he made it big,
Clark Gable was a necktie salesman. I'll sing and you
can swim in the water and get some sun. Natalie
Wood sank like a stone in her big heavy jacket, death
by drowning said Dr. Thomas Noguchi about his
investigation as detailed in his new book* Coroner.
Had Christopher Walken and Robert Wagner quar-

reled, aboard their yacht? Imagine the weight of the water, imagine the manner of death. He meant to go without me, I saw him trying to leave. He tried to sneak out in the storm in the night with Elizabeth sound asleep. He thought we were all asleep. He meant to take that journey by himself, he meant to leave me, and after all he'd said. Some men are just so mean. He said honey oh honey oh honey you'll like it there. But then he meant to leave me in the end. The investigation will continue as detailed by Dr. Don Dotson. Nettie says they will dig up Elizabeth's yard they will put in a pool, everybody who's anybody in L.A. has a pool, you know. Ha ha! I see what he's up to, I read the stars. The investigation will continue as detailed by Dr. Don Dotson and they will find the body in the water death by drowning, and all the dogs will bark. You have to take that lonesome journey by yourself. It's a long hot trip honey but at least we'll get to see the ocean.

"We can't find her." It's Nettie, like a little black crow at Miss Elizabeth's kitchen door.

"Find who?" Lacy almost shouts in order to be heard over the sudden roar of the bulldozer, but then Nettie comes on in, followed by Kate, and shuts the door behind her.

"Fay." Nettie sits down at the kitchen table and starts fanning herself with a newspaper. "She's not over here, is she?" Nettie looks around at all of them. Kate and Theresa look around too, eyes big, holding their tongues.

"Why, you know she hasn't gone anywhere for years and years," says Candy.

"Well, sometimes she'll take a little walk or something, and that's just what she done this time, I reckon, but me and Clinus can't find her no way."

"*I* didn't know she ever took a walk," Sybill says, and Nettie snaps, "Well, I guess you don't know everything."

"Did you all look in the closet?" Arthur asks.

This question makes Kate and Theresa, hovering like butterflies at the edge of the crisis, start giggling. "You all hush," Myrtle says, rifling frantically through the kitchen drawers for a match, since her butane lighter seems to have disappeared.

"Well, we might as well start in on the kitchen stuff, since we're all in here," Sybill says, climbing up on a chair so she can reach the blue china clock.

"How long's she been gone?" Arthur asks Nettie.

"Don't know. That's the thing of it. Last I seen of her was last night, actually, she was watching the *Tonight* show. But the TV was on this morning too, *Good Morning America*. So it could of been real late last night, or it could of been this morning. I'll be damned if I know," Nettie says. Nettie's face is hard and brown as wood, in fact that's what she looks like, a little carved statue, folk art, thrown in among real people. She's different from them. And now she sits and looks beyond them, drumming her fingers softly on the tabletop. Her eyes narrow as she sucks in smoke—what in the world does she see? Nettie looks like one of those smoking monkeys you buy at souvenir stands in Georgia.

"I'll try Clinus again," Candy says, and dials, and lets it ring.

Sybill turns the blue china clock over and over in her hands, and then runs her finger around the smiling sun in its center, and something comes up in her throat, and she starts to cry.

"Nettie, can I have a match?" Myrtle asks, and Nettie gives her one, and then Myrtle can light her cigarette too and look at the scrap of paper in her hand, an old list of her mother's she found in the drawer.

"Well, you know she couldn't have gone *far*." Arthur is laughing.

Nettie stands up and moves to the kitchen window.

It's a grocery list Myrtle has found. It reads: *milk, oranges, eggs, bacon, bread, paper napkins, candles, prescription (Rexall), Metamucil, Ivory soap*, all in Miss Elizabeth's elegant, spidery hand. Myrtle is profoundly moved. It could be *her* list—why, she's made this list a hundred times! Myrtle sees her mother clearly, sitting at the little kitchen desk to write this list, writing with her fountain pen and her head inclined to the side, and then Myrtle sees herself, making her own list, with a Pentel. Making a list every day, hundreds of lists, hundreds of days. Myrtle feels like she's making some kind of a breakthrough, but she can't tell what it is. She has got, as she will tell Don later, *mixed emotions*.

Candy pats Sybill, who holds the clock and cries for her mother.

"Jesus!" Kate says.

"This is all so ironic," says Theresa.

"Did you call Ed Dark?" asks Arthur. Ed Dark is a state trooper they all went to high school with. "Clinus said she'd been talking about a trip," Arthur says. "You don't reckon she could of gotten down here to the bus station somehow, and gone off on a bus someplace?"

"Arthur, don't be silly," Candy says. "Besides, wherever would she go?"

"Well, she gets these crazy ideas," Arthur says, "like all those prayer handkerchiefs that come in the mail from California. You can't tell what she's got in her mind. One time she sent off to buy a square foot of swamp in the Okefenokee, she showed me the deed."

"Sometimes Clinus knows things," says Candy, "but he won't say," and Arthur, looking at her, wonders if Candy knows she's a love child and guesses not. *He's* not going to tell her, that's for sure.

"Clinus don't know a thing about this,". Nettie says. "Clinus is worried to death."

Then Sybill says suddenly, "Nobody ever loved me," and Candy hugs her, and says that's silly, and Myrtle says it's silly too. Myrtle hugs Sybill too.

But Nettie stares beyond them out the window, where Dr. Don and Sean stand together watching the bulldozer dig the pool. All that earth looks startlingly red and raw, against the green. Nettie bites her lip. It don't seem like none of the rest of them is even noticing.

Except for Sean.

He's right there beside his daddy when the bulldozer hits the body or what's left of it, where the old well used to be, he's right there when the big bulldozer operator gets down off the yellow bulldozer and waves frantically at Dr. Don to come over there. Sean has been trying to show his father the gun, and see if he'll let him keep it. "Not now, son," Dr. Don keeps saying, or trying to say, above the roar of the bulldozer, all of which pisses Sean off, the way his father calls him "son" instead of his own name which is bad enough, and the fact that his father won't pay any attention to what he says, which is just typical. Then when the fat guy climbs down off the dozer and leaves it running and waves his arms, Dr. Don takes off at a dead run to see what the old guy wants, like it's something important, more important than his own son.

Idly, so idly that in memory it will always seem like a dream, Sean raises his great-grandfather's silver revolver and points it straight out in front of him. He isn't thinking of anything at all, his mind as clean as a whistle. His father bobs up and down, running across the field, while Sean holds the point of the revolver steady. Dad used to be a jock, he still thinks he's real hot shit. His dad's back goes up and down, up and down as he runs across the dry red clumps of dirt. He's still in real good shape. Sean holds his arm out steadily for a long time, until his arm hurts, and then he pulls the trigger. Bam! It's a huge explosion, a huge satisfying puff of white smoke exactly like you see on TV, and the noise is so loud it seems to ricochet back and forth inside Sean's head like the 4th of July. *Well, that's that.* Sean will remember thinking this, and finding himself flat on the ground with no memory of falling. Smoke hangs all around him. It hurts his nose. He waits for it to clear, to see what has happened.

The first thing he sees is his father, Dr. Don, now running as fast as he can in the *other* direction, back toward him, Sean, and screaming, "Son, are you all right?" Sean says yes, but no sound comes, and then he notices his right hand, which is bleeding. Dr. Don reaches him and kneels and hugs him, hard. "Never fool around with an old gun like that, son," he says. But Sean doesn't even care. He's *crying,* and so is his dad. Whatever else Sean will have to do in this life, he won't have to kill his father, having done it. He can relax some now, and grow another fourteen inches, and take up tennis and girls. His head is pressed into his father's stiff white shirt. Out the corner of one eye he sees the kitchen door and then the cold-pantry door burst open like doors in one of those fancy little Swiss clocks where the people come pouring out right at noon, and Nettie swoops like a bird across the red earth toward him, followed by his mother, screaming, and Candy and Lacy and Kate . . .

"Jesus H. Christ!" This is just about the worst day that Coy Eubanks, the bulldozer operator, has ever spent. It's damn sure the damn worst job. First you run up on a half-rotted corpse and then some god-damn fool teenager shoots himself in the hand. They'll do anything for attention. Coy Eubanks would of walked off the job right then, right that minute, if he hadn't owed a favor to Dr. Don, who cured him last year of venereal warts and helped him cover it up from the missus. Well, everybody's got something to hide. But most people don't have no actual bodies where they're planning to put their pool. Still, if a body *is* under there, you need to get it up. Coy can see that. And he halfway wonders if Dr. Don wasn't *looking* for this body after all, the way he seemed so excited, sketching out for Coy where to dig. Well, you can't ever tell, and in the long run, it don't matter. It's a sight how many people through the ages must have fell down in a well. If it was Coy, though, deciding, he'd of put the pool up a little closer to the house and built in a barbecue pit. He'd never spend this much money and not have a barbecue pit. Well. Ain't going to be no more work done *this* day, for damn sure.

Sean stands unsteadily and walks, supported by Myrtle and Kate, toward the house, while the rest of them go over to look down in Coy's big hole. What they see is bones and bits of bones and clothes, chewed up by the bulldozer, and one good shoe, all of it bearing little or no relation to what was, but everybody knows that's him all right—Jewell Rife. Sybill is sobbing. "Oh, I'm sorry. I'm just so sorry," is what she says. She still carries the blue clock, trailing its cord along through the dirt. Lacy suddenly grabs at Nettie's shoulder, hard, and makes her turn around. "Nettie," Lacy says, "what do you think?"

WHAT do I think? *Lord.* You're asking me? Me that has left one man and buried two? Well, a lot has happened. And sometimes, looking back, I can remember how it went, but I can't recall what it was like, all those years ago. I can see me sitting in that kitchen out in Long Valley, grieving, I can see the high spots of color in Elizabeth's cheeks when she married Jewell. But I can't recall how strong I felt things, how wrought up I got then. Seems like it was somebody else. Life goes by so fast, just like a dream. But I'll tell you about Elizabeth if you want to know.

Elizabeth, and I hate to say it, was a pure-tee fool. Now I don't mean a fool in the sense of dumb. But learning and knowing are two different things. Elizabeth learned aplenty, but she never knew much. Me, I've known more than I wanted to, all my life. And I was here. I saw it all. I saw it coming, and I saw it pass. I know what happened in this house, I've always known what happened here, but I know when to hold my tongue. There's no point hanging dirty linen on the line. You can know it, but you don't have to tell it. Because life is long, and bad times come and go, and you have to hold your tongue and bide your time if you want to go on living in this world. And there ain't any other, and so you might as well.

Elizabeth took things too much to heart. If she hadn't of been *too* good and *too* sweet all those years, she might of seen him coming too, Jewell Rife. She might of known him for what he was. But she couldn't see it until too late, and wouldn't own up to it then, not even to herself, in fact I don't know to this day if she *ever* did, ever let herself know exactly what all went on in those bad years. I doubt it. Because the road, that seemed so twisty and full of holes, straightened out after a time, and she kept on walking it, and holding her head high, and after a while, it was like those years were just a ghost town she'd walked through and then decided to forget. I've not got much patience with that. I'll take it all, whatever comes, it's the way I am. Ain't nothing else coming, the way I see it, so you might as well take what you can get. Take it all. I can't forget a thing, either, or *won't*, I reckon. I'm old as I can be now, and I remember all of it.

You can see how it happened. It was bad times after Daddy died. A lot of drifters came around in those days looking for work, looking for *anything*, I guess, and for a girl like Elizabeth it was hard to judge a man like that, him not being from the county here, and her having no way to place him, or know who his people were. She hadn't been anywhere, or done anything, remember, in spite of the airs she put on. She was a girl who had spent all her days in a house on a hill, mooning. Oh she fell for Ransom McClain, and fell hard, or thought she did, but she couldn't keep him. A man, even a man as mincy as Ransom McClain, don't want a little stuffed doll. There's more to it than pink satin ribbons and sitting in a swing. But she didn't know about that. She didn't know a thing. And so she stayed on in this house, and Fay with her, getting paler, getting older, getting too dressed up to go to town. A few more years and she would of been a laughingstock, a crazy old maid, like Grace Harrison or Miss Mona Pike. She was right there on the verge of it. She stayed on up here, while down below, the hard times hit, and many's the man that was out of work, and the drifters started coming into town.

They had heard tell of work at the mills or the quarry, but when they got here, they found one mill boarded up, that used to be ours, and then the Wilsons lost theirs in 1931, and the quarry quit about then, too. So there wasn't nothing for them to do here after all, and after a while they moved on and a while after that, they just stopped coming. I used to see them standing around the depot, when I'd come into town with Marvin on a Saturday, or standing around the hotel. I was a married girl then. I'd see them standing around there, shifting their feet, their eyes hot and staring. They didn't have a thing, most of them. It was awful. I'd look away real quick, I was pretty then.

But one time, it was right after Christmas, one of them caught my eye, and I found out later who it was. Jewell Rife. I never knew it before I saw him up here later, at Elizabeth's house. But when I saw him that first time, downtown, he stood with one foot up on the hitching rail we still had out in front of the bank then, and the bank was closed behind him, and he was smoking a cigarette and looking out at the street like he owned it, cars and trucks and people to boot. He held his head cocked to the side. He had a yellow-and-brown plaid suit, and no coat. He didn't look like he was cold, though. He had curly black hair. His eyes were light, and kind of far away. He was just watching everything and everybody. Looking for an opportunity. He was big, too, or bigger than most of the men around here. It crossed my mind that he might of been in a circus sometime. He looked like that.

The way it happened was that their gas heater went out up there right in the dead of winter, late January it was, and Elizabeth had phoned down to tell Mr. Bascom and ask him to come up there and take a look at it. Mr. Bascom used to play poker with Daddy, and he tried to see to things for Elizabeth and Fay. When she'd let him. She was so proud, she wouldn't let anybody do much, ever, or even tell me or anybody else if she was to get sick. They could of died up there, and she was too good to let anybody help her. Including me—me most of all, I reckon. But Mr. Bascom was the best-hearted man. He ran the hardware, and fixed whatever needed fixing all over town—wasn't anybody *building* much, in those days—and he'd take some of those drifters in sometimes, and let them sleep in that back room at the store, and help them out if he had any work. Well, he had took in Jewell Rife, who had a definite way about him, everybody said it and it was true, and he took Jewell Rife with him up to Elizabeth's to look at that gas heater. This was one of those old Ruud heaters, and from time to time you had to get them blown out.

I bet he thought he'd died and gone to heaven, Jewell Rife. Think for a minute if you was him, and imagine what-all you saw. Imagine that cold gray afternoon. And here's the house way up on the hill at the end of the long, long walk all lined with the boxwoods, all that land lying around it empty and cold and smeared white with the leftover snow, and inside the house is Elizabeth, to answer the door. It must of been like stepping into a magazine, to answer that door. Because who knows where-all he'd been, or what he came from? In those days men were desperate. It must of been like stepping into a movie, those pretty things of Mama's, and how Elizabeth kept them all just so. But the rooms were big, and cold and drafty, the heater was broke. Elizabeth stood in her long plaid coat with Fay behind her, wrapped up in a blanket. Jewell stood there holding his hat, looking like something wild, looking like all outdoors. But one thing about Jewell was that he always did have the prettiest manners. You'd have to call him a lively man, too, when he wanted to be. "You go ahead and start in on the heater," he told Mr. Bascom, after they'd been introduced. "You go right ahead on, sir, but I believe I'll just take the liberty of building these pretty ladies a fire in the fireplace to warm them up a bit, they look half-froze to me. Ladies, where's your wood?"

"Out back there in the shed," Elizabeth said, her voice shaking. "But that won't be necessary, I'm sure, Mister—"

"Rife," said Jewell. "And I won't take no for an answer."

Mr. Bascom went in the kitchen to look at the heater, and Jewell went back outside and around the house and up to the barn for the wood. He was checking things out, I imagine, and I imagine he liked what he saw. He came back carrying a great load of it like it was nothing, like it was matchsticks, and dumped it all down in the parlor, and moved the Chinese screen to the side and started right in building a fire, getting wood chips all over the carpet. I don't think anybody had made a fire in that fireplace for years and years, not since I could remember. Probably not since Daddy died, in fact, or if they had, I couldn't remember it. Of course I'd been gone two years or more by then.

"Get me some paper," Jewell said, and Fay went scurrying, and then he sent her off to the kitchen for matches. Mr. Bascom came in and out, to see what was going on. And Elizabeth stood by the window holding her coat collar tight at her neck, her eyes as wide and as blue as Mama's Wedgwood plate in the dining-room breakfront. Then he lit it, but he had forgot to open the flue, and smoke came all out in the room and everybody set in to coughing. Jewell reached up in the chimney then and found the cord, and finally pulled it. Mr. Bascom said everybody was coughing, and smoke filled up the parlor. Then Fay got to laughing, and Jewell did too. He threw back his head and just hollered with laughter. Finally Elizabeth joined in, and once she started, she couldn't stop. Her eyes streamed tears, and Mr. Bascom had to pound her on the back and she had to put her arms up over her head. This was what did it, I think. Jewell could make her laugh. Because there had been precious little laughter in that house for years and years. And making a woman laugh can mean a sight more than other things that ought by all rights to be more important. So everybody was laughing, and then Elizabeth and Fay got up by the fire, and after a while Elizabeth took off her coat and Fay took off her blanket, and the parlor started warming up. I bet it was a mess, too. Jewell Rife went in the kitchen and helped Mr. Bascom blow out the Ruud heater, and then they got it started. They made a big loud noise, those heaters, but they worked good. Elizabeth went in the kitchen and put on a pot of coffee, and then they sat down around the kitchen table to drink it, her and Mr. Bascom and Jewell Rife. Mr. Bascom said later that he knew what was going to happen, right then. He said that often since that time, he's rued the day he ever took Jewell Rife up there with him.

Because Elizabeth was like an apple hanging on a tree, waiting for somebody to come along and pick it, and Jewell was the man for the job. He was one of those men that can do just about anything, and can get whatever they want. So Elizabeth was easy for him, easy pickings. Besides, Jewell could of charmed a snake. Now there's nothing wrong with that, but if things come too easy for you, and everything came easy for Jewell, I reckon—he was just down on his luck temporarily, like so many others—why then you don't develop no restraint. You can't say no to yourself when you ought to. But he did have a way about him. Mr. Bascom said he told a funny story there at the table about one of the drifters down at the hotel that mumbled all the time, and wrote things down on little scraps of paper and put them in his pockets and his shoes. He said this fellow thought he had a dog, too, but he didn't. Anyway, I guess it had been a long time since Elizabeth had heard such foolishness. I can see it now, can hear her laughing. She had kind of a silvery laugh. She was always a handsome girl, big and fair like Fay, with the whitest, smoothest skin. Fay came and stood at the door, hanging back and watching. Elizabeth was smiling and Mr. Bascom said it had been years since he'd thought how pretty she was. He looked over at Jewell, and Jewell was taking note, he said. The Ruud heater was roaring away. Mr. Bascom stood up and put on his hat and his coat and his gloves, and Jewell Rife did the same.

"Well, I sure do thank you." Elizabeth was blushing.

"It's been a pleasure," Jewell said. "It's not every day a man gets to help out a lady in distress." He winked at Mr. Bascom, who winked back before he thought better of it. Jewell was like that. You'd find yourself going along with him. Jewell was looking around. "I don't mean to speak out of turn now," he said, "but it looks to me like you've got a lot around here that needs fixing, and I'd be proud to come up here sometime and do a few little no-account things for you, since I've got some time on my hands. Wouldn't take a minute to shore up those back steps," he said. Jewell Rife noticed everything.

"Well—" said Elizabeth. "Well—I can't pay you much," she warned him. She was twisting her hands in her skirt.

"I'm not worth much," Jewell said, and then he winked at *her*. "But I can sure fix them steps."

Elizabeth hemmed and hawed a little, she was flustered, and then Jewell said, "That settles it. I'll see you again directly." He nodded to Elizabeth, and nodded to Fay over by the door, and put on his hat, and they took their leave. Mr. Bascom said that Jewell Rife asked him question after question about Elizabeth, all the way down that long cold hill, and that when he ran out of questions, he started whistling. Mr. Bascom said he answered him, and saw no harm in it, even though he saw real clear what was liable to happen. But he thought it would be just fine. He liked Jewell Rife, thought he was smart and handy, and I guess he thought Elizabeth could do a lot worse. Like everybody else, he thought she needed a man to take care of her. He said he thought Daddy would of wanted it too, and that he did it in Daddy's memory.

This is hogwash. Daddy would of wanted Elizabeth to marry anybody but Jewell Rife, I believe he could of seen right through Jewell Rife in a New York second. He would have wanted me to keep on running the mill, too, which I could of done, or anyway kept it and then leased the land for coal, which has happened since. It's all water under the bridge, now. But we had had a serious falling-out at that time, Elizabeth and me who were as different as night and day anyway, and I had married Marvin Sizemore, a man who was twenty years older than me, because I couldn't think what else to do next.

I got the whole thing up. I was eighteen, Daddy was dead, and Elizabeth had gone and sold the mill and she planned to live right there in that house, it looked like, and polish the silver until the day she died. We had already sold off my horses. Well, I stood it as long as I could, living there with them, and her not wanting me to take any job because whatever I took it in mind to do, she said it was beneath me, and would violate our parents' memory, and then she'd cry, and then Fay used to get all upset and cry too. I stood it for about two months, and then one day I went out in the country with Lucius Knight to look at a horse out at Marvin Sizemore's, that Marvin was boarding for some people, it was a horse that Lucius Knight was thinking of buying. Lucius and I were old friends. This was a pretty little mare, but weak in the hindquarters. We stood out in the field looking at her, it was spring, and then Lucius asked would I mind riding her around once or twice and see what I thought, so Marvin saddled her, and I did. Redbud was blooming everywhere, and dogwood, but the leaves on the trees weren't out yet. Nothing was green but the meadow. The horse kept shying to the left. When I got off I bit my lip and looked down, indicating to Lucius what I thought. The Knights were one of the few families in the county who still had anything at that time, although they were land-poor. "Well I'll think about it," Lucius said to Marvin Sizemore, and we all knew that meant he wasn't interested. I handed Marvin Sizemore the reins and looked at him good for the first time, and that did it.

I don't know to this day exactly what got into me. Marvin's wife had died two years before, leaving him all alone with that little hardscrabble farm. She had died of her lungs. They'd never had any children. Anyway, that little farm was the prettiest place, smack in the middle of Long Valley, with Blue Creek running through it. Marvin had a little white house with a tin roof and a white fence, it sat in the middle of the meadow with no trees at all around it. Marvin's farm looked like a farm that a child might draw. It looked real simple and sweet to me that day, all straight lines. "How have you been getting on now, Nettie?" Marvin said. He talked slow, like all the Valley men. Marvin was spare and faded, light eyes, graying hair, overalls washed so much they were nearly white. Nobody had ironed them for him. "I've been all right, I guess," I said. I looked at Marvin and I looked at the farm. Why not? I thought. I thought, I'm like *this*, this is how I am, I might just as well do this. I looked at him a while, until he started smiling at me.

So I was married, living out there, when Elizabeth took up with Jewell Rife. I don't think I could of done a thing to stop it, if I'd been still there. It was like she was drunk on him. She acted crazy, different from any way she'd ever acted before. She'd hum, and giggle, and blush, and say things that didn't follow whatever she'd said before. Jewell Rife went up there every night for dinner, and every Sunday he took her to church and then they went for a ride in Mr. Bascom's car. Mr.Bascom had asked Jewell to go in with him, and work there, but Jewell said no, that he had some other irons in the fire. He thought he'd just live on Elizabeth's income, was what he thought I reckon, and it's what he did. It made me mad as fire when I found out about it later, because that was my money too, or it could of been, if I hadn't been so bullheaded. Anyway, Elizabeth was in love with Jewell Rife, and everybody in town was talking about it, she was such a spectacle. Everybody *knew* Elizabeth, was the thing of it, because she went to church every time they cracked the door, and went to all those little clubs, and because they had known Daddy, and also you just couldn't miss her, she was a big woman, all dressed up. Some people thought she was a fool, and others said it was a good thing. Everybody had something to say about it. Elva Pope said, "Oh, isn't it *wonderful?*" when I ran into her on the street, and started crying. Everybody watched and waited, to see what kind of a business Jewell Rife might go into, but he confounded them, and didn't go into a thing.

And they *did* get married, bye and bye, in the Episcopal church, and Marvin and I went to it, sat in the back. I was pregnant. Everybody in town went to that wedding, it seemed like, and I felt I didn't have any relation to any of them. We led a quiet life, just me and Marvin, out there in Long Valley.

Elizabeth looked so full of life and joy, she looked like three people, like somebody actually about to

bust right out of their skin. She wore a white satin
suit and a hat with a veil, and he wore a striped navy
suit, grinning from ear to ear, like the cat that swallowed the canary. They ran down the aisle like they
were running straight into paradise instead of the
Hotel Roanoke, where they went for the weekend in
Mr. Bascom's car. I looked over at Marvin. He smiled
that little smile of his, where the corners of his mouth
turned down, and put his hand on my stomach. "We'd
best go on now, Nettie," he said, so we did.

It had almost come my time when she came out to
the farm to see me. She had a boy drive her out there
in the new Packard which Jewell had just bought. I
got the idea she hadn't told him she was coming, and
that maybe she didn't want him to know. Jewell and I
had not spoke above ten words at that time, nor he to
Marvin. We didn't know him at all—I *never* knew
him, really. Anyway it's not clear in my mind, to this
day, exactly what it was that Elizabeth wanted that
day she came out to the farm. I think she was asking
for some kind of help, and I would of helped her if I
could of, she was my sister, but then she turned on
me there at the end. She always turned on me.

Anyway she came right in the house looking everywhere, poking all around to see how we lived—or I
thought that, and maybe I was too quick to take
offense, maybe she was just trying to be friendly. It
was hot, Marvin out in the field, she wore a seer-
sucker suit and highheel shoes. She looked everywhere. There wasn't that much to see, I didn't take a
thing from Mama's when I got married, and Marvin
never had much to begin with. I was in the kitchen
putting soup beans on to cook, my stomach was out
to here. She came in the kitchen. "I'd love a glass of
ice tea," she said, but I didn't have any made up, and

gave her some water. We had two chairs. She sat in one of them and I sat in the other, with my feet splayed out.

"What is it?" I asked.

But Elizabeth wouldn't say. She smiled that kind of a big loony smile she'd been smiling ever since she ran into Jewell Rife, and ran her tongue around over her lipstick.

"I just thought I'd come see you," she said.

A fly buzzed around and around the kitchen. It was dead noon on the kitchen clock.

I hate to beat around the bush. I said, "Now Elizabeth, I've been out here going on three years, and you never came out here before. So something is the matter, I reckon, and you'd best just go ahead and tell me what it is."

She kept looking all around the kitchen at first one thing and then another, darting her eyes every minute or so over at my stomach which was sticking way up under my calico dress. She swallowed hard, and licked her lips, and shut her mouth.

"Things are not—" she started. "It's just not—"

"Not what?" I asked. But she wouldn't say. I got up and turned the fire down under the soup beans and put the lid on. "You're not happy, are you?" I said. "Not like you were at first."

"Of course I am!" Elizabeth stood up and brushed down her skirt and reached for her purse. "I certainly am! That's just like you, Nettie," she said. "All of this is just exactly like you."

I let that go, and watched her. She was all agitated. She went out of the front door and called the boy, who came in bringing a stack of diaper cloths, and told him to put them down. I was mighty glad to have them, which I said. She said goodbye, and the boy drove her off home, raising a cloud of dust which hung in the air for the longest time after they left. I sat on the front steps and looked at it. It came to me that she thought she was some fine princess, visiting poor relations. I got so mad. I stomped all around and went back in and cleaned the whole house I was so mad. There is a streak of pride in the two of us, I see this now, that has run in between us like lightning, and burned up what should have been. So I didn't know what was the matter then, but I know for a fact that the trouble between her and Jewell started that early on.

I had my baby, Lou, and she was the prettiest thing. I remember how in August one time we were laying in the bed, Marvin and me, with Lou in between us, and it was thunderstorming outside, rain drumming on the tin roof, which was how come Marvin couldn't work that day, and the light all pale and watery in our room. We had us a white iron bed. Lou was cooing away. I was so taken up with my baby then that I guess I kind of forgot, for a while, about Elizabeth and her visit. I don't believe I ever did tell Marvin, who was not much of a talking man anyway, about it. If I'd had to guess at the trouble between Elizabeth and Jewell, though, I'd have said it probably had something to do with their personal relations, and with what he might have wanted, or expected, of her—she was not a young woman, Elizabeth, nor used to men.

But then bye and bye she got pregnant too, and had Sybill, and then she had Arthur. I plumb lost track of it here. Because it was at this time that my own baby Lou took sick, and stopped growing any, and Marvin and me carried her to the doctor in town, and then we carried her all the way down to North

Carolina to Duke Hospital in the truck, I recall it like it was yesterday, it was raining then too, and Marvin driving his new truck, and the windshield wipers beating back and forth like crazy and Marvin and me spent the night at the Bull Durham Hotel, they wouldn't let us stay in the hospital with her. We stayed down there three days, and talked to every doctor in the place, and at the end of that time we took her home. She was cooing and giggling on my lap the whole way home. But she had leukemia, and died just seven months later. Her coffin was not as big as a footlocker.

After that, it's hard for me to tell what happened, for a while. Marvin gathered up all Lou's baby things, after about a week, and took them over to his sister's. I sat in a kitchen chair, in the day, and couldn't do anything. At night, Marvin and me would lay in that white iron bed right next to each other flat on our backs but not touching and not talking either, Marvin not being then or ever, as I said, a talking man, and we'd just lay there. You could hear the crickets outside, and the tree frogs, and the train sometimes away off down Long Valley in the night, sounding real lonesome. It was the worst I ever felt, and the most lonesome I ever was, laying right next to Marvin Sizemore in that bed. It was like we couldn't stand to talk, or touch each other.

Finally one morning I got up and told Marvin I was leaving. He stood in the bedroom door in his work pants smoking a cigarette while I dumped the dresser drawers out on the bed and packed up everything I had in a cardboard box. It didn't take long. Marvin looked real old. I used to love him, I thought. "Don't you want—" he started, but I said no. "I don't want a thing," I said. When it's time to go, you'd best get a move on, I think. I have always traveled pretty light. I hauled that box out to the pickup, Marvin standing there on the front porch smoking his cigarette and watching me. It was still early morning. The grass was real green, wet with dew. He watched me while I pulled out and drove off. Now I don't remember this too good except for little things, like that Marvin had his thumbs hooked in his pants loops, watching me go, and that I had planted a bunch of crookneck squash along by the fence and they were blooming. Yellow flowers.

I went on into town and rented a room from Lula Morris in the hotel, and the next day, I paid a boy to drive the truck back out there. Not too long after, Marvin sold that place for nearabout nothing, I heard, and went to live with his sister down in North Carolina, on a tobacco farm. The only thng I kept was a little yellow curl of Lou's hair, in a locket that used to be Mama's. I started waiting on tables at Ed's, and took up with a lot of men. Now I'm not proud of this time, nor do I regret it either. It helped some.

Eventually of course I met Millard Cline who used to come in there every day about eleven o'clock for a piece of coconut pie, and we started running around together. We used to go out on the highway to roadhouses, and dance. I remember dancing by a blue light, and somebody singing "Careless Love." Millard had a weakness, he was bad to drink, but he was a lot of fun. Sweet-natured. After a while, he left his wife and kids for me. So you see how it is. If anybody's passing judgment, I've not got a leg to stand on, I've not got a thing to say. I left one good decent man, and married another woman's husband, and don't regret any of it, to this day. You do what you have to. I quit over at Ed's and started helping Millard with the flower business, and since his wife stayed on in their house of course, we just got us a couple of rooms over the shop there, and lived in them, and were happy. We were real happy. Millard could make you a bridal bouquet, or a funeral wreath, or whatever you fancied in between. He could do anything with flowers. So we were running the flower shop, and going out dancing on Saturday nights, and Elizabeth was really in trouble.

I'd seen Jewell out once myself, with a woman named Mavis Lardner. They left the place they were at, when we came in. I didn't say a word to them. Millard said that Jewell was becoming known around town as a ladies' man, and also that he was known to make trips from time to time, and come back to town flashing money. He used to play the guitar and sing around here at dances. He was so good at it, that those that heard him said he ought to go over to Nashville and make a record, and be a star. But Elizabeth never did go to those dances, or say anything about them to her friends, nor about Jewell's guitar playing. One time he came back with a mink coat for Elizabeth, and another time I heard he'd brought her a diamond ring. Which she wouldn't have, either one of them. She was not that kind of a woman. But Mavis Lardner was seen by somebody's cousin, over in Bristol, wearing a diamond ring that might have been that one. She was trying on clothes at King's.

Anyway, Jewell Rife never did get a job, or a job you could put your finger on, though he did as I said go away on "business." Just what that business was, exactly, nobody ever knew. Except for those records in Bristol. More likely he was gambling. Anyway, they had been married about six years, and Jewell

Rife was showing his true colors at last. Now this was not the strange thing, though. Anybody might have expected that. The strange thing, to my mind, was how Elizabeth acted, which was just like none of it was happening at all. Since she had those two little tiny children, Sybill and Arthur, she stayed at home a lot more, so that people in town didn't see her much, but if you ever did see her, she looked fine. She had Jewell Rife take her to church every Sunday he was here, both of them dressed up fit to kill, and anybody that might of said anything to her about it just shut their mouth. She looked beautiful in those days, and Jewell Rife had his curly hair slicked down like a movie star. Sybill and Arthur had on little suits. Seeing them like that, it was hard to credit what you might have heard or might have thought you'd seen. And I didn't have any regular truck with them then either, since I didn't go to church, which would of been the one place I would of been sure to see them. Millard and me were more apt to lay up in the bed of a Sunday, and listen to the radio. Of course I heard people talking, and knew what they said. But the only thing I knew about it for sure was that every now and then Jewell Rife used to come in the shop, or call on the telephone, and order a dozen red roses sent up to Elizabeth.

So I was surprised that day the phone rang and it was Grace Harrison calling me, her voice so old and thin it was like the rustling of tissue paper. "I remember you, Nettie," Grace Harrison said. "And you were always a good, strong child. You need to see to Elizabeth now, I don't know who else to tell."

"What do you mean?" I said. "See to Elizabeth?" I was talking on the phone in the flower shop which was full of people, people were always hanging around in there talking to Millard.

"Listen," Grace Harrison said, her voice like a little wind way up on the mountain. "Something must be done. He beats her," Grace Harrison said. She hung up, leaving me holding the phone in one hand and a bunch of glads in the other, and all upset.

"Well, go right on up there and see about it," Millard said when I told him, "and call me if you want me, I'll be here," and so I went. Millard said he'd drive me, but I said I'd walk.

She was not expecting me. Nobody up there was expecting me, which is why I saw what I saw, and know what I know. This was early February 1940. We had had one of the awfulest winters we ever did have, and it was still hanging on. The snow was dirty gray and as hard as a rock, pushed up against the new sidewalk all along Main Street. The big stumps where they had cut down those pines looked like something awful sticking up out of the snow as you got on out of town, and all those tacky new little houses that Olan Griffith had built along there looked naked and cold. Olan Griffith said it was progress, to cut down the pines and build those houses in there. He had painted every one of those houses the kind of light green that makes you think about vomit. On the other side of the road, way back, sat Grace Harrison's house, hiding behind her shade trees and her ivy. You couldn't tell, looking at it, if she was home or not. You never could. I walked past Grace Harrison's house and those other big houses, and stopped to get my breath where Main Street does the dogleg, so it looks like Elizabeth's house is smack at the end of the street.

I stood right there with my hand on my side, breathing puffy white clouds out into the freezing air. It put me in mind of summers gone, and better times. I felt a sadness. Also I was not feeling good that day anyway. I was on the rag, and it was a disappointment to me, as Millard and me had been trying and trying to get us a baby, which never did happen. The only baby I ever had was my pretty Lou. Anyway I stood there a while looking up that long walk to the house with the boxwoods on each side of it like so many big round snowballs. The walk was not shoveled off, so I knew I'd have to go around to the side and up the driveway. I was just thinking it was a funny thing how I felt no connection to that house that I'd grown up in, no connection at all. I thought in my mind, *Elizabeth's house.* But I have noted a strange thing in a lot of families, how one child might take after one parent, and the other after the other. I loved Mama, what I can recall of her, but I guess I was Daddy's girl, and even if he did make considerable money at one time, he was a county man with not a highfalutin bone in his body which I could remember. So that house was Mama's, then Elizabeth's, and not ever Daddy's or mine. I never did think, and I don't believe anybody did, *Elizabeth and Jewell's house.* I felt like Jewell was just a fancy storebought dress that she was trying on, which was bound to split at the seams or pucker at the neck or in general *wear out* after a while. I hated to go up there and get into all of it, but blood is thicker than water, after all.

It was getting on for dark and I knew if I didn't go on up there then I wouldn't, and so I went. The driveway had been shoveled, all right, and the Packard was gone. But lights were on in the kitchen, so I kept walking. I figured that Jewell was gone probably, out playing the guitar someplace or doing whatever it was that he did, and Elizabeth was there in the house with the children. I couldn't quite get my mind around it, that Jewell had been beating Elizabeth, in fact I doubted it was true, and thought Grace Harrison had probably made it up. I didn't think Elizabeth would stand for beating. But people had remarked a look of strain on her face, and said how the skin seemed stretched too tight across the bone, and we all knew that Jewell was running around. So I was aware of these things. But one thing about life which I learned from Millard Cline is that even if you know something's wrong, you don't have to deal with it right then. It's best to take your time, and poke around it a little, because the plain truth is that most things will just go away of their own accord. But Grace Harrison had called, it was time I went up there.

I scraped the snow off my feet on the porch steps and then for some reason I just walked on into the entryway, the cold-pantry as Mama used to say, without knocking. I don't know to this day why I did that. There is two doors, see, and usually I'd knock on both of them.

What I saw was awful.

And it was the very last thing I ever expected to see.

First I stood there in the cold-pantry shaking the snow off myself. There was one more door still closed between me and the kitchen, remember, but that was a new door with a big pane of glass that Jewell had put in it early on when he was making himself so useful. So I could see everything. Elizabeth wasn't in there. Fay stood at the sink, her back to me, washing dishes. Of course this didn't surprise me none. Fay was different, no question about it, but she had turned out to be a pretty good hand at helping out around the house, where she could understand enough to do most things. Since she had Fay to help her, Elizabeth never had hired anybody to come in and clean for her, the way most of her friends in town did, not even when Sybill and Arthur were little babies. If she had of hired somebody, if there had of been somebody else up in that house with them, it might have put some checks on Jewell's behavior, and things might not have happened the way they did. But it's easy, looking back, to see something like that, it never comes to mind at the time.

Anyway, Fay was a big strapping girl, twenty-five years old. She looked a whole lot younger than she was, with her yellow hair falling in curls down her back, like a schoolgirl. I know for a fact that Elizabeth tried to get her to keep it pinned up. She had a wide, fair face, with pretty, regular features. She looked like Mama in the face. But there was something missing, which had always been missing, around her eyes. You couldn't put your finger on what it was exactly, but you knew it wasn't there. She was real shy, and looked down a lot when you tried to talk to her. And of course, she wouldn't hardly talk at all. Everybody in town said how good Elizabeth was to her, and I guess this was true, but it was also true that she did a mighty lot of work for Elizabeth. The only thing Fay ever did, that I knew of besides stay up there in Elizabeth's house, was go to the movies. Every time the picture changed, which was once a week, Fay would walk down the hill and go see it, sit through it twice. Coming or going, she'd usually stop by the flower shop, and Millard would give her a flower, or a fancy ribbon, she used to love those, and a Coke. Everybody in town was real nice to Fay, out of regard for Elizabeth, and also because that's the way they are. People here are real nice.

So Fay was washing dishes at the sink, with her hair all down her back. She had on a big old dark green sweater which I think used to be Daddy's, and some kind of a printed skirt, and white socks and house shoes. Now all of this part is burned in my brain, I remember it like it was yesterday. Jewell Rife sat at the round oak table under the hanging lamp, reading a newspaper. Jewell used to be a fancy dresser. That day he was wearing a white shirt, no tie, and dark blue suit pants. He wore his hair a little longer than most of the men hereabouts, kept wearing it in fact like he had worn it back when you might have thought he didn't have the money for a haircut. Well, now he had the money, but he still had those black curls, which popped back up no matter how hard he tried to slick them down. He had his chair pulled up to the table at an angle to it, so his back was to me, too, he didn't have the faintest notion I was there.

For some reason I didn't make a move to let him know it, either. I stood out there in the freezing cold-pantry, and it had grown dark by then so I stood there in the dark, looking through that pane of glass like I was watching a picture-show. There was some music going on which I could barely hear, and this puzzled me, their radio being on a stand in the parlor, and I knew it. So it wasn't the radio. It was a high, thin, singing sound. Finally it came over me, real gradual, that what I heard was Fay singing. She was singing, "Roll out the barrel, we'll have a barrel of fun," which was real popular then. It made me feel faint, and sick-like, to hear Fay sing. I'd scarcely heard her speak since Mama died. Fay's singing kind of stopped me, I couldn't move a muscle. I watched.

Jewell threw down his paper in a heap on the floor and ran a hand through his hair. He was looking at Fay, too. Fay sang, "Roll out the barrel, we've got the rain on the run." Then Jewell banged his hand down on the tabletop, it was so loud I liked to have jumped clean out of my skin.

"*Fay!*" he said.

Fay did everything slow. She wiped off her hands on the front of her skirt, slow, and then she turned around. She had the awfulest look on her face, I hope to die before I ever see anything else like it. That blankness was gone, and I'd never seen it gone before. In its place was a whole new thing, a completely different way for Fay to be. Her lips looked redder, kind of wet, her eyes were shining, her cheeks were pink, her whole face had taken on a *waiting* look. Her mouth was open with singing sounds still coming out of it, but garbled. You couldn't tell the words. The sound was high and thin, strained, like the wind through a barb-wire fence. She was smiling a loose, sweet smile. But her face looked awful, it looked— how can I tell it?—it looked like the end of the world.

"*Fay!*" Jewell Rife said again. He stood up.

While I watched her, Fay backed up to the sink and hiked up her skirt and hoisted herself up there, on the edge of the counter, spraddling her legs. She didn't have on any drawers. Then Jewell was at her, his trousers down around his feet, didn't even bother to take them off, fucking her. That's all. He never kissed her, or nothing. He was just fucking her. And the worst part about it was Fay's face, which I could still see, I could see her face all the time, over Jewell's back, above his white shirt. Her face had changed from that waiting, knowing look into something terrible where wanting and hating went back and forth like the shadows of clouds across a field, back and forth faster and faster, ending up as something awful which you've not got the words to say.

Soon enough, Jewell was done. He flopped his head down over her shoulder, and let his hands drop too, he was breathing hard. Fay stopped making the singing sounds. She was staring straight out over his dark head at the pane of glass in the back door, staring straight out to the cold-pantry where I stood watching. Now I know she couldn't see me, out there in the dark. I don't think she could have seen me at all. But a look came into her eyes for just a minute, it was the strangest thing, like she *could* see me, and like she was a reasonable person after all, a regular girl, a girl with good sense. This look said, *I know what I'm up to. I know.* And it was all pain. This was pain so pure it was like a real thing twisting and yelling in the air between her and me. Then while I still watched, that was gone and gone entirely, nobody home. And nobody's been home since. Nothing there except Fay's sweet blank expression the way it was before he said "Fay!" the way it always was.

Now I can't even remember leaving the cold-pantry or going out on the porch and down those steps and down that long hill, back toward town. I don't know if I made any noise or not, or if I did and if he looked out and saw me. I didn't care. I can't even remember that long walk home. I felt awful, my mind in a whirl like the kind of a wind that blows when a thunderstorm's on the way, and I thought about how excited we used to get when we were little, the three of us, and how we'd run out in the yard and twirl around and around and around in the high fierce wind that came then and turned the leaves of the trees to their silvery insides-out. The way that house sits up on the hill, you could see the thunderstorms coming miles away, all across Long Valley, see the blowing clouds and the lightning and the moving sheets of rain. We used to run out and wheel around and around in that strange wild-smelling air you get right before the rain comes, until Mama came out, too, and shooed us back in the house. I couldn't stand it to think of those days, to think of Fay as a little child, as she was then. It made me feel black and empty, like losing Lou. My mind went around and around, but there was one thing I knew for sure, that I would of staked my life on.

I told it to Millard, who was real nervous waiting for me. He had closed up the shop by then of course, and had been looking out the window for me, and worrying. This is the first thing I remember, in fact, about that long walk home, Millard at the window, against the yellow light. He met me there at the top of the stairs, and hugged me, and sat me down on the sofa inside, and I told him all of it. I used to tell Millard everything. He was good to talk to. I've never told it since.

"The worst part is," I said to Millard, "and I'd stake my life on it, honey, the worst part is that the way it was, you could tell it had happened over and over, it's probably been going on for years. You could tell she was used to him telling her like that, and resigned to it, and you could tell he was used to getting it whenever he said. It was that kind of a thing," I said to Millard, who lit two cigarettes and handed me one. My whole hand was shaking.

"Do you reckon she knows?" Millard asked, meaning Elizabeth.

"No," I said, "or if she does, she don't know she does." I thought this was more likely.

"I'm going to talk to her," I said.

Millard said, "Honey, I don't know if I'd do that or not, if I was you. Things'll either get better, or they'll get worse, and you can wait and do it then." This is how Millard was, and one of the things that made him so easy to live with. And also he'd come right out and tell you what he thought, but he'd never try to tell you what to do. That's the one thing I won't stand for, never have. Everybody knows it.

"Well I am anyway" I told him then. Elizabeth was my sister after all, and so was Fay.

But Elizabeth wouldn't listen.

I came up to her on the sidewalk, two days later, outside the five and dime, she was all dressed up and looked real pretty.

"Hello, Nettie," she said in a way that said something about my old coat, and my hat, and the way Millard and me lived. She looked beyond my face.

So things got off on the wrong foot right then, and me with the best of intentions.

"Listen," I said to her, speaking fast, and keeping my voice low. "Elizabeth, I don't want to hurt your feelings, but there's something I've got to say." People were going by on the street, a lot of them nodding and speaking, and she kept smiling and nodding at them. A little icy drizzle fell all around.

"It's about Jewell," I started, and her face iced over, but she kept on smiling. "I don't know if you know what he's been doing," I said, "but it's not right, and it's time you sent him packing," was what I said. Now I know I did this all wrong, there's ways of beating around the bush to put a person at their ease, and ways to sugar-coat a bitter pill. But those ways are not my way. Once I decide to do a thing, or say it, I go on and get it over with, that's the way I am.

"It's none of your business, whatever you're talking about," she said.

"I mean about him and Fay." I said it plain.

Elizabeth stood staring at me for a minute with the misty rain falling between us. She opened and shut her red mouth. Then it was like she gathered herself up somehow, so she stood about three inches taller.

"Well!" she said. "I never in all my life! I don't have the faintest notion what in the world you might be talking about, Nettie. I can't imagine what you're referring to. I don't have the faintest idea. I am a happily married woman, which ought to be evident even to you, and these insinuations will get you no place. Oh you'd like to see the end of Jewell, I'm sure, you think you might have access to some of my money then. But don't you think for a minute I'll fall for such a trick as that," Elizabeth said.

I was too surprised to say a thing. You'd have thought she really believed it, she spit out those words so strong. Maybe she did believe it right then, for a minute, or maybe it just came to her as a way not to listen to me.

"Listen, Elizabeth—" I started again, but she opened up her red-and-black striped umbrella with such a whoosh, she damn near poked my face.

"I'll thank you to stay out of my business in the future, Nettie dear." Her voice was cold, sugary sweet. "My marriage does not concern you. And if I ever do need any advice, I'll seek it elsewhere, I can assure you. I certainly don't need either criticism or consolation from a two-bit whore." Then she was gone, off up the street, red-and-black umbrella, black suit and hat, all elegant. I stood there looking after her, I saw how it was. Even if she did know it, and I got the feeling she must of had an idea about it by then, she didn't want to hear it. Well, can you blame her? What a thing to know! And her putting on all those airs. As for her calling me a whore, that didn't set too well with Millard, but it never bothered me. I could see why she said it, I know how she thinks, but that is just one of those words that don't mean a thing in the world to me. I can't say I had not given plenty of thought to Millard's wife living over across town, and to his three kids, and one of them retarded. But what's done is done. I went on back in the shop and worked on the books for the rest of the day, and never did see her close up like that again for weeks.

Not until he disappeared, I reckon, thinking back. I mean Jewell.

It was in March, close onto six weeks later. We had been having crazy weather as I recall, hail and some of those early thunderstorms you can get sometimes in March. And it was still bitter cold. Millard had had him a big drunk—he was bad to drink from time to time, he couldn't help it, it was a sickness with him. This happened every three or four months. Then he'd get real sick after it, and I'd have to run the shop, and get somebody to sit up there with him. Well, that's how Millard was, and Millard's daddy before him. But Millard was such a sweet man, I couldn't complain.

So Millard was getting over a big drunk when this all happened. I had been real busy. And the first I knew of it was when Fay came down to the shop all frazzled and wild-looking, a couple of days after the worst one of them early-spring thunderstorms. I was in there alone. "Let me make you a bow, honey," I said to Fay. "Looky here." I showed her some new satin ribbon.

But Fay shook her head back and forth, and seemed all wrought up. She said something about a trip, pulling at my arm. I could tell she wanted me to come with her, so after a while, I closed up and went. Water was running down the gutters beside the new sidewalks, I remember. And several times we had to step over limbs of trees that had fallen across the sidewalk, or walk around. Some men were sawing up one whole tree that had fallen on the Harrison property, but we saw not a sign of Grace. The sunshine was sharp and cold. When we walked around to the side of Elizabeth's house, to go up the driveway, I saw that Fay had left the back door wide open. Now this looked funny, and made a bad feeling start inside my stomach right then. "What's going on up here?" I asked Fay, but she just looked at me sideways and ducked her head, giggling. I went in the cold-pantry, then the kitchen, which was a mess. Dirty dishes all over the sink, sugar spilled out on the kitchen table, the cookie jar broken in three pieces on the floor. Elizabeth would not have left a kitchen that way if her life depended on it.

"Elizabeth!" I screamed.

No answer.

Then I felt this little tugging, tugging at my sleeve. It was Fay, so I let her take me into the parlor. There sat Elizabeth. Fay pointed at her, and giggled, and then started crying. Elizabeth sat on the loveseat, just sat there, hands down slack at her side. She sat staring out the window down toward town, waiting, I reckon, for his return. Her eyes were empty and flat, she looked like she had had a complete nervous breakdown, which I guess she had. I never did figure out exactly how long it was between the time Jewell disappeared and the time Fay came for me. I don't know how long Elizabeth sat there. I do know it was a day or so. She had soiled herself, waiting. Fay and the children had eaten up what was there. The ice-box was empty, they had left things like bread crusts and apple cores everywhere, broken china and cookies all over the kitchen. You never saw such a place. Sybill and little Arthur were rampaging through the whole house, pulling things down, the way children that age will do if they're not attended. Arthur in particular was always hell on wheels, the cutest, most mischievous little boy, but he was shaky and crying that day, and Sybill would not let go of her dolly. Fay kept holding my sleeve. She seemed younger than ever, like one of the kids.

I took a good look around and then I called Millard and told him to come up there. Arthur quit crying and started to squeal. He loved Millard, who would give him a piggyback ride at the drop of a hat. Then I was fixing to dial up Elva Pope and get her to come up there and help me too, and maybe Mr. Camp, who was the Episcopal minister then, but Elizabeth came up behind me and put her hand over the phone. It spooked me, her coming up so silent, when I'd thought she was plumb off her head.

"Nettie," she said, and there was a tone in her voice which told me she might not be as crazy as I had thought, "don't tell anybody else, please."

I put the phone back on the hook and turned around to face her. "All right," I said.

"Jewell has left me, as you see," she told me then, "and Fay is pregnant." Looking at Fay, I could see this was so, in fact Fay had almost got to that point where anybody would notice it. But she was a big girl, and wore Daddy's sweaters around all the time.

"Who all knows it?" I asked, and Elizabeth said, "Nobody." We didn't say whose it was. Elizabeth's hair straggled all down her back, it looked like a rat's nest, her face looked like death warmed over. Although I had hated her putting on airs, it hurt me to see her that way.

"Come on over here, honey," I said, and took her and washed her face in warm water at the kitchen sink, and after I did that, she broke down. "It's been terrible—" she said this over and over. "He does horrible things, he wants horrible things." But she never did say what these things were, and I didn't ask her, either. Her eyes looked like big blue holes poked in her tight white skin. She had not eaten, or slept, I could tell, for some time. I washed her off and got her to put on some clean clothes. I put Fay to making some Wheatena and they all ate that. The kids ate like they were just starving, and Sybill feeding her doll. Millard had got there by then. We made Elizabeth go lay down on the loveseat in the parlor, since we couldn't get her to go upstairs, and before her head touched the pillow, she was sound asleep. She woke up one time, about twenty minutes after she fell asleep, and sat straight up and said that Jewell had gone on a business trip, and that he would be back on Thursday. She said this in a calm, regular voice. Then she laid back down and went back to sleep, moaning and twisting and calling out, and crying. I hate to see a person cry in their sleep, but she would do this for months to come.

Millard gave Arthur a piggy-back ride all over the house. Then Fay helped me bathe the children, who were as dirty as could be, and then I got them to bed and Fay went to sleep sitting up in the wing chair in the parlor, didn't want to leave Elizabeth. Fay slept a heavy sleep like a little child, with her mouth open, head hanging off to the side, pulled forward by her heavy yellow hair.

Now all this sobered Millard up pretty fast, believe me. And wasn't no use him saying not to get involved, we *was* involved, and that was all there was to it. Well, we spent the night up there, of course, drinking coffee and talking about what to do, and ended up sleeping finally for a couple of hours in Jewell and Elizabeth's bed. A person can do anything if they get tired enough. But before that, we cleaned up the house the best we could, and investigated, as Millard called it. It did look for certain like Jewell had planned to go on a trip, as she said. His toilet things were gone from the bathroom, and some of the dresser drawers were pulled out like somebody had packed in a rush. He had not took much that we could tell, just the toilet things as I said and maybe some socks and some underwear. Now since Jewell was gone so much anyway, what puzzled us was how Elizabeth had seemed so dead set, at first, on the fact that he'd left for good this time. We didn't know what to make of it. We figured at the very least that they'd had it out, the two of them, and had a big argument, and then he'd left. Also it seemed funny to us how the Packard was still there, still out in the driveway full of gas, like Jewell had just left it, waiting. But then Millard said that was the real tip-off, probably, that he was taking off for sure, that meant that he had had somebody come for him, such as Mavis Lardner, or got somebody else to drive him over to Buncoe to catch the train. Jewell Rife got around, he knew a lot of people, he could of gotten anybody to come up here and drive him. So he had left the car for Elizabeth, Millard had figured, and then that started us wondering what else he might have left in the way of support.

Precious little, as it so happened. After we left town, which I will tell about directly, Millard went to the bank and explained himself and looked into it, and Jewell had nearabout cleaned her out during all those years he'd been living so high on the hog. He had got him a hundred dollars the day of his trip, that was all, and there was some left in there of course, but nothing compared to what you would have thought, which would have took care of her and Fay for the rest of their lives. Millard said Geneva Vail, one of the tellers, remembered Jewell coming in that day, and getting the money. She said he got a hundred-dollar bill, that that was how he usually cashed a check. She said he was wearing a red-striped tie. Geneva Vail said that Jewell was in a real good humor, and said he was fixing to go on a little trip. Fay said this too, and it was all she'd ever say, when Millard and me asked her about it. Oh, we asked her a lot. She'd nod her head up and down, up and down, and say "Took a trip" or "Took a big trip," over and over, like she was agreeing with herself, and thought she was real smart.

Millard and I did this. We packed up a bag with things in it for the children and Fay and Elizabeth, and I went downtown and gathered up some things for myself, and Millard drove us all over to Buncoe and put us on the train going to Lynchburg, where Millard's aunt lived, this was Mrs. Edna Everhart. Edna Everhart had raised Millard and his two brothers and his sister, her and her husband by then deceased, so he thought a lot of her, and said she would be glad to help out. He had not seen her in years, and remembered her like an angel.

Well, this was not the case. In fact, she liked to not have took us in at all. I don't know what we would of done then! Millard called her on the long-distance telephone from Buncoe, after he put us all on the train, and told her we were on the way, and he said she squawked like a pulley hen. It seems that Edna Everhart had been as sweet as a saint in her middle years and then turned sour with age, as people sometimes will. But Millard said he was sending money, and said he was sending more than he'd planned to, to mollify her, so finally she said, all right. But she was not friendly at the outset and just about all she ever gave us to eat at first was hominy grits. She wouldn't let me cook, either, but later she got to like us and wanted me to fix her ham and red-eye gravy all the time. She'd dip snuff and listen to baseball on the radio. She was real interested in baseball, wouldn't hardly let you listen to the war news. So it was all right once we got there, we stayed for close onto four months, until Fay had the baby and Elizabeth got over her nervous breakdown.

Getting to Lynchburg, though, was something! I won't forget that trip as long as I live. Sybill and Arthur were real fretful, and anything you said to Sybill, you had to tell her dolly too, or she wouldn't do it. Fay was so excited about the train, she just loved it, and got up and walked back and forth, if you didn't watch her. She was real big. Elizabeth wore all black. She was playing it to the hilt by then, hard at work grieving. She sat and stared out the window at Virginia passing by, and cried real softly into one of a number of linen handkerchiefs she'd brought along for the purpose. She said her reputation was destroyed, and she was "ruined." She wouldn't eat a thing. But Fay ate everything in sight, all the fried chicken we'd brought, and all the pies, and kept wanting me to buy her some more popcorn and Coca-Cola. Everybody on the whole train was looking at us. I'd walk out back on the platform from time to time, and smoke me a cigarette, and take a little nip of the bourbon Millard had poured into a bottle for me to bring. I thought we'd never get there.

But we did, and even if Edna Everhart herself took some softening up, her place was just about perfect for what we needed, some miles from town, with no close neighbors. All she said, to those that came by, was that she had decided to take in some boarders for the spring and early summer, and introduced us. We tried to keep Fay out of the way so Edna Everhart wouldn't have to introduce her too, and she didn't have to. As her time got closer and closer, Fay got sweet, and quieter. She used to sit for hours on Edna Everhart's back porch in the glider, with both hands on her stomach, feeling that baby move, and a smile spread out all over her face. This was a good time for me and Elizabeth too, we got on better than we ever had and Lord knows, than we did ever after. At first Elizabeth got all dressed up in black every day, and sat in a rocker in the front room and cried.

Now this cut no ice with Edna Everhart. "Why don't you get up and play hearts?" she said. Edna Everhart was wild for cards, and had not got to play any while her husband was alive, he was against it, so she wanted to play all the time.

But at first, the only thing Elizabeth would do was cry. Next, all she'd do was talk.

"Nettie," she'd say, picking at my sleeve, "Nettie, listen here—" All the stories she told then were about how much Jewell Rife had loved her, and how fine a man he was, until bye and bye his leaving had turned into something fine and tragic that showed his "nobility," which she called it, although she was real vague as to how all this worked. After we heard on the radio that the Nazis had invaded Denmark and

Norway, and gone into France, it got even wilder, her saying that Jewell had gone off to Europe to get in the war, and then finally that he'd died in it, a hero.

Millard, who came over there to see us three times, said as far as he could tell, it didn't much matter what Elizabeth thought about where Jewell was. He had not showed back up at home, and nobody knew a thing, so Elizabeth's guess was as good as anybody's. Millard said everybody in town was buzzing with it, swearing that they weren't surprised a bit, and that they'd known all along it was coming. People will always say that, like it's important. Millard had put it out that Elizabeth had had to leave for a rest cure because she had had a nervous breakdown, and people said they had seen *that* coming, too. Millard said that the rest of us had just come along for the ride. Well, nobody questioned any of it, except to sympathize and ask, when were we coming back? Millard told them, when we were ready to. He said everybody felt real sorry for Elizabeth. She had a lot of friends in town there as I said, she was a well-known woman. Not a soul had heard from Jewell, or knew where he might be, and Mr. Bascom came by the flower shop one day to see Millard and cry like a baby, and say that he felt terrible, and it was all his fault. Well Millard set him straight on that, right away. But he was the best-hearted man, and he felt awful.

Then Mavis Lardner came to town, and came to see Millard too, which surprised him, since he really thought, as he said, in his heart of hearts, that Jewell had gone off with her. But it wasn't so. Jewell had told her a pack of lies, she said, all flattery and nonsense. He had let on like he wanted to go off with her *sometime*, and said his marriage was nothing but a social convenience, and said he'd take her to Florida.

Florida! He told her to keep on working, where she worked there in Bristol, and save her money. But then it had been ever so long since he had come over there to see her, so she had called a friend of Jewell's up on the telephone, and found out that he had left town. Who was this friend? Millard asked, because several men that Millard didn't know had called up and asked for Jewell since he'd left, and wouldn't leave a message. Mavis wouldn't say.

Millard said she sat in the back of the flower shop smoking cigarettes, as mad as a wet hen, and thinking of what to do next. Finally she went in her purse and got out a little green chamois sack which turned out to have a big diamond ring in it, and tried to give the ring to Millard, for Elizabeth. "No, you keep it, honey," Millard told her. Then Mavis got mad at *him*, and threw it across the flower shop and ran out the door crying. Everybody in there dived for the corner then, and set to searching, and directly the little Prince boy came up with it, and Millard gave him a quarter for it.

"And here it is," Millard said, telling me all this on the back porch at Edna Everhart's house where Elizabeth and Edna were playing double solitaire.

"Let me see it," said Elizabeth, throwing down her hand.

Millard stood up and gave it to her. Elizabeth took it and put it on her finger, and held up her hand. Elizabeth had real white hands with long skinny fingers, she used to call them artistic. Anyway, she put this ring on the ring finger of her right hand, and held it up, and turned it this way and that way in the sun. It was a dinner ring with one big round diamond set in the middle and little ones all around it. Fay came to stand behind her. "Pretty," Fay said. The baby had dropped by then.

"Oh!" Elizabeth drew in all her breath in one great rattling sob, and took that ring off and put it in the green bag and just left it right there on the table, and ran upstairs and went to bed, and cried for the rest of the afternoon. Millard put the ring in his pocket, and later he put it in the bank in Elizabeth's safety deposit, and whatever has happened to it now, I couldn't tell you. Elizabeth, who turned against me later, never said. Anyway, she cried all that afternoon. Me and Millard took the kids and Edna Everhart for a ride in the car, and got everybody some ice cream in town, and Millard gave Edna the snuff he'd brought her, and the two rosebushes, which we planted for her in the side yard, and when the kids took their nap, we went out in the pine forest beyond the field and lay together on the soft pine needles, they smelled so nice. I cried hard that day when Millard left.

Because I liked it out at Edna Everhart's farm, for a fact I did, and when I think of those months now they seem slow, and blue somehow—you could see more of the sky, I reckon, the mountains being further off, and blue themselves. Elizabeth and me were close. At first she talked, as I said, and then she quit talking and cried—cried buckets. Now you'd think a woman wouldn't mourn a man the likes of Jewell Rife, but this is not true. She had loved him, and she mourned him, the way you'll mourn whatever it is you've gotten so attached to, no matter how bad it might be. Sometimes the worse it is, the more you'll mourn it. Be that as it may, this time passed too, and in late June, Fay had the baby.

Her water broke first thing in the morning, in the kitchen, and she stood there looking down at the floor not knowing what it was. I don't know if she would of come to tell us, or not. We were in there scrambling eggs. Elizabeth took her back to the bedroom and I lit out for town in Edna's old Ford, for the doctor. This was old Dr. Brown, Horace Brown, who was expecting me to come for him any day. We'd had him out there to see to Fay already. Edna knew him, and said he could keep his mouth shut. He was looking at somebody's throat, but when he finished that, he came on with me.

Now we had a hard time with Fay. She was scared, and couldn't understand, and kept trying to get up off the bed. She yelled so loud that Elizabeth had to take Sybill and Arthur and leave, it was scaring them. But it didn't take long, Fay was a strong, big girl, and here came the baby. Old Dr. Brown cut the cord and cleaned her off and looked her over good. She was fine. He had seen it all in his day, you couldn't surprise him none. He was real old. "Well," he said, "this is one fine little baby, and I reckon you girls have figured out what you're going to do next."

But the truth was, we hadn't. We had kind of been avoiding it. What I had thought, was that me and Millard would take it to raise. But Elizabeth, in that way she had of thinking things so definite in her mind that it was like that's how they already were, had decided that baby would be hers, and she would raise it. She had it all set in her mind. Nothing I could say would sway her. I kept trying to talk to her about it until Dr. Brown ran us out of the bedroom, and then I kept trying to talk to her about it on the porch. I do pretty much as I please, and always have, but every time I have come up against Elizabeth, forget it. That's the long and short of it. Once she got something in her head, she couldn't hear a word you said. She wouldn't even argue with you. She just looked at you. Her eyes would go flat, and her mouth draw out tight in a thin little line.

She only said two things, which made me mad as fire because they made a crazy kind of sense. I had been saying how I had lost Lou, and wanted a baby. "Now Nettie," she said, and her voice was pure reason, "I'm sure you and Millard will have your own children. Even if you don't, Millard has got three of his own already, which you took him away from, and that's enough. Furthermore, nobody in town has got any idea whether I might have been pregnant or not, when we left home, but nobody would believe that you were. You saw people all the time. And Millard would have told people by now, if you were." Of course this was true, Millard being a talker.

"But this baby is Fay's," I said. "Why can't we just say that, and I'm raising her?"

Elizabeth shook her head slightly, like she couldn't believe how stupid I was. *"Nettie,"* she said, very gently, "Nettie, *what would people think?"* I just stared at her, this being the very last thing in my mind.

"People are going to think whatever they're going to," I said finally.

Edna Everhart was out there on the porch stringing beans and trying to listen to the ballgame. She kept turning the radio up. But Elizabeth had set her mouth in a line, she stood staring off at the mountains. I really let her have it, then. I asked her what she expected to live on, anyway, with no job and no husband and two children already, and most of her money gone, and said that she couldn't expect me and Millard to wait on her hand and foot for the rest of her life like we had been doing for the last four months. I asked her just who did she think she was.

"It's always money with you, isn't it, Nettie?" Elizabeth said. "I'm aware that my funds are somewhat depleted, of course. But I'll certainly be happy to pay you what I can for your services, if that's all you're interested in. I must say I'm surprised at you, however, although I suppose I shouldn't be."

"*What?*" I hollered. Oh, I was mad!

"Girls, girls," said old Dr. Brown, coming out.

"I wish all of you would just hush," Edna Everhart said. "It's the bottom of the eighth, and DiMaggio hasn't got a thing off this Auker. He won't even get up again unless . . ." She turned the radio up real loud.

Elizabeth said something I couldn't hear.

"What?" I said. I went closer.

"This will be my baby," Elizabeth said. She looked at me steady then. "Because it is my right. You know who her father is."

Now this was the one thing I never thought Elizabeth would say—and she never said it again, afterward—and it was the one thing I couldn't argue. She meant that this baby was part hers, because it was Jewell's, and since keeping it was the closest she could get to keeping him, she intended to do so. Some people are bound to hold on to what hurts them. The radio announcer said, "Rolfe moves off second . . . the first pitch to Joe . . . he lines it to left . . . Yes! Extra bases! Rolfe scores . . . the Yankee Clipper has stretched his hitting streak to thirty-eight consecutive games!" Edna Everhart banged on the arm of her chair. "Damn!" she said. Elizabeth sat down in the rocker and started to rock and fan.

"I'll drive you back to town," I told the doctor.

By the time I came back, Elizabeth was sitting there holding the baby, and Sybill was holding her dolly. Elizabeth looked up at me, her face all firm and glowing. "I've decided to name her Candace," she said.

So I gave up.

I went on in the house and called Millard.

Now some of what she had said was true. I did think I'd have my own baby bye and bye, for a fact. It was years before I'd give up on that. And it was also true that Millard and me was struggling to make ends meet.

So this is how it all fell out, exactly the way Elizabeth wanted.

Except for Fay. You couldn't reckon with her, of course, or plan on what she'd do. She was up and around in a day or so—it seemed like having a baby came natural to her, like having a cold, and didn't hurt her the way it does most. But it had made a powerful impression. She was quieter than ever, and crazier—more confused. And she seemed real sad, and did not want to be around Elizabeth, nor did she like to be around the baby. Whenever the baby cried, Fay cried, but after her breast milk had dried up, it was easier dealing with her.

Millard came and got us in Elizabeth's car, and took us back. When we left, old Edna Everhart was real sad. So Millard and me came back for her two weeks later, and brought her to live with us, where she wouldn't be so lonely, and she stayed with us for the next four years, until she died. She used to love to make wrist corsages. She taught Fay to play cards. Oh yes—Fay came to live with us too. She showed up the day after we all got back, with her clothes in a paper bag. She's been with me ever since.

Elizabeth never discussed Fay's coming. Nor would she let me help her out much, when I tried to, with Candy. She had turned on me then because I had helped her, and because she had told me the truth out loud. It's not a good idea to let people show you too much, or tell you too much, or they'll hate you for it. I know this now, but I learned it too late, when everything had already happened.

And as for what people thought, people in town I mean, they just knocked themselves out trying to do for Elizabeth. Nobody could do enough. He got her pregnant and left her, that's what they thought. And there she was up there all alone, with those sweet little children—you can see how it went. Poor, poor Elizabeth! I have to admit I wondered, later, whether Elizabeth was that calculating, to have figured on the impression she wanted to make, returning. I don't think so. Elizabeth was a proud woman with a will like a piece of iron pipe, and the ability to see and hear exactly what she chose to, but she was not conniving. A conniving woman would have seen through Jewell in the first place, remember, or would have figured out how to keep him, and keep him in line.

Anyway it wasn't long before Verner Hess, who owned the dimestore, had gone up there and married her. He was a sweet, slight man with red hair, maybe six inches shorter than Elizabeth. Millard knew him from the Moose Lodge. Verner had always had a yen for Elizabeth. He used to tell Millard she was a "fine figure of a woman," Millard said. He used to try to court her, way back in the days when she had a broken heart from Ransom McClain, but she wouldn't give him the time of day, then. Now she said yes in a month. It may have been that what-all had happened had knocked her off her high-horse just a little. It may have been that she looked at Verner and saw, for once in her life, the light of day. For Verner was a good, steady man who would take care of her, and take good care of those kids. It was the smartest thing Elizabeth ever did, to marry Verner Hess, who was crazy about her. They had the wedding up there in the parlor, with nobody much present except for Verner himself and his real old parents and Elva Pope.

Millard and me were not invited.

Nor did we care, or even know about it until later.

It was a snowy day in December 1942 and Millard closed the shop up early, I recall, and came on up-stairs, and Edna and Fay and the two of us sat around the card table all that afternoon, looking out the window at the snow, and drinking some wine, and playing hearts.

"*Nettie*," Lacy says again, pulling at her. "*Nettie, what do you think?*" Lacy's pretty face looks a lot like Elizabeth's used to, Elizabeth after she cut her hair and married Verner and turned on Nettie because she had depended on her too much, all those years ago. Elizabeth had that same pretty fairness, those wide-spaced blue eyes. And why not? This is Elizabeth's daughter, after all. This is not Nettie's daughter, Nettie has no daughter now, but she has a lot of people to look after and a service station to run with a row of tomatoes behind it that need to have the suckers on them pinched off directly, so they'll bear good. Nettie's got things to do, and Fay to find, with Lacy pulling at her sleeve. It's always something.

If it's not one thing it's another, Nettie thinks, and then of all things here comes Roy Looney driving up in his VW bug with Clinus sitting right there big as life in the front seat beside him white as a sheet, you can tell he's scared to death. Lord knows what in the world has possessed them to come over here in the middle of the day like this, and leave nobody minding the store. Roy's driving real fast. He swings off the paved driveway and lurches across the graded red dirt toward where they stand, all of them watching him now, Myrtle and Candy holding on to Sean, who's bleeding. "Watch it now, watch it!" shouts Dr. Don. Dr. Don begins jumping and waving his hands. Roy Looney grits his teeth and drives on, he's still coming. Clinus, the gray curls sticking out under his Yankees cap, looks terrified. His eyes are big and round, like doll's eyes. "What in the world!" says Candy. "I don't think I can stand one more thing," Myrtle says faintly, and Sybill says, "Myrtle, that's just like you!" Roy Looney slams on the brakes and his VW stops abruptly, rocking. "It's just a flesh wound," Dr. Don assures Myrtle, looking at Sean's hand. Roy Looney jumps out, slams the door behind him, plants both feet wide in the fresh red dirt, clasps his hands before him, and clears his throat. He wears his Texaco shirt with his name, Roy, on the pocket. He looks like a boy in a play, ready to speak his piece.

"I'm real sorry to have to tell you," Roy says, "that Miss Fay has gone and shut herself up in Clinus's old Chevrolet out there, that he was working on, and died. It was the heat that killed her, it looks like. Bert barking was what put us onto it. I'm real sorry," Roy Looney says. "I'm real sorry I have to tell you this." Roy looks at them all carefully, one by one, and then his gaze returns to rest on Theresa, blond lissome ironic Theresa, who stares right back at him. Sparks fly.

"Well, son, come on in the house," Dr. Don says. "I'm sure you did all you could. It's not your fault. There wasn't a thing you could of done if you didn't know she was out there. Get Clinus out of the car and come on in for a minute."

"Yessir," says Roy Looney.

"Come on, honey," Candy says to Clinus.

A play, a play, this is all like a play, or a movie, Lacy thinks, feeling herself move outside herself and hover someplace right above them all, so that she can see the wide green field, the bright blue sky, the pile of red dirt and the hole with Jewell Rife in it and big Coy Eubanks still standing there beside it, scratching his head and looking disgusted, and Lacy can even see the butterflies on all the blue flowers by the fence, and she can see all of them, herself included, this odd gaggle of disparate family teetering here on the brink of the past while all around them, it's just another pretty day. Full June. Suddenly, for no reason at all, Lacy feels like writing her dissertation.

"I think we could all use some ice tea," Candy says, leading Clinus back to the house, but Nettie sinks like a stone to the ground right there where she is, a little black stone, and cries, and tries to push Lacy away.

"Come on now, it's time to come," Lacy says from her sudden great distance.

But Nettie grabs Lacy's arm then, hard, Nettie's fingers biting into her arm like claws, and says, loud enough for them all to hear: "She must of done it, then, Fay. Why sure. She done it all along, and to think I never knew it, all these years." So the mystery is solved, but it's more of a mystery than ever. Because Nettie won't say any more, or explain it, not even when they sit her down at the kitchen table with iced tea. Nettie says, "*She* didn't know it either. I mean Elizabeth." And that's all. That's all they'll ever know. Sybill says, "I think it's time to call the police," but Dr. Don says, "Let's not be too hasty here now, Sybill, this is a family matter after all," and calls Gurney Fletcher first, instead. He's a reasonable man. Candy says she doesn't think that even she can do much with Fay. Coy Eubanks drinks three Cokes in a row and goes back out and starts up his bulldozer again, working down the hill, grading the new driveway. "Isn't he *cute*?" Theresa whispers to Kate, meaning Roy Looney, who's loading Arthur into the back seat of the VW now, Arthur's having kind of a crying drunk. He loved Fay. And he remembers finding Mavis Lardner finally, in Lexington, Kentucky, a married woman with grandchildren, so old you couldn't even tell her hair had once been red. "Listen, honey," she told Arthur then, "your daddy might not of been much count, but he was sweet, and could carry a tune." Roy Looney walks back to ask Theresa, before he leaves, if she'd like to go see *Trading Places* on Saturday, and she says yes. Don is planning everything. There'll be two quiet, tasteful burials, that's *it*. It can be done. You have to think positively, and act decisively. Whatever comes up, Don can handle it. The sky's the limit, he's on a kind of a roll. He told them he'd get to the bottom of this, and he has. Well, why not? That's the question to ask, instead of Why? *Why not?* You have to think positively. There's even a cure for acne now—Accutane, of course it does have some side effects. There will always be side effects. Dr. Don writes out several prescriptions for Valium and hands them around. He sends Seán down to the clinic with Myrtle, to get his hand bandaged. Candy leaves too, heading out to the One Stop, taking Nettie and Clinus, who refuses to speak to Sybill on the subject of Depression glass or willoware or anything else. Clinus acts real upset, rolling his big round eyes. Clinus's eyes are wild and strange: their enormous flat blueness broken sometimes suddenly by a darting flash of pain, like lightning, a sudden crack of horror. With a retarded person, you can't tell how much they know, or what they feel, or see. Candy holds Clinus's arm as she guides him out to her car. Sybill gets her things together. She's ready to go back to the Holiday Inn; she wants to call Betty, who just won't believe it! Then she wants some peace and quiet, and a glass of Mateus in the motel's Jolly Roger bar. On her way out the door, Sybill notices Myrtle and Don's oldest daughter Karen, who looks like she's pregnant, getting out of a car with her smart computer boyfriend, and passes Jack—crazy Jack—on the front porch, poised to ring the doorbell, bringing Lacy some flowers.

"*H*ow bad is she showing?" Judith Wilkes asked, on the afternoon of the wedding, about Karen. Not that it was any of Judith Wilkes's business, but she went to high school with Karen, so she thought she ought to know. Candy started to say something sharp to her, which she never does to her ladies, but she had a clippie in her mouth right then and by the time she got it out, she had thought better of it, and said, "Right much." Why not? Everybody knew it anyway. Myrtle and Don had decided on a small poolside wedding, mostly family, under the circumstances, but everybody in town knew the circumstances by then, just like they knew about Jewell Rife's bones found down in the well and Fay dying out at the One Stop in Clinus's Chevrolet. Not only did they know it, but they had just about forgotten it by then, especially since that young nurse was raped not a foot from her own apartment a week ago Tuesday, and the guy that did it was still at large. This was at the London Bridge apartments off the bypass, next to the new public library. The apartments with the fancy bridge across the creek and the red double-decker bus that runs back and forth to town. It's mostly singles that live out there. If it was family-oriented, as Martha Rockbridge said, somebody would have been home, would have been around, and seen it. But those apartments discourage families, and pets. Anyway, now everybody was talking about the rape, and even Karen Dotson pregnant was old hat. She'd been home, and she'd been showing, for over a month. Myrtle and Don might as well have had it at the country club and invited everybody. There's no such thing as a little bit pregnant anyway. Those that didn't know it, would. And then they'd forget about that, too, in time, and get onto something else. That's the way folks are.

The only one interested was Judith Wilkes, because she went to high school with Karen, and because she's never done much of anything since. Judith Wilkes lives with her mother who has arthritis, and teaches home ec at the high school, and that's it. That's the story of Judith Wilkes. She was jealous. Candy felt sorry for her, so she gave in and told her some more about it, while she put in Judith's body wave. Candy said that Karen was close to five months pregnant, and that after the wedding she was going right back to Winston-Salem where she had been living with her boyfriend, who is a computer genius, for three years, and finish up her degree in folklore from UNC-G, and then stay home with the baby for a while before she started to look for a teaching job. Candy said Karen's fiancé made plenty of money, so she didn't *have* to work. "I'll bet he does!" Judith said. Her eyes popped out a little, she looks like a Pekingese.

Candy was wrapping the rollers in end wraps. All she ever uses for permanents is Zotoz Warm and Gentle, that's the best.

"Are they going to live in the *same place* they lived in when they were living together?" Judith wanted to know then, and Candy said yes.

"I just wouldn't want to do that," Judith said. She sucked in her breath, a habit she has. Candy put the plastic bag over her head and pinned it tight in the back, and took her over and gave her some heat. She set the timer for ten minutes. You have to be careful if it's an old lady or somebody with high blood pressure, you can't set the heat up so high. But Candy was trying to rush Judith a little without her noticing it, so she could close up and get to the wedding herself. And so Judith could get on back to her mother, poor thing—Candy doesn't like to do her too much, anyway, because she's the kind that won't let herself look good, scared to try anything new. With those pop eyes, she needs some hair down on her forehead, and around her face, and not that tight curly look she's had for so long. Well, some people want to look good, and some don't. It hurts Candy, though, to give somebody a permanent or a cut and have it not look good, and send them out on the street not looking any better than they did when they came in. It's not right. She has dreams about it.

An oval face is the perfect face, but Candy can count on the fingers of one hand the ladies she does that have got one. Most times, nature needs help. Like if they've got a round face, you want to give them some height on top of the head, and flat around the ears. A square face, and you lift it up off the forehead, bring it forward at the sides and jaw. A prominent chin—go for bangs.

Take Sybill. Candy had done Sybill at ten o'clock that morning, and done her friend Betty, too, who had come down to the wedding with her, and Sybill went out looking like a million bucks. Sybill never looked better in her life. The reason was, she came in acting real friendly—Candy was surprised when she called in the first place—and said, "Okay, Candy, here's your chance. I'm just *tired* of it," which is exactly what you always want to hear, and almost never happens. First Candy got Lydia to shampoo her good, and put on a Spun Sand rinse, Roux Fancifull, it's old but nothing ever has come along yet to equal it for color. That was to blend in the gray and soften her. Then Candy feathered it all around her face, and blew it dry instead of using rollers, and showed her how to do it herself, and sold her a round brush so she could. Sybill was smiling at herself in the mirror. Candy turned her around and showed her the back. "Well, what do you *think?*" Sybill asked her friend Betty, and Betty said, "Girl, you've never looked better in your life." It was true. Sybill looked ten years younger. Then Candy gave Sybill's friend Betty a deep side part, to offset that long thin nose, and she looked good, too. Then both of them went on up to Myrtle's to help with the flowers and other decorations.

Myrtle and Don say Sybill's been a real big help with the wedding. She always did know how things ought to be, exactly like Miss Elizabeth. Sybill knows for instance whether or not bridesmaids can wear big hats at a seven-o'clock wedding. They can. So Sybill got these beautiful picture hats made at Thalhimer's, in Roanoke, for the bridesmaids, and brought them down in her car. Everybody in the beauty shop went out and looked at the hats, in the parking lot behind the drugstore, before Betty and Sybill took them up to Myrtle's.

Candy had done over Myrtle the week before. Myrtle had wanted some more Ash Blonde mixed in with the Golden Blonde, so the gray would start showing through. A new look, since she's going to be a grandmother. But the one Candy really wanted to get her hands on, and didn't, was Karen, the bride. Karen hasn't cut her hair in about three years, it's stringing all down her back and looks awful. It's too thin for her to wear it that long. Candy would take off about a foot of it if she got a chance to, and give her a blunt cut. Also those split ends are going to get worse and worse as her time comes on—all the protein in your body goes straight to the baby. Still, Karen is pretty, she's always had a glow about her, like Myrtle.

Candy did two more shampoo and sets that afternoon, waiting for Judith to take, but she takes slow, and then Miss Elva Pope sailed in like the Niña, the Pinta, and the Santa María all rolled into one, to get her hair combed. Miss Elva comes in once a day for Candy to do this, she says it hurts her arm to lift a brush. And every three weeks, Candy shampoos her. She won't get it done any more often than that because she thinks it'll give her bronchitis. When she comes in to get her hair combed, it might be any hour of the day, and she expects Candy to drop everything, and fit her in. But she is a sweet old lady, who was Miss Elizabeth's friend. So Candy got Judith Wilkes out from under the dryer and had her sit there until she finished up Florence Hatfield who has been getting the same French twist for twenty years, she's another one that you just hate to see walk out the door and own up to doing her, and Florence Hatfield's ten-year-old granddaughter Beth that she is raising since her mother—that's Florence's daughter—has fallen into a depression.

"You wait right here," Candy said to Judith and Florence, "while I finish up on little Beth here and comb Miss Elva."

"That *hurts*," Beth said, which was not true, as Candy flipped her bangs. When Candy was done with Beth, she looked as cute as she could, and Florence gave her two quarters to go up to the Rexall for a Coke. Candy has her own Coke machine right here, but she figured Florence wanted to get rid of Beth for fifteen minutes. Florence is real sweet, but there's a limit to everything. You like to feel like you can say what you want, in the beauty parlor. Then Lydia took out Florence's rollers while Candy did Miss Elva.

Miss Elva held her chin up high and looked hard at herself in the mirror. She's a kind of a fierce old lady, like Miss Elizabeth was. Nobody knows how old she is, or what she does with herself outside of church and the ladies' poetry society and coming over here once a day to get her hair combed. She has wispy blue curls all over.

"For the wedding," Miss Elva announced, "I shall wear pink."

"That's a good color for you," Candy said, fluffing her up in the back to cover her bald spot.

Florence said that in her opinion, Karen Dotson was going to have a girl. She said she could always tell, and hadn't been wrong once. She said that the way she does it is, if you can tell somebody's pregnant from *behind*, it's a girl. You carry a boy up high in the front, and he doesn't wrap all around you like a girl will.

"That's *ridiculous*," said Miss Elva, snorting through her long nose. "It's all in the hands of God."

"Well, you can also tell by amniocentesis," Judith said. "That's when they take a needle and—"

"I *know* what it is!" snapped Miss Elva. "A crime against nature, a sin against God. That looks real pretty," she said to Candy in the mirror, and gave her a quarter, which is what she does every day. But Candy wouldn't care if she was paid or not. Then Miss Elva went zooming out. Lydia was giggling, she'd been giggling all day long. Candy was pushing it by then, she had to go home and change, she'd be lucky to get to the wedding at all, never mind cleaning up the shop. She got Florence up in the chair and started to comb her out.

"What are you giggling about?" she said to Lydia. Lydia is so thin and gawky, she looks like somebody drew her with a pencil.

"Well . . ." Lydia said. Lydia always says "Well . . ." through her nose, and stretches it out real long. It'll kill you to talk to her. "Well, I forgot to tell you that Kate came in here while you were gone up to Myrtle's at lunch, and got me to take a piece right here, in the top of her crown, and dye it pink."

"Dye it pink!" Candy said. She dropped her brush on the floor.

"Unh-huh," Lydia said. She was sweeping up hair, and cutting her eyes over at Candy, and giggling and looking guilty.

"Well, did you do it?" Candy asked.

"Unh-huh," Lydia said.

"I bet it looks awful" said Florence.

"It's the 'in' thing," Lydia told her. "Everybody's doing it, look at *Vogue*."

"Myrtle is going to just die." Candy was getting tickled herself.

"Now, who did this?" Florence wanted to know, and Candy said it was Lacy's daughter, her niece, and Judith said was that the weird one, that wore the hat.

"Hats are 'in,' too," Lydia said.

"Well, I never!" said Florence. She kept twisting this way and that, looking at Lydia. Candy thought she'd never get her done. She decided she'd just go on and close up the shop after she finished with Judith, and then come back in here after the wedding to straighten up. She knew she wouldn't get any more work out of Lydia *that* day, she was too flighty. "You go on, hon," Candy told her, and then she finished Florence, who was outlining another theory of hers that if you exercise too much during pregnancy your baby won't have pretty features, but Candy wasn't listening, thinking back on her own wedding which took place in a JP's kitchen in Cheraw, South Carolina, under a bare hanging lightbulb on a string. Candy was pregnant, too. And it was winter. She wore a red wool skirt and a cardigan sweater set. Lonnie was just a kid. They were both kids, Lonnie was a kid when he died. At least she has Tammy Lee, who has his eyes. And then there was Gray Justice who said he'd marry her, and didn't, and is now a lawyer someplace in east Tennessee. Candy was thinking, *It could of been worse. At least when I was at my wits' end Darnell Blossom, who had the Beauty Barn then, said, "Well, Candy, why don't you come in with me, you have always been good with hair." I have, too. I am. But I believe one wedding was enough for me.* And speaking of weddings, Candy remembered all of a sudden that Tony should have been here by now—he was coming in for Karen's wedding, driving up from Florida with a new girlfriend for them to meet. A law student, just like Tony—well, girls do everything these days. Candy's all for it. She doesn't even object to men doing hair, fags or not, fags have got to make a living the same as anybody else. A lot of beauticians resent it, but Candy doesn't. She thinks a person ought to do what they're good at. Finally Lydia left, and Florence settled down, and Candy covered up her eyes and sprayed her. She went out the door hollering for Beth.

That left Judith Wilkes, who sucked in her breath and said, "Well, I think a person ought to get done at a reasonable hour if they take the trouble to make an appointment."

Candy just smiled at her. "Relax, honey," she said. "You're not going anywhere."

*A*ND the wedding goes off without a hitch. It's just perfect! All the things that might happen, don't—Karen *likes* the bridesmaids' hats, for instance, when they arrive in tissue paper in the back seat of Sybill's car, along with Sybill herself, and thank God Myrtle ordered them, since they cover up the top of Kate's head. Karen didn't want hats for the wedding, didn't even particularly want a wedding—she and Karl, her boyfriend, spelled with a *K*, said they would rather take the money and buy a new Apple computer and two bikes, but Myrtle has convinced her older daughter to give in and be gracious, since after all she *is* pregnant, and so she ought to want to please her daddy. Even the thunderstorm which was forecast for 6 p.m. has failed to materialize, the very threat of it reduced to whimsy, to an extravagant puffy pile of pink clouds around the sunset, clouds that look exactly as though they have been expressly ordered for Karen's wedding. And Dr. Don is not only pleased, he's delighted, standing by the punch bowl with his arm around his wife. Of course it's a huge expense, when you think about it—an Apple computer and two bikes wouldn't begin to cover the cost of a wedding. And in a way, it's crazy to spend six weeks getting ready for something that takes ten minutes. But Don wanted Karen to have a proper start in life, he believes in that, and his heart swelled to bursting when he walked her around the side of the pool to where Karl stood with that young Episcopal rector whose name he can never remember but who certainly knows how to do things right. Of course Don wishes they had stuck to the prayerbook, but once Karen and Karl gave in to the idea of a wedding at all, Don didn't quibble. And the poem Theresa wrote for the occasion was pretty enough, although Kate and Lacy told Myrtle it was "sappy." Well, why not? This is not Chapel Hill. This is Booker Creek, where Don and Myrtle will live for the rest of their lives in this house on the hill at the end of town, and even Myrtle likes it now.

Her big glass coffee table looks wonderful in the living room for instance, along with the antique wing chair and the Chinese screen and the stereo system tastefully built into what used to be the bookcase. Her wicker set looks wonderful on the screen porch, which used to be the cold-pantry, the overhead fan turning lazily around and stirring the leaves of the hanging ferns and the trailing begonias. Myrtle has begun to speak knowledgeably of crown molding and pie safes, and has been heard to say that an old home should be "maintained rather than restored." She has also decided to go into real estate, just as soon as she gets this wedding over with. Why not? She clearly has a knack for it, it's fun, all those years of home-making have paid off, she knows just what a woman looks for in a house. Plus she can talk to anybody. Myrtle, staring up at the pink fleeting wispy clouds turning darker now as the sunset fades and night comes on, cannot quite recall whatever she must have been thinking of, or how she felt last year. In her mind's eye she sees Gary Vance for an instant, like a tiny man viewed through the wrong end of a telescope, in his strange white suit against the darkening sky.

People are coming up the hill now, parking at the bottom and walking up for the reception, everybody who's anybody in town, and Myrtle looks with satisfaction at the long linen-covered tables laden with everything imaginable to eat. They had the reception catered, from Buncoe, an undertaking that involved three huge Negroes and a refrigerated truck, and was worth every penny it cost. Just look at the shrimp trees there, at either end of the table! But Mary June Grimes made the cake, she's made every wedding cake for every serious wedding that ever happened in Booker Creek for fifteen years. It's all she does. You have to ask her. She expects it, and has lots of friends. She makes the layers and sections one at a time and freezes them, and then brings it all to your house and assembles it there; the frosting takes hours. It's exhausting to have to listen to Mary June while she frosts it. But worth it, too—you can't get married here without one of her cakes. The wedding cake sits on a card table by itself, near the diving board, and it, too, is perfect.

"You need to get in line now," Sybill tells Myrtle and Don. "They're almost here," as indeed they are, the tide of people surging up the hill now, exclaiming over the new curving driveway and the patio and the pool, and all the flowers. The flowers are really something, towering freestanding arrangements of glads as big as trees, placed strategically about the edge of the patio, and three floating arrangements of red roses in the pool, mounted on Styrofoam, anchored in place by weights. Only the sparseness of the green grass beyond, on the hillside, with the red dirt showing through, indicates that all of this is new. But daylight is fading fast, nothing but a kind of pearly luminescence hanging in the air now, and soon it will be full dark, so you can't see how thin the grass is. This is the last long moment after the wedding, before the reception starts, this is the lingering last of the light.

"You all come on over here now and get in line," Don calls to Karen and Karl, who come, and take their places. Karen is pretty, dimpling and plump in her pregnancy, veil askew. Even her dress looks lovely, although she insisted on making it herself out of one of Miss Elizabeth's old lace tablecloths. Myrtle finally said she *could* do it, if she wouldn't tell anybody except the family, and so she did, and she hasn't. Kate and Theresa and Karl's sister, the bridesmaids, wear pink, as does Miss Elva Pope, who is first in line.

"I'm going to hit the lights," Sybill says in Myrtle's ear and then she's gone, off toward the house, Betty following. Sybill likes to say, "hit the lights," she likes the urgency of a wedding, the intricacy of the timing, the general need for some precision all around. Which she, thank God, has been able to supply! Myrtle and Don could never have managed all this without her. "Speed is of the essence here in more ways than one," she told Betty, who hooted, but it was true. And Betty is having a big time at the wedding, too. Sybill feels a lot better in general now that her headaches have disappeared, even though Edward Bing has, too. While she was down here at her mother's funeral, he up and married his secretary, a dizzy blonde. Sybill can't imagine why an old man like Edward Bing would want to do such a risky, undignified thing. But in her heart of hearts, she was relieved. Sybill pushes her way through the crowd and goes up on the screen porch and reaches under some wicker to plug in the lights.

"Aah!" goes everybody.

This is very satisfying to Sybill, who thought of these Japanese lanterns in the first place, and bought them at Western Auto in Roanoke. They hang all along the chainlink fence at the edge of the hillside, making the whole scene look like a kind of festival, which it is. Betty sends Sean around with two Bics, to light the candles, and then Sybill plugs in the underwater pool lights too, so the pool gives off a soft blue mysterious glow right in the middle of the whole reception.

"Aah!" everyone goes again.

This is also satisfying to Sybill, who goes to stand at the edge of the patio, hands on hips, and cries a little, there where nobody can see her. This is not sad crying, though; and it comes up from the bottom of Sybill's heart, for just no reason at all.

Even Arthur looks reasonably decent, drinking champagne with that Mrs. Palucci. "Hello, Arthur," Sybill says, and Arthur hugs her. Either he's drunk, or ebullient, or both—with Arthur, it's hard to tell. He keeps one arm tight around Mrs. Palucci, who looks imposing in a sort of turquoise jumpsuit. Arthur is now an ex-house sitter, with a new career. This new career is working at the One Stop, where big things are going to happen. Mrs. Palucci, it turns out, is tired of sick people, and has always wanted to run a restaurant. She also said, "What about a motel?" and

Arthur finds himself fancying it. Arthur envisions himself in a little office, saying "Howdy, where you from?" to strangers. This plan seems to be fine with Nettie, who is not much interested in her business anymore. Nettie spends more and more time these days in her garden or just sitting out there in a lawn chair smoking Camels, and staring off into the smoke. If they turn the One Stop into a motel, she'll have plenty of people to talk to, it'll pep her up. Mrs. Palucci is peppy, all right. When Sybill said it sounds as if this plan will require a lot of get up and go, which Arthur has never been noted for, Mrs. Palucci defended him publicly on the spot, saying, "Well, Arthur is putting a great deal of energy into his courtship, at any rate." Which is true. Arthur can't get over it himself. He loves Mrs. Palucci and hates Sybill, for a second, as they all stand together looking at the pool, not because Sybill has said that he lacks get up and go, but because Sybill has seen his father's face, even under water.

"Where's Buddy?" Mrs. Palucci says suddenly, and then she and Arthur go off to find him, her turquoise jumpsuit lost to sight in the growing crowd. Everyone's eating and drinking a lot; the noise level rises, but Lord, it's hot, and seems to be getting hotter. Mrs. Palucci and Arthur search the fringes of the crowd for Buddy, her son, looking for such things as hoses and rocks, which Buddy is drawn to. He's been busy sabotaging stuff, already. For instance he broke the icemaker on Myrtle's new refrigerator not ten minutes after he got here, but Myrtle doesn't know it yet. Myrtle stands in line and smiles, shaking hands, kissing people on the cheek. Kissing people on the cheek is a new thing, it's just hit town. Mrs. Palucci and Arthur search the bushes around the house, calling softly, "Buddy, Buddy—" Arthur thinks it would be interesting to hang around this kid, Buddy, and watch him grow up. There ought to be some interesting moments, over the years. Arthur thinks of his own girls, that he loves so, and kisses Mrs. Palucci behind the boxwood.

Everyone's drinking a lot, the receiving line has broken up, Kate can take off her hat at last, and Theresa can rush back to stand next to Roy Looney. They're in love. In the six short weeks she's been dating Roy Looney, Theresa's whole outlook on life has changed. In fact she wrote a new long poem named "Irony Sucks," last week.

Lacy finds this amusing, or bemusing, it's hard to say, just as she finds it amusing that it was she who suggested this band, Ernest Dodd and the Rhythm Masters, who have finished tuning up, finally, and are playing the "Tennessee Waltz." Myrtle and Don wanted something more like Lester Lanin, some tasteful little combo, but Karen stuck to her guns and said well, as long as she was going to have a wedding, after all, she wanted some kind of traditional music. And there's nobody more traditional than Ernest Dodd and the Rhythm Masters, with their big black cowboy hats and those black shirts with all the glitter. What will Myrtle and Don's new friends from the Racquet Club think of this music? The Rhythm Masters are playing "The Yellow Rose of Texas" with lots of enthusiasm. Lacy drinks champagne. She's writing her dissertation, and will be teaching a course in the fall, at Durham Technical Institute. It's a start, anyway. Great Books. Lacy cannot imagine what she'll say to her class: "Okay, this is a *great book*." Still, it's clear that since they've hired her, she must know something. And Jack? He's still living with Susan, his graduate assistant, but he takes Lacy out to dinner every Thursday night. On these occasions, Jack is charming, attentive: a beau. Lacy smiles. She doesn't know what will happen. God, it's hot.

That's the only thing wrong here, it's so damn hot, the men are taking off their jackets, and suddenly, too, there is dancing, which Myrtle and Don did not expect. The Rhythm Masters are catching on. It's so *original*, for Myrtle and Don to have such a band! Karl and Karen are first in the hastily cleared space, joined by others. The newlyweds have just declared their intention to stay at the party, rather than "go away." They can't be convinced to leave. "It's a real good party, sir," Karl told Don. And watching them dance, pregnant Karen so light on her feet and her computer husband so handsome, Lacy, a little drunk already, says to Myrtle, "You know, don't you, Mother would just *die*," and Candy remarks, "She did." But Sybill says that's nonsense, Mother would be tickled pink, everything has gone like clockwork, which it has, thanks to her, and Don, winking at Candy, asks Betty to dance, and won't take no for an answer. Betty hasn't danced in eleven years, but she's not bad. Sean is shooting off some fireworks on the hillside, and Candy explains to Myrtle, over the racket, that Tony bought them on his way up here, passing through South Carolina. They're legal in South Carolina. Tony's new girlfriend seems real nice. Nettie grins, and says goodbye, she's got to get back to the One Stop, but the truth is that cut flowers always make her think of Millard Cline. Besides, she's had all the bourbon she needs. Nettie hums on the downshift, driving the pickup off into the night. Clinus didn't make it, of course, but he put a special sign up in honor of Karen's wedding: KAREN AND KARL, TODAY

IS THE FIRST DAY OF THE REST OF YOUR LIFE. It is, too. That goes for everybody. The Rhythm Masters play "You picked a fine time to leave me, Lucille." Everybody's drunk, and dancing. Candy dances with Mr. Constantine, Mrs. Palucci dances with Don, and Betty, now that she's started, won't quit—she'll dance with anybody. The Rhythm Masters sing "You're Ruining My Bad Reputation."

Tomorrow, nobody will remember exactly who was the first one in the pool, but soon it's full of churning bodies, pale flashing flesh beneath the water. Karen and Theresa, all wet, do the cancan at poolside, red roses in their teeth. Lacy's Bill is diving: a flip, a back flip, a jackknife, a swan. "Aah," goes everybody. The Rhythm Masters attempt "Mule Skinner Blues," which means they get to yodel. Lacy is pretty drunk; she smiles and shakes her head. Bill, diving, is darling. Old Ernest Dodd is darling. Strange that Lacy can't remember his son, the Dodd boy, at the lake, especially since he was sweet on her. But then suddenly Lacy has an idea of him, outlined against the blue water, braced against the pull of the rope, his bright open face a shining blur in the rushing wind.

ABOUT THE AUTHOR

Lee Smith is the author of five novels, including FAIR AND TENDER LADIES and ORAL HISTORY, and a short story collection, CAKEWALK. The 1988 winner of the John Dos Passos Prize for Literature and twice winner of the prestigious O. Henry Award, she teaches at North Carolina State University in Raleigh and lives in Chapel Hill with her husband and children.